OPERATION STORM CITY

JOSHUA MOWLL

WALKER BOOKS
AND SUBSIDIARIES
LONDON · BOSTON · SYDNEY · AUCKLAND

For Sonya

INTRODUCTION

A Note to the Reader

Dear Reader,

At a little after 6 p.m. on the 24th March 2006, I met an antiques dealer outside the Man Mo Temple in Hong Kong; he'd contacted me after reading my two previous volumes, *Operation Red Jericho* and *Operation Typhoon Shore*, and was insistent he had something to sell me – and that it was "something Tembla".

If you recall, my principal source of information for the books published so far had been my great-aunt's archive concerning a secret society of scientists and explorers, hidden in a series of cellar chambers beneath her house in Devon. I'd unexpectedly inherited this, along with the title President of the Honourable Guild of Specialists, on her death in 2002. The fifth and final archive chamber has at last provided me with enough material to complete the trilogy, although gaining access to it was something of an adventure in itself.

When I sledgehammered through the final cellar wall, I discovered not a chamber but a passageway, blocked at intervals by doors with complex puzzle locks. To progress, I was forced to investigate clues Great-Aunt Rebecca had hidden throughout the many thousands of MacKenzie archive files I already had access to. I'm now certain these puzzles were a test, set by my great-aunt to ensure that I understood all of the Guild's history and background; only when my knowledge was sufficiently advanced would the heart of the Guild mysteries be revealed to me. After many months' intensive research, I cracked the final clue and the last archive was mine.

In 2006 I set out on a research trip to China and India, hoping to substantiate the extraordinary claims made in the new material I now had in my possession, and to piece together the chain of events described in the next tranche of my great-aunt's diaries.

First I journeyed to the Chinese region of Xinjiang, formerly Sinkiang. On a cold morning my hired Bactrian camel plodded up a preposterously high sand dune – a tricky ascent for which my Uighur guide charged me a considerable premium – and I reached what I believe to be the location of Ur-Can: the fabled Storm City. My guide and his camel seemed anxious to move off, and he said in broken English, "Bad place... Desert djinn."

HUNTING FOR UR-CAN, SINKIANG, CHINA

From the barren wastes of Takla Makan I travelled by train and aeroplane to the mysterious rendezvous in

OLD SILK ROAD CITY, CHINA

Hong Kong. The antiques dealer was there outside the Man Mo Temple. He seemed fidgety, and I noticed he checked the street several times before approaching me – I was carrying a copy of my book so he would recognize me. He hurried me to a trinket shop in the Cat Street market, and ushered me into a cramped back room overflowing with extraordinary objects for sale: swords of every vintage, wax seals, snuffboxes, Buddha statues, and any number of prancing horse carvings. The air was heavy with incense and, for the briefest of moments, I felt as if I were back in 1920 and that perhaps

ON THE TRAIL OF BECLA AND DOUG, LUCKNOW, INDIA

SINKIANG – A WILD AND BARREN PLACE

Becca and Doug would appear from behind the curtain covering the door.

My contact was in a hurry. He pulled an astounding object from a rough wooden box: it was a gyrolabe. I'd seen illustrations of them in the Guild histories, of course, but I'd never believed I would see one of the original artefacts and I was rendered speechless for several seconds. I knew by now that this was a gravity device, the initiator of an ancient machine powered by the substance known as zoridium – all of which had shaped the lives of Becca and Doug through the events recounted in my two previous volumes.

I noticed there was something wrong with the gyrolabe: the polar nodes were scorched and burnt, and as I turned the contraption to the light, it was obvious that the metal was twisted and distorted as if it had been exposed to great heat. The antiques dealer offered to sell it for a surprisingly low price, so I bought it without delay and with the briefest of goodbyes we parted company.

Closer scrutiny back at my hotel revealed certain unexpected aspects to my new purchase: this gyrolabe wasn't, in fact, Tembla – it wasn't even especially old! It did, however, fit exactly with what I'd learnt back at that strange archive in Devon, and with the story I'm about to recount in this third volume of Becca and Doug's adventures.

Yours sincerely,

Joshua Mowll.

OPERATION STORM CITY

LOCATOR MAP

THEATRE OF OPERATIONS – ASIA

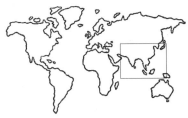

(MA 351.14 ASIA)

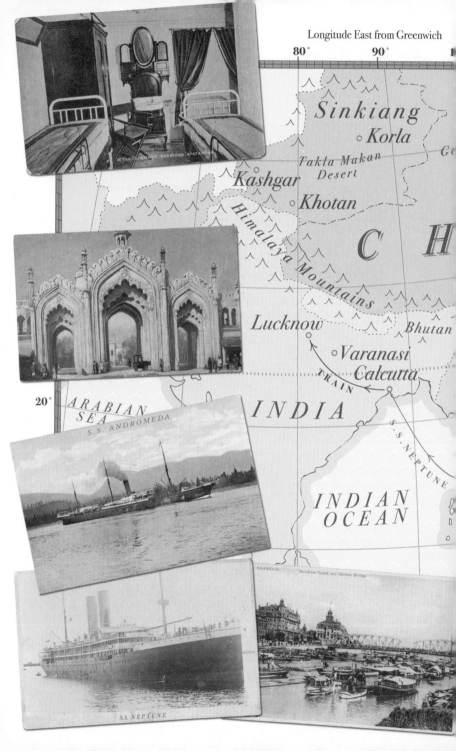

80°   90°

Sinkiang
○ *Korla*

Takla Makan Desert

Kashgar
○ *Khotan*

C H

Himalaya Mountains

Bhutan

Lucknow

○ *Varanasi*
Calcutta

TRAIN

20° *ARABIAN SEA*

S.S. ANDROMEDA

I N D I A

S.S. NEPTUNE

INDIAN OCEAN

SHANGHAI   *Soochow Creek and Garden Bridge*

S.S. NEPTUNE

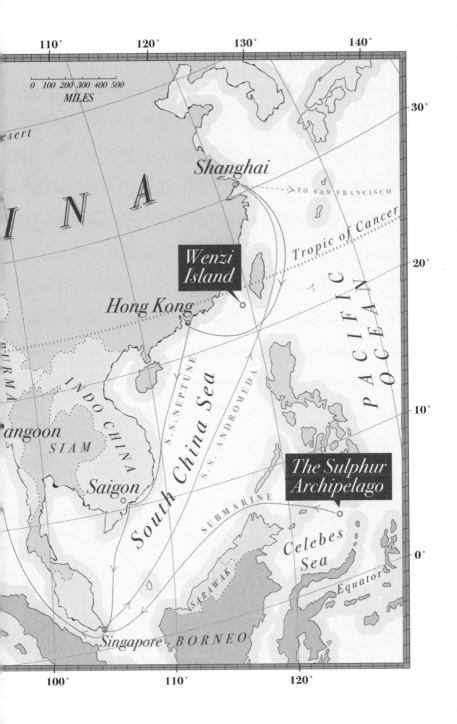

OPERATION STORM CITY

But whence do all these legends come? ...To these fabulous, these adventurous tales I gave the eager ear of a child. I had fallen under the spell of the weird witchery of the desert.

Sven Hedin, *Through Asia* (1898)

CHAPTER ONE

Cutting from the 20th June 1920 edition of the *Lucknow Times*.

Son and daughter of Lucknow family feared lost at sea

Absence detected at Yokohama

YOKOHAMA, JAPAN, Tuesday – Douglas and Rebecca MacKenzie, residents of The Lodge, Lucknow, have been reported lost, presumed drowned, at sea. The children were sailing from Singapore to San Francisco aboard the steamship Andromeda. Their cabin was found empty by the chief steward when the ship docked at Yokohama.

Mr and Mrs Hamish MacKenzie, parents of the lost children, were themselves reported missing last year when they failed to return from a cartographic expedition to the Sinkiang region of China. This new tragedy has caused much concern within Lucknow society.

A rope ladder had been found tied to the stern stanchion by crewmen shortly after the ship left Shanghai. No action had been taken at the time, the captain believing the matter to have been of no consequence. He later speculated that one of the children might have gone overboard accidentally, prompting the second to attempt a rescue using the ladder. The children's pet Bengal tiger was also found to be missing.

31st July 1920
The Lodge, Lucknow, India

The Lodge was a preposterous name for such a large and grandiose house. Douglas MacKenzie's old home seemed more monumental than ever in the moonlight as he edged along the branch of the mango tree to better view it with his binoculars. The broad, two-storeyed building had been constructed some one hundred and fifty years before by the British East India Company as the hunting lodge for the Lucknow regional official, and later purchased by an Indian noble. On his death it was handed down to his son, Maharaja Amar Singh, a vivacious young man who had become the MacKenzies' landlord.

Doug remembered the last time he'd been in his old home, many months before, when he and his sister Becca had been dragged by their ear and pushed into a taxi by Aunt Margaret, for the start of a journey that had led to Shanghai and their adventures aboard the research ship *Expedient*.

He felt surprisingly little sadness at seeing his home again, but it reminded him how desperately he missed his parents. They were lost on a secret expedition to the desert wastes of Sinkiang in China. And now he and Becca were about to break into their own home to try to find their parents' expedition papers. Their plan was to follow their trail deep into the Sinkiang; this was why they'd returned to Lucknow, and neither of them wanted to linger here among the memories any longer than they had to.

"Do you see anyone?" whispered Becca, from below. The Duchess gave a low growl and paced back and forth. Becca tried to calm her, but the white tiger pulled at her lead restlessly. "Duchess, settle."

Doug lifted the binoculars and scanned the familiar facade, searching each of the lit windows.

"Oh, Becca, there's Bhanu – he must have got his old job back. He's taking the telegram to … to a man who must be Bergstrom. It fits."

While on board *Expedient*, Doug and Becca had read a message from a man called Bergstrom, a resident of Lucknow who was also a member of the Honourable Guild of Specialists. Their first task on arrival earlier that day had been to reconnoitre The Lodge. There was a stranger living there, who they suspected might be Bergstrom. To test out their theory they'd sent a telegram addressed to him at The Lodge.

The telegram boy cycled past, his tyres crunching on the gravel.

Becca looked up nervously. "Is Bergstrom taking the bait?"

The front door opened, casting light on the car parked under the portico.

"Shh, here he comes…"

Bergstrom strode out and climbed into the back seat as Bhanu put the starter handle into the front of the engine and fired up the motor.

"Get behind the tree!" hissed Doug as the car set off, the spill from its headlamps momentarily illuminating their hiding place.

"Can you see anyone else in there?"

"No. We're safe," he said as he swung down from the tree. "Leave the Duchess here. We can't have her going wild if Bergstrom gets back sooner than we'd hoped."

They tied the tiger's lead to a branch and raced across

The Lodge

The grand architecture of 'The Lodge' always reminded Doug of a squat, poorer cousin to Washington DC's White House. The opulence of their Lucknou home contrasted starkly with the MacKenzies' thrifty lifestyle; they lived in a handful of rooms, the maharaja's exquisite furniture veiled under dust sheets. Known only to Doug, these sheets also concealed several chipped vases and a headless statuette which had once been the casualty of a lively game of indoor cricket.

"THE LODGE", LUCKNOW

the lawn and round the side of the house. Doug opened the window beside the back door using a method he'd perfected two summers before. Once inside the house the two MacKenzies stopped and looked at each other. They were back in their old home. How many times over the last few months had they dreamt of this moment? Yet without their parents it was incomplete.

Becca broke the spell. "Come on. Once Bergstrom realizes the director of the HGS isn't at the railway station, he'll be back, wondering who sent the fake telegram."

Their parents' study was along the corridor. A pair of stout desks faced each other, stacked high with the same books and papers that had been there when they left.

Doug was immediately suspicious. "Bergstrom's changed nothing."

Becca circled the room, running her hand along the polished edge of her mother's empty chair. She pulled the nearest pile of books towards her and scanned the author names: Stein, Hedin, Prejevalsky – weighty tomes from which a profusion of bookmarks sprang, all annotated in her mother's neat handwriting: *Takla Makan Desert crossing; Myths of lost cities; Qui'l'bharat, storms, dust clouds*. For a

STEIN (*pictured with his dog, Dash*)**, HEDIN AND PREJEVALSKY**

These men were pioneers in the exploration, mapping and study of the Sinkiang region of China. Sir Aurel Stein (1862–1943) was an Englishman, Sven Hedin (1865–1952) a Swede, and Colonel Nikolai Prejevalsky (1839–88) a Russian. Their perilous expeditions were the first to investigate this enigmatic region, whose hostile climate had been a natural barrier between east and west crossed only by the traders of the Silk Road. This vanguard of modern explorers produced the first accurate surveys of the region and discovered archaeological evidence of cities which had flourished there over a thousand years before.

moment, Becca wondered if her mother could still be alive, or whether she was in fact as dead as the air in the unused study.

Doug interrupted her reverie. "Father's map chest," he said triumphantly. "There, below *The Ambassadors*. His maps of China should be in the third drawer down."

Becca sighed, glancing up at the reproduction of Holbein's painting. "I'll never want to see that picture again after all this."

"Here. These are the ones. Chinese Turkistan," Doug said as he pulled open the drawer. "Central Asia ... Cathay ... Kashgar, Korla, Khotan ... Sinkiang ... more Sinkiang..."

"Take all of them." Becca's voice was suddenly severe. "Leave nothing."

"Becca. Something's bothering me. If Mother and Father *were* members of a secret society, where are all the secrets?" Becca looked about her and could see what Doug meant. "We've been in this library a hundred times. Did you ever see any mention of the Honourable Guild of Specialists?"

"No. But then I never looked before."

Doug unlocked the grandfather clock case with its small key. His tongue clenched between his teeth, he felt upwards inside the case towards the mechanism just as their father used to do.

A memory flickered through Becca's mind. "But you could never open that lock before!" she exclaimed. "You used to try all the time."

"I've become a lot more experienced since then. It's a reverse lock. Anticlockwise to lock; clockwise to unlock."

"Father used to do whatever you're doing to the clock at the end of each day."

"I know. That's why I'm doing it. He always said he was adjusting the pendulum, but that's a lot of old rot; I checked in a – got it!" Doug pulled out a well-worn key. It was dainty, with a bow grip into which the letters HGS had been carved.

Becca looked around the room with a keen eye. "Let me see the key."

Doug threw it to her.

Her eyes fixed on a sturdy five-shelf bookcase fronted with a pair of lockable glass doors. "There."

"Why?"

"Because this key is just like the one already in the door – only this one has HGS on it."

They examined the bookcase for a second, secret keyhole, but found nothing. Doug opened the glass doors and caught the musty waft of old books. He pulled one out and flicked through it, unsure if they were on the right track. It was a collection of plays by Christopher Marlowe. "Ah, *Doctor Faustus*."

"We haven't got time for Elizabethan drama," snapped Becca, snatching the book from her brother and slamming it back on the shelf.

"It moved," breathed Doug. He pressed downwards. The shelf moved fractionally. He looked more closely at the join where the shelf met the side of the bookcase. "There's no bracket here. No support. There are some wear marks, as if…"

He closed the doors and relocked them. "Becca, perhaps the answer is staring us in the face. Use the HGS key this time."

She quickly swapped the keys and unlocked the doors again. Doug pushed down on the shelf but it moved only fractionally.

"Maybe it's another reverse lock, like the clock," Becca suggested.

This time a satisfying click could be heard deep within the bookcase. They opened the doors and pressed down hard on the shelf.

The engraved key.

(MA 00.524 RM)

The shelves were on a continuous carousel loop; a new shelf appeared at the top as soon as one disappeared from the bottom. The first of the hidden shelves glided down to eye level. It contained a neat set of red leather-bound books entitled *History and Gazetteer of the Honourable Guild of Specialists*. More shelves slid by crammed with books and manuscripts from a hundred centuries and in as many different languages. One shelf was less cluttered than the others, but Doug, fascinated with the mechanism, spun it until the carousel had completed an entire revolution.

"The secret Guild papers were here all along," said Becca. She revolved the carousel back to the half-empty shelf. It was labelled SINKIANG – EXPEDITION NOTES & PLANNING. "Looks like they took most of this stuff with them."

With shaking hands they spread out the remaining papers. There were bills and receipts for equipment, and loose scraps with notes on subjects as diverse as how much camels might cost in Kashgar and the price of a new set of walking boots.

"Not exactly top-secret stuff, this, is it?" sniffed Doug.

Towards the bottom of the pile, there was a neatly folded sheet of tracing paper, a slender folder, a leather-bound book and some handwritten notes. The book was Volume XXIV of the *History and Gazetteer of the Honourable Guild of Specialists*.

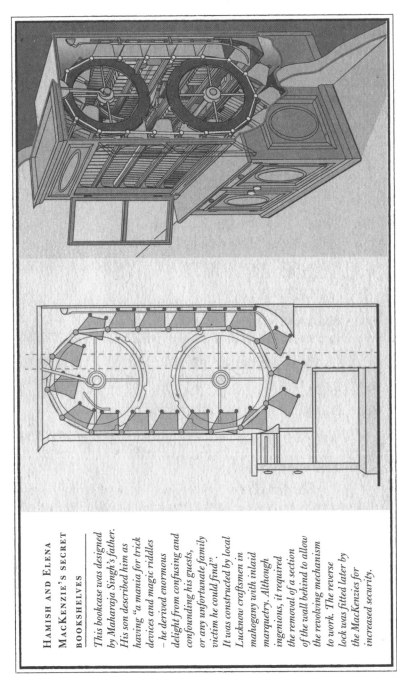

HAMISH AND ELENA MacKENZIE'S SECRET

BOOKSHELVES

This bookcase was designed by Maharaja Singh's father. His son described him as having "a mania for trick devices and magic riddles – he derived enormous delight from confusing and confounding his guests, or any unfortunate family victim he could find". It was constructed by local Lucknow craftsmen in mahogany with inlaid marquetry. Although ingenious, it required the removal of a section of the wall behind to allow the revolving mechanism to work. The reverse lock was fitted later by the MacKenzies for increased security.

Tucked into one of the pages of a chapter entitled 'The Tembla Cult – Death Rituals' was a single loose photograph showing four hexagonal sections like bolt heads, slightly recessed into some sort of flat panel. The scale was difficult to establish but each of the four hexagons had six different symbols engraved around its edge.

"Twenty-four symbols – and none the same."

Becca flicked the photo over and saw written in faint pencil: *Picture 476: Ur-Can hieroglyphs.*

Doug snorted. "Where do you think the other four hundred and seventy-five snaps are?"

"Not here," she replied forlornly. "Why did she leave it, though?"

"They left in a shocking hurry," said Doug. "She could've forgotten it."

"It looks important."

"Well then, perhaps it was safer here. I expect she copied all those symbols down in a notebook, anyway."

While Becca pondered the mystifying picture, Doug carefully unfolded the sheet of tracing paper. "This was drawn by Father. One of his preparatory sketches for a map, I think."

Becca tucked the photograph back in the book and glanced at the sketch. Not a single city or place name was marked on it. Her attention turned to the handwritten pages; she skimmed through them looking for any mention of the Sinkiang expedition, but there was none.

Inside the folder was a Guild report. "*General Nicolaus Pugachev,*" Becca read.

"Hang on – wasn't he mentioned in the message Mother hid in her correspondence box?" said Doug excitedly.

Becca read out the short paragraph:

"*Born 1886. Made his name in the Russo-Japanese war 1904–05. 1905–07 studied Oriental history and languages at the University of Moscow, although it is thought he was there as a spy to monitor anti-tsarist political activity. Decorated with the St George Cross for military service in 1915. Considered a superb soldier. Sources say he was on the point of dishonourable discharge from the Imperial Russian Army for flaying alive one of his fellow officers who he claimed held anti-tsarist sympathies. However, his dismissal was interrupted by the Bolshevik uprising. His wife and five children are believed to have been shot by Bolsheviks fifteen miles outside Moscow in June, 1918.*"

"Blimey," Doug remarked with a sniff.

"Put all of this in your bag. We'll look at the rest of it later. We need to clear out of here before Bergstrom gets back. And I'd … I'd like to see my bedroom again. Just quickly."

"Your bedroom?" Doug hesitated, knowing from the tone of his sister's voice that she was set on this detour whether he liked it or not. "Get a move on, then. I'll keep a lookout down here."

As Becca ran towards the stairs, Doug relocked the bookcase doors and wandered across the chequered marble floor into the main hall. Their house-sitter had turned the small parlour into his own study. From the papers on the desk – mainly letters and bills relating to supplies of telescopes and lenses – it seemed that Bergstrom was an astronomer.

After several minutes Becca appeared looking sad and reflective; she was clutching a book. "Found out anything?"

"Bergstrom's a stargazer," replied Doug.

"What?"

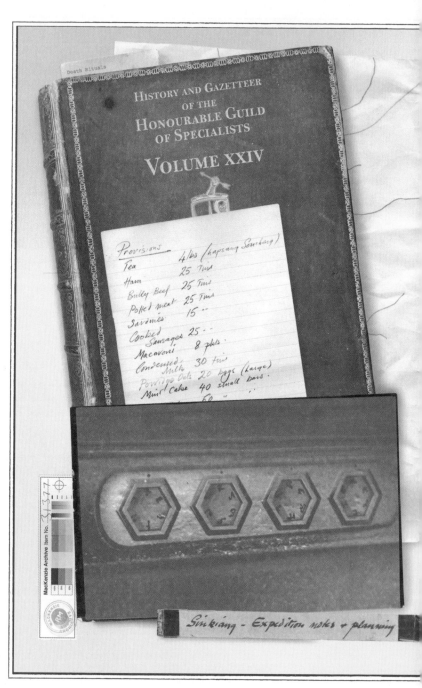

HISTORY AND GAZETTEER
OF THE
HONOURABLE GUILD
OF SPECIALISTS

VOLUME XXIV

Death Rituals

Provisions
Tea   4 lbs (Lapsang Souchong)
Ham   25 Tins
Bully Beef   25 Tins
Potted meat   25 Tins
Sardines   15 ··
Cooked
  Sausages   25 ··
Macaroni   8 pkts
Condensed
  Milk   30 Tins
Porridge Oats 20 bags (large)
Mint Cake   40 small bars
               60 ··

Sinkiang - Expedition notes + planning

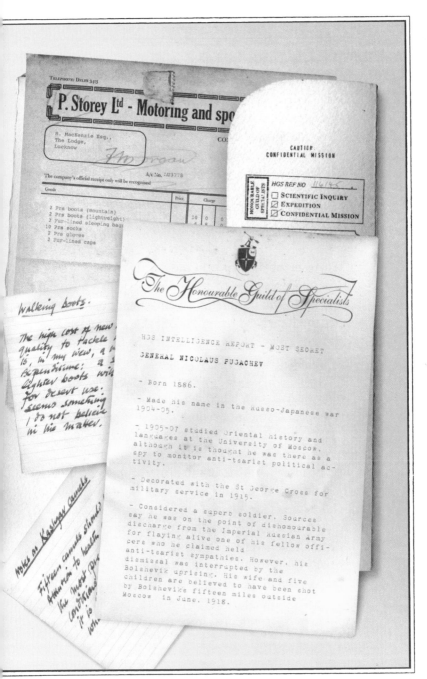

TELEPHONE: DELHI 3413

P. Storey Lᵗᵈ - Motoring and spo

R. MacKenzie Esq.,
The Lodge,
Lucknow

CO

The company's official receipt only will be recognised

A/c No. LU3778

Goods	Price		Charge	
2 Prs boots (mountain)				
2 Prs boots (lightweight)	10	0	0	
2 Fur-lined sleeping bags	6	0	0	
10 Prs socks				
2 Prs gloves				
2 Fur-lined caps				

CAUTION:
CONFIDENTIAL MISSION

HONOURABLE GUILD OF SPECIALISTS

HGS REF NO 116/45

☐ SCIENTIFIC INQUIRY
☑ EXPEDITION
☑ CONFIDENTIAL MISSION

Walking boots.

*The high cost of new
quality to tackle
is, in my view, a
expenditure: a s
lighter boots wil
for desert use:
seems something
I do not believe
in the matter.*

Notes on Kashgar camels

*Fifteen camels should
attention to health
the most (pro
conditions
it is
wh*

The Honourable Guild of Specialists

HGS INTELLIGENCE REPORT - MOST SECRET
GENERAL NICOLAUS FUGACHEV

- Born 1886.

- Made his name in the Russo-Japanese war
1904-05.

- 1905-07 studied Oriental history and
languages at the University of Moscow,
although it is thought he was there as a
spy to monitor anti-tsarist political activity.

- Decorated with the St George Cross for
military service in 1915.

- Considered a superb soldier. Sources
say he was on the point of dishonourable
discharge from the Imperial Russian Army
for flaying alive one of his fellow officers who he claimed held
anti-tsarist sympathies. However, his
dismissal was interrupted by the
Bolshevik uprising. His wife and five
children are believed to have been shot
by Bolsheviks fifteen miles outside
Moscow in June, 1918.

"Doctor of Astronomy, I think. Scientist, anyway."

"Is that his diary?"

Doug looked at the book beside the table lamp, and nodded. He didn't like the coldness in Becca's voice.

"Have you checked it?"

"No ... it didn't seem right."

"Right? None of this is right, Doug, but we need to find out as much as we can." Becca opened the diary and began to search through its pages.

"Did you find what you were looking for upstairs?" tried Doug.

"What I'm looking for is in the deserts of the Sinkiang, and the thought of going there fills me with something close to panic. But if it means we can come back here with Mother and Father and return to normal, then I'm prepared to do it. Every nerve in my body says it's the most dangerous thing we'll ever do. Doesn't that frighten you too?"

Doug sniffed. "Well, I hadn't really given it much thought ... other than getting there. But I think Bergstrom might be on our side – you know, with the HGS. If he was Coterie like Pembleton-Crozier, surely he would have ransacked the house looking for information?"

Becca paused at a date in the diary. "If that's so, Doug, why is Bergstrom meeting with Pembleton-Crozier and Capulus in seven days' time?"

"You're not serious. Where?"

"The Bhul Bhulaiya."

"What – the labyrinth?" cut in Doug.

"Yes, at seven in the morning. Maybe Liberty will answer our telegrams now. She's got scores to settle with both of them. Capulus," continued Becca thoughtfully. "I wonder if he isn't the key to all this. He sold Mother the Tembla hieroglyphics from Ur-Can. He *must* know where it is."

The crunch of car tyres on gravel made them look up.

"Time to go," whispered Doug, adjusting the weighty bag of papers on his back. "Quick – out the kitchen window."

The MacKenzies slipped into the shadows of the garden, untied the Duchess, then ran towards the side wall where they'd climbed in. They were halfway there when a second car drew up, and with a shock, Doug saw their landlord, the maharaja, step out and greet Bergstrom warmly.

"I feared I'd be late," said Bergstrom, his voice cutting clear through the night air. "Someone has been playing games. I've been sent on a fool's errand."

"Bergstrom, my friend, it is no matter," said the maharaja. "You are here now, and you are nobody's fool."

"Come. Let's dine." Bergstrom ushered his guest towards the house. "There is much to discuss."

"Your news is indeed most alarming. And the night drive has sharpened my appetite," laughed the maharaja. "Your letters have intrigued me greatly; I hope my advice was of use. Now, how is The Lodge holding up? You know, I've always had a fancy to retire here when I'm old. The fortress is too far from the centre of things…"

Their voices faded as they entered the house.

"Let's get closer," whispered Doug.

Becca gripped his arm and pointed. He could see the outline of two figures, also trying to hide in the shrubbery. The Duchess growled and squatted down, sniffing for a kill.

From Doug's sketchbook: The Duchess sees off the intruders.[1] (DMS 7/07)

"Duchess, no!" hissed Doug. But the animal crept forward towards the intruders. Doug grabbed her lead and tried to slow her down, but she wasn't to be stopped. The two Indian men leapt up and fled, scaling the garden wall at speed.

The commotion attracted Bergstrom's attention, and his face appeared at a downstairs window. Doug and Becca lay flat on the ground, hoping the darkness would cover them. Bergstrom stepped outside with a pistol in his hand and looked about. After staring into the gloom for almost a minute, he went back inside, then closed and locked the door.

"That was close," sighed Becca.

"Let's get back to the shop. The Duchess wants her dinner."

---

1 The picture above is from one of Doug MacKenzie's sketchbooks. Most of Doug's sketches were drawn from memory (or, often, partly imagined), and may not be accurate representations of the people and events in this account.

CHAPTER TWO

The Rampal bookshop was one of Becca's favourite places in all the world. Mr Rampal and his wife had been family friends for as long as she could remember. He had supplied many of the hundreds of books in their parents' library. His shop lay in the very centre of the city, and his insist-

From Doug's sketchbook:
The Rampal bookshop. (DMS 7/05)

ence on giving anyone who dropped in "a little cup of tea" made him not only one of the best liked and best read people in Lucknow, but also one of the best connected.

Such was the bookshop's popularity and renown that the Rampals let two guest rooms above the shop. Becca and Doug had set up camp there as soon as they'd arrived. It had seemed a natural choice, and they'd been warmly welcomed. Mr Rampal had, of course, heard of their parents' mysterious disappearance, though it was not in his nature to pry into why Becca and Doug had arrived by train from the south with a white tiger for company, asking for lodgings.

At breakfast the next day, in the room behind the shop, Shriman Rampal poured tea for his two guests.

"We should like to stay for a week," said Becca. "Will that be convenient?"

Mr Rampal

In 1857, aged 7, during the First War of Indian Independence, Shriman Rampal carried water to the Indian forces besieging the British garrison in the Lucknow Residency. When he reached the age of 97, Mr Rampal finally saw the British leave India for good as the British Raj crumbled. He celebrated by saying: "All good things come to those who wait … and I've waited longer than most."

The bookseller remained silent, carefully placing the teapot down on an embroidered table mat.

"We can always stay in a hotel," Doug said, filling the silence. He cast a glance at his sister, and continued. "We have a meeting next week."

Mr Rampal's thin eyebrows shot up. "A meeting? I see…"

"Yes, at the Bhul Bhulaiya."

The bookseller nodded. "And where are you intending to go after you have been to this meeting?"

"China," stated Doug matter-of-factly. "Our parents are there. We're going to find them."

"Ah yes, I suspected that was the reason behind your travels. You don't think you are a little young for such an expedition?"

Becca sipped her tea then answered curtly, "Mother and Father have been missing for over a year now. We want to find them."

"Naturally, naturally. Your parents are particular friends of mine; I miss them a great deal. But do you not think you should be … at school?"

"Mr Rampal, I'd like nothing better than to go back to school, but the inability of … of our parents' employers to launch any sort of proper attempt to find them means we've had to take matters into our own hands."

"Your parents' employers," echoed the bookseller. "I see… And do you know where in China they were exploring?"

"The Takla Makan desert region of the Sinkiang, I think, judging by what my mother was reading."

"Oh, Stein, Hedin and so forth, of course – I should have guessed." Another pause. "Do you know what Takla Makan means?"

"No idea," said Doug, stretching. "Don't care much either. Just as long as it's where it says it is on the map."

"What does it mean?" pressed Becca.

Mr Rampal didn't answer. His thoughts had moved on. "Travelling is a dangerous activity. You are young and unchaperoned. What if you are beset with dangers? When I read accounts of exploration, the writers are invariably *beset with dangers*."

"We have the Duchess. She'll scare anyone," said Doug.

"She doesn't scare me particularly, I'm sorry to say," said Mr Rampal, looking down at the tiger slumbering on the floor. He gave her a gentle pat.

"We've been sending telegrams to a good friend of ours, a pilot adventurer, asking her to help us," said Becca.

Mr Rampal nodded.

"You won't tell anyone we're off to China?" asked Doug. "You see, we're meant to be in America at Aunt Margaret's…"

"Conspiracy *and* lodgings?"

"You remember Aunt Margaret. She came in here when she was looking after

AUNT MARGARET

Fondly known in MacKenzie circles as "the old bat", she was the devoted elder sister of Fitzroy and Hamish. As children, they ran wild in the Scottish ancestral home inventing elaborate games of global exploration and adventure. An illness contracted in late childhood (Becca records rumours of tuberculosis) prevented travel with her brothers. Her life's ambitions thwarted, she moved to America, where she cultivated a passion for romantic fiction and collecting portrait paintings of Spanish matadors.

A DAMSEL'S KISS DENIED
BY
MISS AUDREY DULARD

*He was an Italian Count in disguise;
she the lowly Neapolitan seamstress.
— But can a damsel's kiss be denied?*

A Damsel's Kiss Denied
*by Miss Audrey Dulard. Published
1918 by The Gauntlet and Lace Glove
Press, San Francisco.* (MA 239.19 MAC)

us, wanting all those diabolical novels."

"This Margaret is the pilot adventurer who is going to help you? She didn't look the type for such, ah, intrepid pursuits."

"No, that's Liberty. Aunt Margaret is the obstinate old bat who was – I mean *is* – our guardian. You must remember her? What was that book she was so hot on, Becca?"

"*A Damsel's Kiss Denied*, by Audrey Dulard."

"That's the one!" laughed Doug. "She made us read a chapter aloud every night after dinner. It was rotten."

"Ah yes." Mr Rampal nodded, a sudden hint of mischief glinting in his eyes. "I remember now. The lady in question was fond of romantic novellas, yes, yes. I still have a few volumes of Dulard waiting to be collected. A woman of limited horizons – Dulard, I mean, not your aunt. If you have your aunt's address I could forward the books?"

Becca looked suspicious. "We left San Francisco quickly. I don't have her address."

Mr Rampal let this lie hang, his expression leaving Becca in no doubt that he didn't believe a word of what she'd just said.

"So, may we stay next week, Mr Rampal?" she asked again.

"We had better ask the boss. Padma?" called out the bookshop owner.

His wife nudged the door open, carrying a traditional

Lucknow breakfast of nihari and naan on a polished mahogany tray.

"Our young guests would like to stay a week. We have no one booked for the rooms?"

Mrs Rampal smiled, and it was clear their accommodation was secure.

"You never told us what Takla Makan means," said Becca.

"There are two translations, meaning roughly the same thing." Mr Rampal broke the naan bread and took a mouthful. "The first is 'the place you enter but never leave'." He leant forward, making the joints in his chair creak. His wise old gaze flicked between Becca and Doug. "The second is one you should consider carefully before leaving the safety of Lucknow. Takla Makan is more generally known as the Desert of Death. Are you sure you still wish to go there?"

Becca's diary: 1st August 1920
The Rampal bookshop, Lucknow

The events surrounding Mother and Father's disappearance are, by degrees, falling into place. How much we've learnt since we were last in Lucknow. And how much now depends on our getting to the Sinkiang.

I've spent the morning going through the material we took from the secret bookcase at The Lodge. Unfortunately, there's almost nothing about the expedition to Sinkiang. No route, no planning notes, nothing to show us where they thought Ur-Can was, or how they were going to get there. What's more, there's no trace of Mother's translation work on the Tembla hieroglyphics. They must have taken the rest of the contents of the shelf with them. It's possible they left so little here in Lucknow because they knew the Guild had been infiltrated by the Coterie.

I believe their hasty departure for the Sinkiang was prompted by discovery of the revived Coterie. I'm more certain than ever that they went to Sinkiang to find Ur-Can. Wherever they are, what Mother and Father can't know is that all four gyrolabes are now found. If the gyrolabes are brought together and Ur-Can is located, the threat to mankind – if all the ancient warnings are to be believed – will be enormous.

I'm excited at the thought of being able to see or even meet the mysterious Russian known as Capulus, but this is tempered by the knowledge that Liberty thought him a dangerous piece of work. Whether he's worse than Pembleton-Crozier is impossible to tell. Capulus isn't a member of the Coterie or the HGS as far as I can work out, and I still don't know how he fits into this puzzle, yet he seems to have access to all the secrets they seek in the deserts of China.

I do hope our telegrams have reached Liberty. Ever since we jumped ship at Shanghai, we've been sending them to all the branches of da Vine Oil, in the hope they will know where she is. Something tells me we're going to need her, and I can't help feeling that the clock is ticking.

Doug sauntered into the bookshop late that afternoon with the satisfying feeling of having spent a lot of money – a large chunk of the proceeds from selling some of the gold bars he'd "rescued" from Sheng-Fat's junk at Wenzi Island. He carefully put his backpack down on the table, and undid the reef knot holding the drawstring.

"You know, sis, it's good to be back in Lucknow. I've missed the old place."

"Did you get what we need?"

"Well, I managed to find a good chronometer. I knocked the price down as it has a cracked face." He lifted the brass clock from his bag, and shook it. "Works fine, and doesn't rattle. Victorian. Solid."

"What about a new compass?"

"It's a hand-bearing compass. Military job. Much more accurate than my pocket version. It has all the degrees marked off, and a proper sighting line. Makes mine look rubbish."

"No sextant?"

"Not much luck there. The man in the shop said he'd ask around for me."

"Good. It'll give you time to read this." Becca handed him a book: *Navigation by Sun and Stars – A Beginner's Guide*. "Mr Rampal doesn't mind you borrowing it as long as you don't mark it. It looks like a complicated process if you ask me. Are you sure you're up to the task?"

"Charlie showed me the basics aboard *Expedient*. I just need to brush up a bit." Doug flicked through the pages filled with a mass of complex exercises, mathematical sums and equations. "What are you going to be doing while I'm learning all this?"

"Reading too. Mr Rampal has lent me all the books he has on the Takla Makan Desert."

"Right. Guess what – I was followed!"

"By Bergstrom?"

"No. By two Indians. I gave them the slip near the Residency. I think they're the same men the Duchess chased at The Lodge last night. Can't be sure, though."

"They didn't follow you here?"

"No. I'm not stupid, sis."

"What were you doing on that side of town anyway?"

"Oh, just meeting some old friends at the Bhul Bhulaiya. We'll need them if we're going to spy on Bergstrom's meeting undetected."

Becca nodded. "Doug, listen, I've been reading that book in the file. The Guild *History and Gazetteer*. It sounds as though there could be Tembla descendants alive today. They may know things the Guild doesn't."

Doug sat down to take off his shoes. "Go on."

Becca read out loud:

"Tembla Hieroglyphic Discoveries.

    In 1690, our illustrious guildsman Ezekiel Zedd claimed to have secretly observed a Tembla burial ritual while staying at

the house of a man named A'mbarr during his expedition to India. The precise details of this ritual are unknown, as Ezekiel died of typhoid in Cairo before he could return to Firenze to report his discoveries to the board.

    What we know of this burial ritual originates from the few sentences Ezekiel penned on his deathbed. He describes 'ancient Tembla secrets being passed upon the lips from generation to generation at a ceremony of elaborate custom'. What these secrets are has been speculated over by Guild historians ever since. Three symbols were illustrated by Ezekiel, although their meaning is unknown. They are reproduced here (fig. 45)."

EZEKIEL ZEDD

A leading light of the HGS's seventeenth-century push to trace Tembla history, Zedd spent most of his life in Italy, where he combined research for the Guild with soldiering for the dukes of Savoy. He left for Asia in late 1689.

Becca showed Doug the three symbols.

CHAPTER XXII
THE TEMBLA CULT—DEATH RITUALS

TEMBLA HIEROGLYPHIC DISCOVERIES

In 1690, our illustrious guildsman Ezekiel Zedd claimed to have secretly observed a Tembla burial ritual while staying at the house of a man named A'mhar during his expedition to India. The precise details of this ritual are unknown, as Ezekiel died of typhoid in Cairo before he could return to Firenze to report his discoveries to the board.

Tembla Death Symbols — *Fig. 45*

What we know of this burial ritual originates from the few sentences Ezekiel penned on his deathbed. He describes 'ancient Tembla secrets being passed upon the lips from generation to generation at a ceremony of elaborate...

EZEKIEL ZEDD'S DRAWINGS OF TEMBLA HIEROGLYPHS

This page of the Guild's History and Gazetteer shows the symbols observed by guildsman Zedd during a Tembla death ceremony in India. Ezekiel ensured that his notes and sketches were forwarded to the Guild's headquarters in Firenze, Italy, as he lay dying of typhoid in Egypt.

"The way they're laid out, it looks as if there's a symbol missing," said Doug quizzically. He reached over and took the book. "Hang on. We've seen these symbols somewhere recently. Chuck me the photo from The Lodge, sis." His eyes darted between the book and the photograph. "Here. Engraved around these hexagonal shapes."

Becca leant in closer and studied the photograph.

"The three symbols are all here but along with ... let's see..." Doug counted. "Twenty-one others. These must be connected somehow. Perhaps it's a code."

"An incomplete code, though." Becca jumped up in frustration. "How are we ever going to understand a word of this, if Mother didn't leave any translation?"

CHAPTER THREE

The monsoon rains have been lashing down all day, making Lucknow atrociously humid. The weather somehow suits my mood. It's taken me a few days to write down my feelings about going home that first night in Lucknow. I felt numb there, angry that Doug and I were forced to break into our own home like criminals.

I went up to my old room, and it was just as I'd left it. I sat for a moment on the bed, gazing around in the half-light. I tried to remember what it had been like when we all lived there, and the safety I must have felt without even knowing it. I couldn't. Too much has happened and too much has changed. All those books on music seemed to belong to another person. I needed some reminder that I was still Rebecca MacKenzie, so I took the first book I could find – Jane Eyre *– and left, closing the door behind me. I wonder if anything can ever be the same again?*

While we're waiting for Bergstrom to meet Pembleton-Crozier and Capulus, we're both preparing ourselves for the expedition to the Sinkiang. A drum sextant was found by the Scientific Instruments shop five days ago. It's a compact model and comes with a leather case and strap ideal for travelling light. Doug immediately set to work exploring its features.

He has applied himself completely to learning from Navigation by Sun and Stars – A Beginner's Guide. *He's been mastering the exercises one at a time, and writing copious notes – Captain*

MacKenzie would be proud. Every noon he's been on the roof terrace above the shop "shooting the sun" to test his new-found knowledge. Initially he placed Lucknow somewhere off the east coast of Africa, but over the week his proficiency has increased, until yesterday lunchtime he managed to locate Lucknow on the right page of the atlas, and at the right longitude and latitude! My confidence grew when he managed to do this again today.

Jane Eyre must wait for happier times; I've been reading all I can about the Takla Makan Desert. The Sinkiang is a vast and mysterious place by the reckoning of all of the explorers who've been there. Myths abound of lost cities buried under the ever shifting sands. Stories of treasure and gold, of death and strange phenomena are common. None have mentioned Ur-Can, however.

The Bhul Bhulaiya[2] was a vast four-floored labyrinth built into the vaulted roof of the hall of the Bara Imambara to the northwest of the city. Doug was fascinated by this enigmatic building and had spent two previous summer holidays studying the architectural mysteries of its interconnecting stairways and endless dingy passages. The design was so complex that his attempts to map it had failed spectacularly.

During that time, he'd become friends with Omar, the eldest son of the Bhul Bhulaiya's head guide. Omar knew the building like the back of his hand, but gave none of its secrets away, though he'd once mentioned a second labyrinth

From Doug's sketchbook. (DMS 7/16)

2 A labyrinth designed to help defend the fort – any enemy foolish enough to enter would quickly become disorientated and lost.

A 1918 souvenir card – the reverse reads (in Doug's handwriting): One of the biggest vaulted galleries in the world, built without a single pillar or girder to hold up the roof. Lethal! (MA 295.73 LUCK)

built below ground that had been shut for safety's sake. Doug had never even been able to locate the entrance to this and Omar wouldn't show him. However, Omar and his five brothers were a friendly bunch and had been pleased to see Doug again when he'd called in on them to ask for help.

On the morning of the meeting, Doug and Becca reached the front gate at first light, where Omar was waiting for them. Becca remembered him immediately.

"Pleased to meet you again," she said, returning his smile.

"Good morning, Miss Rebecca. This way. Yes please. Douglas says you want to keep this visit a secret," said Omar, narrowing his eyes.

"Yes."

"No problem. No problem. There is no better place in India for secrets than the Bhul Bhulaiya. All my brothers work for me. No one will pass through the gates unnoticed. Be assured!"

"I've done these sketches of Pembleton-Crozier," said Doug. "When he shows up, I'd like him followed wherever he goes."

Omar took the drawings. "But this man is here already. He has a friend. See him." He pointed at two men walking through another gate into the next courtyard.

"We're late!" said Becca. "I knew we should've been here earlier."

"The gates only opened five minutes ago. Omar, we must catch up with them, but without them seeing us."

Omar led them through the first courtyard; they took the steps up to the second gateway two at a time using the shadows as cover. The two men were walking quickly towards the labyrinth's arched entrance to the left of the Imambara. Becca grabbed the binoculars from Doug's bag and identified the men as they paused to remove their shoes. "That's Crozier all right … and Bergstrom. They're laughing together. They *must* be in league, Doug."

They waited until the pair had gone into the labyrinth, then raced across the courtyard.

"We have to find somewhere to hide before they reach the gallery. From there they'll have a clear view of all the gateways and courtyards."

"There is plenty of time." Their guide smiled as they too reached the doorway leading to the labyrinth and took off their shoes.

"Give them to Omar," Doug instructed Becca. "He'll hide them."

"These are bad men, Douglas?" asked Omar.

Doug pulled up his lucky socks. "We believe so, yes."

Omar nodded.

"Can you get us to a place where we can watch without them knowing?"

"No problem, no problem. But you must be silent now. Even a whisper can be heard from a great distance in the labyrinth."

They climbed a stone staircase rapidly, turning right through an archway at the forty-fifth step, then entered the labyrinth. Doug felt a shiver of anticipation. They soon reached its first puzzle, a bizarre set of four staircases arranged in a cross, descending to meet each other. Omar stepped down to the centre of this crossroads then ascended to the right, and set off into the darkened heart of the maze.

The tunnels were little broader than a man's shoulders. It was soon dark, but Doug tried to memorize Omar's every change of course. It was impossible. Eventually they turned a left-hand corner into the barrel-vaulted gallery of the complex's cavernous one hundred and sixty foot long central hall.

Omar stopped and pointed to the figures on the other side of the gallery. Bergstrom and Crozier were in a lookout point that was aligned with the two gatehouses outside. Doug focused his binoculars on Crozier, who was skulking about in the shadows looking shifty and nervous. He carried a pine box with him, and an artist's portfolio.

Omar pointed down to the ground floor, where his youngest brother was waving at him.

Crozier and Bergstrom - in league !

From Doug's sketchbook. (DMS 7/19)

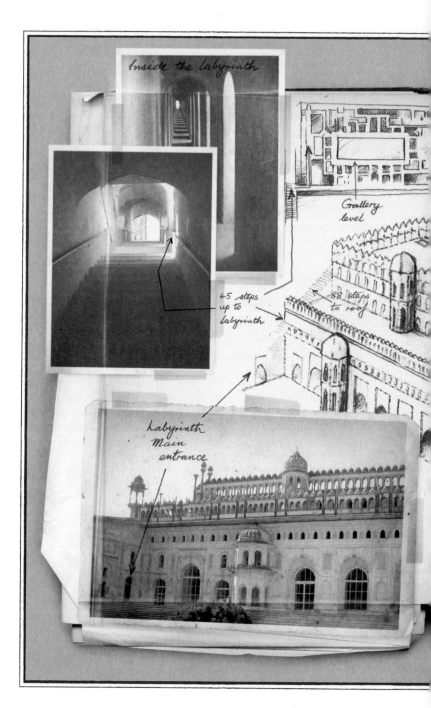

Inside the labyrinth

Gallery
level

45 steps
up to
labyrinth

88 steps
to roof

labyrinth
Main
entrance

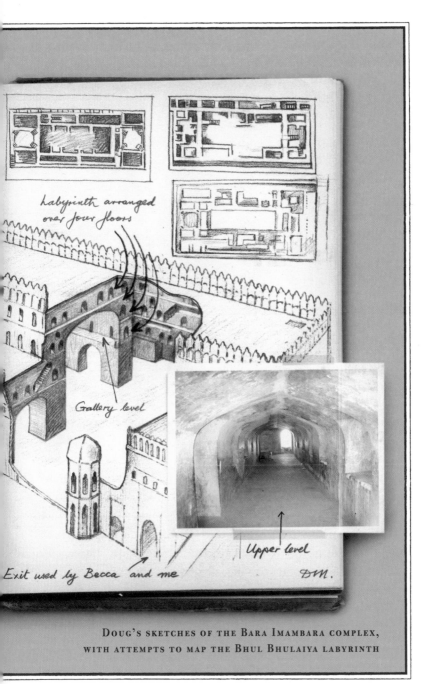

labyrinth arranged
over four floors

Gallery level

Upper level

DM.

Exit used by Becca and me

DOUG'S SKETCHES OF THE BARA IMAMBARA COMPLEX,
WITH ATTEMPTS TO MAP THE BHUL BHULAIYA LABYRINTH

OGEE ARCH

(Pronounced oh-jee.*) A concave arc fitting into a convex arc – introduced to world architecture from the Middle East in the fourteenth century. Also known as the "keel arch" for its resemblance to a ship's keel.*

They drew back into the shadows of one of the doorways and waited. Omar had chosen well. They had an excellent view of the central hall – and their enemies. All they needed now was for the mysterious Capulus to show up.

At ten minutes to seven a man arrived, guided by another of Omar's brothers. They spoke briefly in Urdu, their words echoing upwards, but the new arrival paused at the ogee-arched entrance, uneasy at walking deeper into the building. At first Doug wasn't sure this was Capulus as the man wore local costume and the fluency of his language was impressive. But his cautious entry into the silent hall lent him the air of a skilled hunter, and he kept close to the edge of the room, his eyes searching for Pembleton-Crozier.

The Englishman hung back in the shadows high above him and called out, "Capulus." The word echoed several times. "Capulus … Capulus…" Doug looked across. Pembleton-Crozier was tucked into one of the many archways of the gallery level, cautiously peering down. "Have your guide bring you up to the labyrinth."

"Why should I do that?"

"Because I have come to offer you a gyrolabe."

"Show me." Capulus's Russian accent was barely detectable.

Crozier pulled a gyrolabe from the pine box, and stepped out from his hiding place into the gallery. He held the ancient gravity device high so Capulus could see it.

"Come up. I have a business proposition to put to you."

Becca clamped her hand to Doug's ear and whispered, "What's going on?"

Doug shook his head. He was equally puzzled.

As Capulus made his way to the labyrinth's entrance, Crozier and Bergstrom walked briskly to the end of the gallery and waited. They were now very close to Becca and Doug, who drew back deeper into the shadows. They could hear Crozier chuckling. "I do declare the Russian dog's taking the bait."

As Capulus approached the gallery, Crozier called out, "Walk to the opposite end. I'd like a good distance between us."

"After our last meeting, Pembleton-Crozier, I'm very much in agreement. Why have you brought me here?"

GYROLABES AND ZORIDIUM

The four gyrolabes were ancient gravity devices powered by zoridium.

Zoridium, also known as Daughter of the Sun, is a highly volatile chemical reputedly discovered by Russian scientist Professor Zorid in the early twentieth century. Pembleton-Crozier was known to be mining zoridium ore at a remote island in the Celebes Sea in order to fuel a new wave of zoridium-based science and weaponry.

"Because I've heard you know where Ur-Can is. And Ur-Can is a place I'd very much like to find."

Capulus smirked. "Ha, I know all about your Guild secrets and how much you want Ur-Can. Alas, how slow you are. General Pugachev and I found it, oh, several years ago now."

"I understand General Pugachev is interested in capturing Moscow and booting the Bolsheviks out of Russia. I have

CAPULUS

Guild papers suggest that Capulus's real identity was Viktor Sergeyev, an intelligence officer well connected to the Russian court of Tsar Nicholas II. He escaped Moscow in March 1917, just as the ruling Romanov family were put under house arrest. He was reported to be heading south, driving a truck filled with confiscated material from the original Coterie of St Petersburg.

designs for weapons that would turn his little army into an extremely dangerous force. If he plays ball with me, he could be building snowmen outside the Kremlin by Christmas." Crozier held up the portfolio. "I want to show him some of our zoridium-based special projects. These weapons are unlike anything that has ever graced a battlefield before."

Capulus gave a laugh of derision. "Mm, I've heard something of your Coterie's scientific antics. But you're too late, Crozier. We are on the verge of a military enterprise that will make your weapons seem laughable by comparison."

"Really?" Crozier was intrigued. "Then I'm sure we can be of use to you, Capulus."

The Russian shook his head. "No, no. We don't want you or the Coterie of St Petersburg interfering in our plans."

"Very well, old boy, then I'll take this away again," said Crozier calmly, stooping to put the gyrolabe back in its box.

Capulus held up his hands. "Let's not be so hasty, Crozier. Very well, the gyrolabe will buy you a meeting with my master, General Pugachev; then it's up to him whether he reveals to you the location of Ur-Can. Is the gyrolabe charged with Daughter of the Sun?"

Crozier smiled. "I'm generous, Capulus, but not that generous. Shall we try a walking exchange? I'll leave my presents at this end of the gallery, then we'll walk round and swap ends in plain sight. We'll always have the width of the room between us."

"I shall telegraph ahead to the general," said Capulus, taking a pencil and notepad from his pocket and writing something down. "Go to Korla and find this man. He will guide you to Pugachev."

Capulus placed his note on the floor, his eyes never leaving Crozier.

"I shall walk clockwise with my friend Bergstrom. You do the same," said Crozier, putting the gyrolabe on the gallery floor with the portfolio of arms designs.

Bergstrom and Crozier began to pace away.

The gyrolabe was less than thirty feet from Becca and Doug, glinting in the gloom, unattended and irresistible. Becca bounded out of the recess and grabbed it, then sprinted back into the labyrinth.

From Doug's sketchbook: Becca grabs the gyrolabe. (DMS 7/26)

"This way!" shouted Doug as Crozier spotted them.

"Those infernal children!"

"A trick – I knew it!" Capulus called out.

"Those two are nothing to do with me."

Becca and Doug ran as fast as they could through the arch and back into the tunnels, with Omar following.

"Which way, Omar?"

"Left, left. Down the steps."

Doug tripped, but he didn't slow as he crashed round the corners. He followed Becca blindly, praying he wouldn't lose her. To his horror, she ignored Omar's instructions and led

them back to the gallery level, where Omar's brother was standing looking confused, holding Capulus's note. Becca grabbed it and stuffed it in her pocket.

"Omar! Get us out of here."

Omar pushed past. "Right, left, right, left..." he called out as he ran.

They rounded the corner at a sprint and reached a crossroad of tunnels, just discernible in the gloom. Omar turned right, and ran into a shadowy figure leaning against the wall and out of breath.

In the darkness Doug tripped over Omar and landed on his side; Becca, still grasping the gyrolabe, managed to slow

From Doug's sketchbook:
The dark figure in the
tunnel. (DMS 7/27)

enough that she didn't get entangled. She dragged Doug up, fearing they had bumped into Capulus or, worse, Crozier.

When the figure spoke, she knew it was neither.

"Wait. Are you Rebecca and Douglas MacKenzie?" Bergstrom whispered.

"What's it to you?" asked Becca.

"Shh! I am a friend of your parents, Hamish and Elena. You have to get the gyrolabe away. I'll hold Capulus and Crozier off. When it's safe, get out of here and meet me at the Residency."

They heard footsteps running towards them. They were trapped.

"Quick, hide round this corner."

Something in Bergstrom's voice convinced Becca that he was on their side. She shoved Doug and Omar forward into the dark passageway.

"Julius?" asked Bergstrom. "Is that you?"

"Of course it is. Have you seen those MacKenzie brats? I want my gyrolabe back."

"They just ran past; I couldn't stop them. Straight ahead. We mustn't let them get away."

As the two men moved off, Doug wiped the sweat from his face and let out a long breath.

They waited perhaps a minute, the distant sound of birds and traffic filtering through to them over the roar of their beating hearts. Crozier had been less than six feet from them. If it hadn't have been for Bergstrom, they would have been discovered.

"This way," said Omar in a steady voice.

"We may have shaken them off, but they could be waiting for us outside."

"Omar, there must be other ways out of here," pleaded Becca.

"Yes, yes. But not for tourists."

"We're not tourists!"

Omar hesitated for a moment, then nodded. "Very well. I will lead the way."

He moved quickly. At first Doug thought he'd be able to keep track of the route, but he soon became completely disorientated. After five minutes bumping through the maze, they reached what seemed to be a gloomy dead end.

"You must never try to look for this place," said Omar, still in a whisper. "You promise?"

The MacKenzies nodded. Their guide crouched down and ran his hand along the wall, pushing open a small door that had been painted to look like a stone.

"Down here," ordered Omar. "Watch your heads, please. Very dark."

Once the secret door was shut they stopped to catch their breath. They were at the top of a narrow spiral staircase. Doug let out a laugh. Becca grinned back at him – they had a gyrolabe, and now they'd get away.

Omar forged ahead into the darkness. They descended at speed down well-worn steps. At what Doug judged to be about ground level the staircase stopped at a landing. Two passages led off in different directions.

"This way. We go right. The door here leads to the courtyard."

"Where does the left go?" asked Doug.

"Not even I have been down there. It is the entrance to the second labyrinth."

CHAPTER FOUR

The sunlight seemed intensely bright after the gloom of the tunnels. Doug cautiously peered out at the courtyard. He could see Pembleton-Crozier and Bergstrom arguing furiously at the entrance to the labyrinth at the other end of the building's long facade.

"We'll have to make a run for it," he whispered. "Once we're through the front gate we can split up and meet back at the bookshop."

"I'm going to the Residency," said Becca. "I want to speak to Bergstrom. Find out what he knows."

"Let's worry about that once we've got away."

"If we're running, we need to travel light. Omar, can you look after this." Becca handed him the gyrolabe. "Please guard it with your life, and take it to the Rampal bookshop this afternoon when everything is quiet."

"Yes. No problem. No problem."

"Thank you for all your help, Omar. And thank your brothers for us."

Doug quickly paid Omar double what had been agreed, then opened the door wide, set off down the steps and broke into a sprint. Becca followed. It didn't take long for Crozier to catch on. He gave chase, Bergstrom following more slowly behind. Becca gritted her teeth and ran as hard as she could, her bare feet slapping the rough stone of the courtyard.

They made it to the first gateway with a good lead on their old adversary, but more steps slowed them as they descended to the next courtyard. They hurdled a low hedge and skirted the edge of an ornamental pool. Ahead was the main three-arched gateway and the street outside, already busy with traders selling fruit and produce from handcarts.

Doug suddenly found himself hitting the ground hard; Capulus had come from nowhere and stuck his foot out to trip him. Becca swerved, then stopped short: Pembleton-Crozier's wife, Lucretia, was sitting at the wheel of a green Rolls-Royce waiting outside the gate with its engine running.

Becca veered away as Crozier and Bergstrom raced towards her shouting, "Get the gyrolabe!" Lucretia drew a pistol and aimed it at Capulus, who ran for a truck parked on the other side of the road. Doug, recovering, rolled away and jumped up. Crozier and Bergstrom came after him, but he ducked away, grabbing his sister's shoulder and making for cover behind one of the carts.

Capulus started shouting orders at the waiting truck. Six armed Indians who'd been hiding in the cargo area flung back the blue tarpaulin and gave Capulus covering fire with their rifles. Their aim was as confused as the situation, some targeting Bergstrom and Crozier, the others aiming for Lucretia, who revved the engine and shouted for her husband to get in. Bergstrom reached out to grab the car door, but was struck by a bullet and crumpled silently to the ground.

"Leave him!" ordered Lucretia.

"The MacKenzies, they've got the gyrolabe," gasped Crozier, flattening himself on the back seat.

"They weren't carrying anything," snapped Lucretia. "We must leave. We're outnumbered."

Shots from Capulus's men slammed into the Rolls. Lucretia planted her foot on the accelerator, spun the wheel,

From Doug's sketchbook: The shoot-out. (DMS 7/31)

and sped away in a cloud of dust. The truck roared off in pursuit. Doug peered out from behind the handcart as the dust eddied and settled. Bergstrom lay slumped in the road clutching his side, a patch of blood spreading on his waistcoat. Becca and Doug crept closer.

"I'm all right. Is the gyrolabe safe?"

"Yes."

"Clever. Clever like your parents. Quickly now. We must get away before the authorities arrive."

Even as Bergstrom spoke, Doug heard the distant sound of

GUN BATTLE IN LUCKNOW STREET

•

WITNESSES SOUGHT BY POLICE

•

Lucknow police are urgently investigating a street battle near the city's Roomi Gate yesterday. Witnesses report gun fire between a Rolls-Royce motor car and a goods vehicle. A third car, also believed to be involved, was seen driving an injured man away from the scene at high speed.

The police remain utterly mystified by the unusual incident, but have recovered several spent cartridge cases and identified traces of blood. Witnesses with any further information are requested to contact the police forthwith.

•

INDIAN METALS AND

Cutting from the 8th August 1920 edition of the Lucknow Times. (MA 295.53 LUCK)

a police whistle. From nowhere, Bergstrom's car pulled up, driven by Bhanu.

"Master Douglas? Miss Rebecca?" exclaimed Bhanu, his jaw dropping. "What are you doing here? But it's good to see you."

"Bhanu, it's good to see you too. But can you get us to a hospital?" said Becca.

"No," gasped Bergstrom. "Not a hospital. Not to The Lodge, either. Crozier is sure to go there. Where are you staying?"

"At the Rampal book-shop."

"Of course, of course, an excellent choice." He smiled weakly at them. "Then let us take refuge in learning."

Mrs Rampal cleaned the wound, but she wanted to call a doctor.

"You have brought trouble to my shop," Mr Rampal chided. "The police are sure to come here. Gun battles? Bullet wounds? I am a peaceful man, a man of learning!"

"Mr Rampal, my apologies, but I could think of nowhere

safer," wheezed Bergstrom. "And now I must ask a further favour. I need to speak to Rebecca and Douglas in private. This is of the utmost importance. We will be leaving your shop within the hour, I assure you."

"I will oblige if you allow me to send for a doctor," insisted Mr Rampal.

"Please call this man," replied Bergstrom, writing a name and number down in his notebook with a shaky hand and tearing out the page. "He will send someone immediately."

"Oh," said the bookseller, clearly impressed. "But he is not a doctor."

"He has his own doctor. He will also smooth over any problems you may have with the authorities."

"Very well, very well. Mrs Rampal…"

The bookshop owner and his wife left, closing the door behind them.

"There is much to tell you, but I must be quick," said Bergstrom. "Pembleton-Crozier really does want to make a deal with Pugachev. You've thwarted his plans."

"But who *are* you? Why have you helped us? Are you Coterie or Guild?"

"So many questions. I've been living at your old house; I came to Lucknow after your parents disappeared."

"We know. We read one of your messages when we were aboard the *Expedient*," said Doug.

"You've sailed on the *Expedient*?" asked Bergstrom in surprise.

"Of course – we were there when the captain attacked Wenzi Island,"[3] said Becca, slightly piqued.

Bergstrom mopped his brow with his bloodied handkerchief. "Quite remarkable. Then you must know that I saved the *Expedient* from certain dis—" He winced. "Disaster."

3 The Battle of Wenzi Island, as documented in Book I.

"I don't remember you saving us from anything," said Becca indignantly.

"Yeah, we saved ourselves more like," added Doug.

"No, no, don't you see? I invented that message from the board authorizing the attack on Wenzi Island, and I paid for the *Expedient*'s fuel in Shanghai out of my own pocket. If I had asked for authorization from Firenze, then Operation Red Jericho would have been doomed from the outset. The Coterie's penetration of the HGS is so comprehensive that any attack authorized by the board would have been known to them. They would have warned Crozier and Sheng-Fat. Did Sheng-Fat know of the attack?"

"No ... no, he didn't," Becca admitted.

Bergstrom nodded. "I, like your parents and Captain MacKenzie, am one of the few remaining true members of the Guild. We are just a handful now."

"So how come you're so friendly with Crozier?"

"The Coterie think I work for them. I am a fox dressed as a hound, or is that a wolf in sheep's clothing? I'm never too sure." He chuckled and brought himself up short with pain.

"You need to see a doctor," said Doug.

"No. We must leave this shop immediately. It is not safe here. There is one man who can help us, and I'm certain he will come to my aid."

The shop's doorbell chimed.

"Your guardian angel travels fast," remarked Becca suspiciously.

There was the sound of muffled voices.

"Is it the police?"

After a few moments, there was a knock on the door. Becca and Doug froze, unsure if they should make a run for it. Then the door flew open to reveal a dishevelled, dark-haired woman in a battered flying jacket.

"Liberty!" chorused Becca and Doug. They suddenly felt much, much safer.

"Not Bergstrom's guardian angel, but ours," laughed Becca.

Liberty walked over to Bergstrom and made a cursory inspection of his wound, then turned to look at her old friends, shaking her head. "Well, Douglas and Rebecca MacKenzie, I see y'all have

From Doug's sketchbook. (DMS 7/38)

started without me. Trouble sticks to you two like flies to a windshield, don't it just? Crozier do this?"

"Lucretia," said Doug.

"It was gonna be one or the other. They both in town?"

"Yes. Capulus too."

"A threesome. My. They all owe me, every single darn one of them." She turned back to Bergstrom. "Liberty da Vine, pleased to make your acquaintance. You need to see a quack."

"Everything is in hand," he said, somewhat taken aback.

"You got our telegrams, then," said Doug.

"Yep, and if y'all send me one more of those blasted wires,

I'll wring your necks with it. What's all this guff about an expedition to China? You two should be at school. Where's the skipper? I bet he don't know you're here."

"Well, um..." Doug mumbled.

"You." She wagged her finger at Bergstrom. "Ten to one you're in this Honourable Guild of Screwballs."

Bergstrom looked too dazed to answer.

"Yeah, you look the type. Turnin' into a hobby of mine, spottin' y'all. Just like Crozier and that crazy captain. See, I ain't too disposed to gettin' involved in any more of their capers. I've been locked up with a bunch of singin' loonies, had a finger chopped off by a Chinese pirate, been shot by one Limey lunatic and lost my plane to another, and been darn near seared alive by a volcano – y'all want me to go on?

"Darn nerve of you, Becca and Doug, askin' me along for another helpin'. Like I haven't had enough. Like *you* haven't had enough! Please, for the love of all things good, it's time to go back to America and your Aunt Margaret, and start actin' your age. You're still children! Why don't y'all go back to ridin' bicycles or whatever kids do these days?"

"Bicycles?" Doug thought back over everything that had happened in the last few months. Bicycles seemed a bit dull in comparison. "We're going to China to find our parents. I'm not sure we can get there on bicycles. We need a pilot, and you're the best there is, Liberty."

"Don't y'all start on the flattery, Douglas MacKenzie. I've come to take you to America. See, I've been in touch with your aunt, and I've made her a promise. Here, read this." She pulled a letter from her flying jacket.

The letter read like a terrible betrayal. Their old friend Liberty had sold them down the river.

LETTER FROM AUNT
MARGARET TO
LIBERTY AND ORDER
OF SERVICE FROM
DOUG AND BECCA'S
"MEMORIAL" IN
SAN FRANCISCO

Fairlawns Hou
Clipper Stre
San Francisc

Dear Miss Da Vine,   July 2 1920

Thank you for taking the time to find me here in San Francisco. I could not believe my eyes when I saw the message sent to me by Rebecca and Douglas. I'd quite given them up for dead, believing them lost overboard from the steamship "Andromeda". Your suggestion that you should go to India to locate my errant neice and nephew and repatriate them to my ... has occupied me Constantly ...

... unannounced ... is true I did ... and Rebecca as ... much agree to your ... ternative. ... Some information ... ecided I shall ... e paints, has ... all else ... ow, whom ... , that he is ...

Currently undertaking a search of the Chinese deserts with members of his crew and what he describes as his "Shanghai allies", with the aim of finding Douglas and Rebecca's parents. I can only hope he discovers Hannah and Elena alive, for all our sakes.

I enclose a cheque for Areson $1,500, on account, to cover your costs and expenditure. I must warn you from the off that I shall not stand for any unnecessary extravagance; anything I deem inappropriate will be deducted immediately, without further discussion. We shall remain in touch through the offices of Da Vine Oil as dis...

Yours Sincerely,

Margaret Mackenzie

🜨

MEMORIAL SERVICE
FOR

REBECCA AND DOUGLAS
MACKENZIE

"But how did you find her?" asked Doug.

"There aren't so many Margaret MacKenzies in San Francisco. Poor ol' goat had given up on you for dead. She was worried half to death when the shipping company listed you as missin', presumed drowned."

"We can't go back to her. We so nearly know where our parents are. We can't give up now, Liberty!" pleaded Becca.

"Aunt Marge says the captain's gone to look for them. He's mountin' his own rescue mission to the Sinkiang. Hand-picked some of his crew and set off with those Sujing Quantou guys. Y'all think they need two kids along for the ride?"

There was another knock on the front door. Mr Rampal, in a state of alarm, rushed in and spoke to Bergstrom. "A car has arrived. We must get you into it immediately."

A very well-tailored Indian entered the room, flanked by four others in matching uniforms.

"Get me up to speed here," said Liberty. "Are these the good guys?"

"Yes," said Bergstrom. "They come from the man who will help us."

Without a word they carried Bergstrom to a waiting car. Liberty, Doug and Becca jumped into Bergstrom's own car, with Bhanu at the wheel, and followed them out of Lucknow at top speed.

Chapter Five

Maharaja Singh, the MacKenzies' old landlord, was Bergstrom's influential friend; Becca had recognized the blue silk livery of his staff immediately. They had visited his palace for a sumptuous summer party when they were younger. Now they drove up the dusty road to its vast fortified gatehouse at breakneck speed.

As soon as the cars stopped, the four assistants carefully lifted Bergstrom onto a stretcher and carried him inside to the waiting doctor.

The maharaja's butler, a dapper Englishman wearing a tailored black suit and white gloves, stepped up to Bhanu's car and opened the passenger door with a flourish.

"Good day, sir, madams. My name is Snave." His manner was ludicrously formal. "Would you care to follow me?"

This seemed to tickle Liberty no end. "What *is* this place? The Lucknow Ritz?"

The butler swooped low in a bow. "This is India,

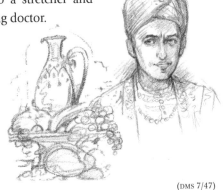

(DMS 7/47)

Maharaja Singh

His somewhat eccentric dawn exercise regime included an hour of Scottish folk dancing or "reeling". For his annual trip to his tailor in Savile Row, London, he travelled with a retinue of 150 servants, each entrusted with a single item of his fabulously eclectic wardrobe. He was a particular favourite in Parisian society, where he was known for his encyclopedic knowledge of European aristocracy.

madam, and India is always full of surprises, don't you find? This is no common hotel, nor guest house either. With respect, I cordially welcome you and your companions to the royal fortress Ari."

Becca regarded him dubiously and stepped down from the car.

"Are you for real?" exclaimed Liberty, summing up Becca's thoughts exactly.

Snave arched his right eyebrow theatrically, then turned and led them through the main gateway into a large elegant courtyard. Ahead lay a stone pavilion set within a garden of flowers, topiary hedges and ornamental ponds, which rippled with the soothing sounds of birdsong and fountains. An ornate staircase led up to the pavilion, a long single-storey building with arcades of marbled columns inlaid with semi-precious stones which glinted opulently in the sunlight. Vivid silks blew scarlet and azure in the morning breeze, shading the maharaja as he reclined on a couch piled high with cushions, his nose deep in a copy of the *Ramayana* of Valmiki.[4]

"Ah, good morning," he called. "Good morning to you all. Rebecca and Douglas I know, but…"

"Liberty da Vine. I'm their … chaperone."

"You are most welcome. And how is our patient?"

SNAVE

Convicted for diamond smuggling in 1912, Obadiah Arthur Snake [sic], was offered a reprieve by enlisting in the British Army to fight in the First World War (1914–18). Records show that in 1915 he was discharged on medical grounds after being wounded at the Battle of Neuve Chapelle, France. His war experiences reformed him, and in 1916 he changed his name to Snave and journeyed to India to begin a new life.

4 Thought to be the oldest written form of the ancient Sanskrit epic the *Ramayana*, which tells the myth of Rama, whose wife is abducted by the demon king Ravana.

From Doug's sketchbook: The maharaja's palace. (DMS 7/45)

"Bleedin'," said Liberty bluntly. "I hope your quack knows his business."

"Oh, Dr Theobald is top-notch, top-notch. Forgive me for not meeting you at the gates, but I do so quail at the sight of blood," confided the maharaja.

"Yeah, well, we're not stayin' long. Just stopped by to drop off Bergstrom, then we're bound for America."

Becca pulled a face.

"America? How … interesting. You'll stay for breakfast first. Tell me, Rebecca and Douglas, how are you? Such terrible news about your parents. Simply unthinkable to be lost in the Sinkiang."

"We were going to mount a rescue expedition to find them, but our plans seem to have been changed." Becca scowled at Liberty.

"Indeed? Mr Bergstrom didn't mention that you were back

in the country. How did you end up caring for him this morning?" enquired the maharaja.

"We bumped into him at the Bhul Bhulaiya," answered Doug with a sniff.

"You were there?"

"Yes, we..." Becca thought quickly. "We found out about a meeting he was attending, and thought we should go. We believe Capulus – the man he was meeting – may know something about our parents' expedition."

The maharaja smiled enigmatically. "You would like to speak to Capulus?"

Becca's face lit up. "Very much."

"Just like your mother – impetuous in the pursuit of answers." The maharaja caught Liberty's angry glare. "Alas, Capulus is a dangerous fellow, and you are bound for America, so there is little chance of it. Come – all this talking is making me hungry. Let us have some breakfast."

"So, you observed the Bhul Bhulaiya meeting?" said the maharaja, picking a grape from the gilt fruit platter.

"Yes, what of it?" replied Becca.

The maharaja casually spat a seed into a bowl beside him. "I believe Pembleton-Crozier was offering a gyrolabe and some weapon designs in exchange for the location of Ur-Can."

"How do you know that?"

"Bergstrom informed me last week."

Doug, also munching grapes, took his cue from the maharaja and spat a seed towards a bird bath just outside the pavilion. It was a perfect lob shot that hit with alarming accuracy, sending ornamental doves fluttering and cooing into the sky.

Becca absent-mindedly slapped her brother's arm, her thoughts on The Lodge and how their parents had always been friends with the maharaja. "Are you a member of the Guild as well?"

The maharaja chuckled. "Let's just say I'm a *friend* of the Guild. Your father has asked me to join on a number of occasions, but I'm not a scientist, or even much of an explorer. I like to read; I like to live well. No, instead I help the Guild when I can. Loan them houses, help arrange meetings…"

"What do you mean?" Becca's tone was sharp.

"Bergstrom was forced by Pembleton-Crozier to broker the Capulus meeting—"

"And you know Capulus?" Becca interrupted.

The maharaja nodded. "Capulus wanted me to help him once. I didn't like his manner much, so I sent him packing. Bergstrom, however, works as a double agent. The Coterie – you've heard of them? – believe he works for them, but his allegiance is to the few remaining true HGS members: a dangerous position that sometimes necessitates dangerous decisions. Bergstrom is a brave man. If he hadn't gone along with the meeting today, Pembleton-Crozier would have been suspicious. I made contact with Capulus, and together Bergstrom and I set up the rendezvous. I suspected all along that Julius was after the location of Ur-Can. What did Capulus tell him, by the way?"

Becca remembered the note in her pocket. "He wrote down a name. Here it is," she said, finding the piece of paper. "Someone called Dante. He told Crozier to find this man in Korla, and that he would guide him to Pugachev."

The maharaja frowned. "Then the crisis is deepening.

My friend Bergstrom told me that Crozier has discovered the southern gyrolabe."

"Actually," said Doug, "*we* found it. Crozier stole it from us. Up until this morning, he had two of the gyrolabes. We managed to grab the eastern one in the labyrinth. But he must have the southern one stashed away somewhere."

"Do you have the eastern gyrolabe with you?"

"No," said Becca suspiciously. "It's in safe hands. In Lucknow."

The maharaja rubbed his chin anxiously.

Doug sniffed hard. "Our uncle, Captain MacKenzie, told us that the location of Ur-Can is encoded in cipher on the gyrolabes. The HGS has detailed drawings of all four gyrolabes apart from the southern one, so by now Pembleton-Crozier and the Coterie must surely know where Ur-Can is."

The maharaja replied distractedly, "Well, in theory, yes. If Pembleton-Crozier has the fourth gyrolabe, then he can find Ur-Can."

"So why hasn't he?" asked Becca.

"You assume Crozier and the Coterie can read the Tembla symbols of the cipher. But in that respect we are safe. There is only one – perhaps two – alive who can read it."

"Who?"

"My uncle. And your mother. The Guild have long known that I'm one of the few living descendants of the priestly sect from whom Alexander the Great's men took the gyrolabes."

"So you're Tembla?" asked Becca excitedly. Doug's eyebrows shot up at the directness of the question, but Becca held the maharaja's gaze.

"Yes, indeed," answered the maharaja solemnly. "A few of us remain who can claim this direct descent."

"That's how you know so much," remarked Doug.

"I know very little, to be truthful. It is my uncle who knows the most. I never took much interest in it all when I was young. To me it was just a lot of old family stories which I never believed could be true – until Capulus contacted your mother offering her the hieroglyphics from Ur-Can. That moment was a revelation; it jolted me from my complacency." He seemed to be chiding himself, angry at his previous lack of conviction. "Here was proof. From that moment I helped your dear mother as best I could, and began to develop a passion for the subject I'd scoffed at for far too long."

"So you understand the Tembla language as well?"

The maharaja grimaced. "Unfortunately no, Douglas. I have some copies of Tembla hieroglyphics in my library. They are connected to one of your ancestors, a Duncan MacKenzie. Do you know of him?"

Doug thought back to the headless skeletons on South Island. "We've met. Or rather, we found his skeleton."

The maharaja raised an eyebrow. "What an extraordinary life you two lead. Back in … let's see, yes … 1721, Duncan sought the help of one of my Tembla forebears named A'mbarr and showed him some hieroglyphs and what he thought were Ha-Mi transla-tions of them. Duncan had found them at a place called Ayor-Nor in what is now known as Sinkiang, China."

"There was a battle there in the Ha-Mi Wars," said Doug, leaning closer.

"A'mbarr confirmed they were Ha-Mi translations of Tembla hieroglyphics,

An engraving of A'mbarr.

(MA 239.88 MAC)

copied from the walls of Ur-Can. He was much perturbed by this discovery. He and Duncan went in search of the Tembla mines mentioned in the translation and were never seen again. A'mbarr left the hieroglyphics in the library here.

"Now your mother enters the story. She explained to me how she had been sold photographs of Tembla symbols by a Russian called Capulus. At first she doubted they were genuine, and asked my opinion. I searched our library and was shocked to find that some of Capulus's hieroglyphs were exactly the same as those Duncan had discovered. What's more, there was a half-page of translation in Duncan's handwriting. From this your mother was able to slowly build her understanding of the Tembla language. It was her Rosetta Stone moment."

Becca rummaged in her bag and pulled out the grainy photograph of the Ur-Can hieroglyphs. "Have you seen this before?"

The maharaja looked at it and shook his head. "No. Not this one. Only my uncle would know how to read this. But he's always been suspicious of the Guild's motives. I'm afraid he will not help…" His words trailed off as he examined the photograph.

Doug was confused. "Didn't your uncle help Mother with the translations?"

"No. What's more, he is angry with me for assisting her. However, he may weaken when he hears the southern gyrolabe has been discovered."

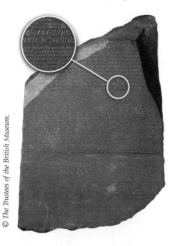

THE ROSETTA STONE

Discovered in 1799 at Rosetta, Egypt: an ancient Egyptian stele dating from 196 BC carved with text in both Egyptian hieroglyphics and classical Greek. This facilitated a breakthrough in the translation of ancient hieroglyphics.

The maharaja took a sip of lassi and ran an elegant hand through his hair. His expression was that of a man reluctantly accepting a challenge. "Rebecca. Douglas. You must understand this. We suddenly find ourselves holding the fate of the world in our hands. We must go to Varanasi and speak to my uncle. Perhaps he will see reason and help us."

"Wait up, Raj," said Liberty. "We're headin' for Calcutta and a boat home."

"If you are bound for Calcutta, then Varanasi is en route. I shall launch an expedition of my own to Sinkiang; I have a contact who will help. I shall telegraph him immediately and fly to Sinkiang after we have spoken with my uncle."

"Fly to Sinkiang? I'd sure like to see you try," chuckled Liberty. "The Himalayas are slap bang in the way."

"Do not concern yourself, Miss Liberty. I think your plan to return these young MacKenzies to America is an admirable one. You can take my train on to Calcutta, where tickets will be waiting for you aboard the finest ship sailing for America."

"Good," said Liberty. "I'm glad we're singin' from the same hymn sheet."

"Rebecca. Douglas. Will you allow me to see the gyrolabe you captured today?"

Becca saw an opportunity. "Of course, Maharaja. On one condition…"

"Aha, a bargain?"

"Yes. You must tell us about the Tembla. Who they were and how they came to be so clever, and yet so old."

The maharaja laughed his assent. "You are so like your mother… Snave?"

"Sir?"

"How is the patient?"

"Resting, sir. The wound is dressed. The bleeding has stopped, and the doctor is satisfied that Mr Bergstrom is not in danger."

"Excellent. We shall visit him, now the blood has been cleaned off. And, Snave – telephone the railway station and have my train prepared for Varanasi. We travel east tonight."

"We came to say goodbye, Mr Bergstrom. Are you feeling any better?" asked Becca.

"Not better, perhaps, but more comfortable."

"I must ask you a question." She showed him the hieroglyph photograph. "Have you seen this before?"

Bergstrom nodded. "I was aware of the photograph, if not its meaning. This triggered the expedition to Sinkiang. Your mother and father wrote to me about it."

Doug butted in. "The maharaja plans to show this and the gyrolabe to his uncle in Varanasi. Do we let him?"

"You must. Time is running out. Capulus and Pugachev have located Ur-Can, and Crozier is on their trail. Now the Guild is compromised, the maharaja and Captain MacKenzie are the only people who have a chance of stopping them."

"Did our parents tell you their plans for the expedition?" asked Becca.

"Pass me my jacket," said Bergstrom.

Doug did as he asked. Bergstrom pulled out his wallet and extracted a thin piece of paper. "Here. Read this. It's the last message I received from them."

Becca took the paper and read aloud:

"GUILD INFILTRATED BY REVIVED COTERIE OF ST P. TRUST ONLY SELF, FITZROY MACKENZIE, BORELLI AND VANVORT. OUR TRANSLATIONS INDICATE UR-CAN LOCATED AT KAREZ, DAOTANG. WE GO TO KORLA TO FIND DANTE, WHO WILL ARRANGE MEETING WITH GENERAL PUGACHEV. WE BELIEVE PUGACHEV IS PLUNDERING UR-CAN AND CAPULUS SELLING US THE EVIDENCE: WHY? WE MUST SECURE UR-CAN FOR HGS. WE STOP EN ROUTE TO SEEK AID OF WESTERN SUJING QUANTOU. EXPEDITION DEPARTURE IMMINENT."

"If you know all this, why on earth didn't you send out a search party?" Becca's voice was shrill.

Bergstrom sighed. "I couldn't do it on my own. Fitzroy was away, and if I'd told the Guild, I would've effectively told the Coterie as well. It was safer for your parents if I did nothing." He wheezed. "Now events have overtaken us. As soon as you've seen the maharaja's uncle you must clear out of India."

He clutched Doug's arm. "It isn't safe here. I believe Capulus and Pugachev to be even more ruthless than our friend Crozier. Capulus will stop at nothing to get the gyrolabe now he knows it's available. I don't know what Pugachev's up to in the desert, but I do know the man is insane in his pursuit of power."

Bergstrom coughed, his face contorting with pain. "Go to America with Liberty. I know you want to find your parents, but you must get out of India with the gyrolabe before Capulus or Crozier

BERGSTROM

Carl Bergstrom, astronomer and physicist, was an Australian by birth. He specialized in researching the strange gravitational properties of zoridium.

finds you. Once you get to America, hide the gyrolabe somewhere safe – it's the best thing you can do for your parents."

"But why would the maharaja launch a rescue mission
now, and not when they went missing?" demanded Becca.

"It is not for your parents that he goes to China. It is to
save the secret of Ur-Can."

Becca's diary: 7th August 1920

*How can Bergstrom have held that message from our parents and
done nothing with it? For all this time? I'm furious with the man,
and the skewed logic of the Guild, working for this "greater good"
while our parents languish in some dark corner of the desert! And
Liberty's just as bad – how can we go back to America now? I've
told Doug that we must give her the slip as soon as we can.*

*We were driven back to the bookshop to collect our things.
I returned all the books I'd borrowed from Mr Rampal, who was
frosty after this morning's events – he wagged a finger at me and
said, "Mr Bergstrom made a bloody mess on my kitchen table." I
apologized and paid the rent we owed, offering him a little more for
the trouble we'd caused. He handed me a hessian sack containing
the gyrolabe and our shoes that had been delivered by Omar. Mr R
also pushed a book into my hands, explaining that it was a translation my mother had ordered before her departure for Sinkiang:*
Imperial Expeditions in Sinkiang. *I offered to pay, but he made
a present of it to me, I think by way of a peace offering. I hope one
day, when all this is over, I'll be able to return it to him in person.*

CHAPTER SIX

"The steam locomotive was built in 1908 for my father at the Nolan foundry in Glasgow," enthused the maharaja as he led his guests through the ticket hall of Lucknow Junction Station. A broad path opened in the throng filling the hall as the Duchess stalked ahead. Many people screamed and fled at the sight of the tiger but the maharaja was not put off by the commotion. "How I love this building – it is like a temple to progress!" he expounded, gesturing upwards at the many cupolas. "Wait until you see my train: eight carriages long, each handcrafted by the finest European artisans!"

His extraordinary palace on wheels lay waiting at platform nine, the engine sending a plume of smoke into the orange dusk of the dying day.

"Is it an 060?" asked Doug, craning to see the driving wheels of the locomotive.

"Never mind that," hissed Becca. "Look for a way off this thing."

All of the windows on the train were tightly shuttered. Each carriage bore the maharaja's coat of arms, painted in vermilion and turquoise, and edged in gold leaf so that it glinted like a jewel. They clambered up polished brass steps and boarded the last carriage, which proved to be the guards' quarters; six men stood to attention as the maharaja opened the door.

He greeted them jovially, then turned to Doug. "If you don't have a ticket, these are the fine fellows you will answer to."

"Ticket? You didn't say anything about a ticket."

"Get a move on, Doug," snapped Becca. "He's joking."

Doug looked at the rack of Lee–Enfield rifles and was glad to hear it.

"This way, ladies and gentlemen," Snave directed with a flamboyant hand gesture. "Guest accommodation towards the front of the train."

Liberty sniggered.

They passed quickly through what appeared to be the maharaja's private carriage. The next door was opened by a servant, and they entered a world of unfettered luxury. The saloon car was dripping with chandeliers and Venetian mirrors and packed with elaborate furniture; overstuffed leather armchairs, couches piled with velvet cushions, and tables covered with European newspapers and cigar boxes gave the carriage the ambience of a gentlemen's club.

"Mahogany panelling throughout, do you see?" continued the maharaja. "And when the train begins to move, a twenty-five-volt dynamo running from the wheels powers these fans hanging from the ceiling."

In the dining car a chef was setting dinner places on a polished table. They walked through into the second section of the coach, which was a well-equipped kitchen.

"Just being in a kitchen makes me hungry," said the maharaja, nibbling at a cucumber sandwich from a silver platter. Doug swiped a couple himself, much to the amusement of his host. "A bit peckish, Douglas?"

"Starving," said Doug, gulping down the minute triangles in a single mouthful.

"We shall dine in an hour," said the maharaja. "Snave will show you to your berths."

The next carriage held the guests' quarters.

"This is your room, Miss Rebecca. Master Douglas, you are next door. Miss da Vine, the one after that."

"When do we reach Varanasi?" asked Becca.

"Oh, the journey is overnight, miss," answered Snave. "We shall be there for breakfast."

Becca pushed the panelled door open, walked straight over to the window and tried to open it. "This doesn't work," she complained, tugging at the handle.

"Don't you go gettin' ideas, now, coz," muttered Liberty.

"All the windows are sealed for security reasons, Miss Rebecca. If you need more ventilation you can pull this lever; it opens an air duct. The airflow is very refreshing once the train is in motion, I assure you."

Doug was intrigued. "Lethal – just like the vents on the *Expedient*."

"The whole thing looks like the *Expedient* to me," said Becca, eyeing the mahogany bed and gleaming brass oil lamps. The Duchess paced in and settled with a yawn, making herself at home. "The Duchess seems to think so too."

"I have taken the liberty of supplying you each with some new attire," explained Snave. "The maharaja is a stickler for manners and cleanliness. If you require any further assistance, please ring this bell."

The engine's steam whistle sounded, and the train

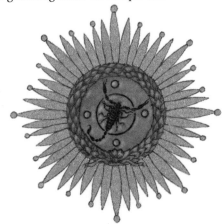

MAHARAJA SINGH'S COAT OF ARMS

The Tembla compass symbols are clearly seen in the inner circle of the coat of arms. The scorpion motif signifies the Tembla descendants' fiercely protective attitude towards their age-old secrets.

moved off. Immediately the ceiling fans began to turn, blowing a refreshing breeze into the carriage.

"See, Becca, no need to open the windows," said Liberty.

Becca looked nonplussed. "Doug – I'll keep the gyrolabe with me, if you don't mind."

"Here, take it. I'm off to see if my berth has a bath."

"No, you're not," she said, pulling him into the cabin and slamming the door in Liberty's face. "There's work to do."

Becca studied the Guild history and *Imperial Expeditions in Sinkiang*, scanning the pages for anything that might be useful. She reread Bergstrom's message again in frustration. Doug was slumped in an easy chair, fiddling with the ventilation lever on the wall, switching it on and off several times to test its efficiency. He then turned his attention to the two fans hanging from the ceiling. These were equipped with individual speed controllers, so he ran the fan positioned over the Duchess up to half-power a couple of times, making the tiger's fur shimmy. She lifted her head and growled languorously.

Then he decided on a complete test, running both fans at full power with the ventilation duct set to OPEN. They sent a blast of air downwards with such ferocity that it almost blew the book out of Becca's hand.

"Doug! Will you... *Please turn them off and help me!*"

Doug left the fans running. He wasn't going to be shouted at.

Becca's face reddened with fury. "You know, sometimes I wonder if you really care."

Doug stared into his sister's eyes with indignation, but

then he saw that beneath her angry veneer she was just fright-ened, lonely, and on a train leaving home. With a pang of recognition, he knew he felt exactly the same.

He cut the power to the fans. The reassuringly regular rhythm of train wheels against track could be heard again. "I can't help you," he said calmly. "There are only two useful books, and you're reading both of them; and there's only so many times I can look at a photograph of symbols I don't understand. I want to have a bath."

Becca stifled a rare sob. She turned and put her head in her hands. "What if they walked into a trap?"

"Mother and Father?"

"What if Capulus or Pugachev engineered the whole thing? Look at this part of the message: WE BELIEVE PUGACHEV IS PLUNDERING UR-CAN AND CAPULUS SELLING US THE EVIDENCE: WHY? WE MUST SECURE UR-CAN FOR HGS...

"Why was Capulus selling the Ur-Can hieroglyphs to Mother? Just for the money? Or because he and General Pugachev wanted to find out the secrets of Ur-Can, and couldn't decipher them on their own? Perhaps he lured them there. He knew they'd go eventually, to find it for the Guild. Capulus said he knew all about the Guild secrets at the Bhul Bhulaiya. Do you remember?"

Doug nodded. "I still don't really understand why Bergstrom did nothing."

"I don't know. I think he feels guilty, though. That's why he gave us the message."

"Can you imagine him in the desert? He's an overweight stargazer. Not exactly an adventurer... Sorry, sis."

"Not your fault Bergstrom did nothing."

"No, I mean for the fans."

Becca smiled and handed Doug the Guild history. "Once you've had a bath, can you copy Zedd's hieroglyphs into your sketchbook? We can show them to the maharaja's uncle; see if he can make any sense of them. Then see if you can find Daotang or Karez on Father's maps."

"I remember your father explaining to me that historians of Europe and America barely teach Indian history," said the maharaja. "But ours is a fascinating legacy. Our traditions remain unchanged and unbroken back to the age before writing—"

The train's brakes slammed on, sending crockery and fine silver cutlery flying, before it screeched to a halt with a judder. Soup slopped onto Doug's dinner jacket. He quickly mopped it up with a napkin and adjusted his bow tie. Becca had washed but hadn't dressed up. Liberty hadn't bothered either, so the two of them looked entirely scruffy in the opulence of the surroundings. The maharaja had ignored this slight on his generosity with good grace when they'd entered the dining car.

Snave appeared. "Cow on the line, sir. Nothing to be concerned about. We didn't strike it."

"Cow?" said Liberty. "Lasso the darn thing and get us movin'."

"Cows are sacred animals, Miss Liberty. To lasso it would cause much offence." The maharaja smiled. "Such incidents are a common occurrence in India."

Becca saw her chance. "And the Tembla?"

"Oh, yes. Our bargain…"

"We've travelled so far, sir, and it would help to know as

much as we can before we sail for America. It's also a pleasant change to find someone willing to talk about this stuff."

"Now, first you must understand that the Tembla are very, very old. When do you think modern man appeared? Hunting and gathering?"

"About ten thousand years ago, isn't it?" sniffed Doug.

"Mm, your western scientists have alighted upon that period. What if I was to say that modern man first appeared *two hundred* thousand years ago?"

Doug winced. Nothing he'd ever read put the age of modern man back that far. "I thought, well, according to Mr Darwin, that we were a little bit primitive two hundred thousand years ago."

"Western science's understanding of mankind's evolution is far from complete, Douglas. The ancient Tembla civilization developed on the site of the Toba, in Sumatra, around seventy-five thousand years ago. Within two thousand years they had developed complex scientific ideas, based on their ability to harness local volcanic resources and coal to create simple steam-powered devices."

"Steam power? That long ago?" said Doug, incredulous.

"Yes! Why not? What is a steam device, after all, except a lid fitted tightly over a cooking pot? You must forget the notion that scientific technology has led us a straight path from hunting and gathering to being pulled along by steam trains. There is ample time in the calendar of modern man to have allowed several cycles of technological development and decline.

"My family speaks of four ages of Tembla civilization. The first was a time of agriculture and ignorance, when the people took only what they needed from nature to live simply.

"The second was the dawn of the Tembla enlightenment,

when the first machines were developed to aid agricultural production.

"In the third age mathematics and science progressed rapidly, driven by the Tembla's need to improve their machinery. Within two hundred years, these developments took the Tembla from a completely agricultural society to an industrial, technologically advanced city state."

The maharaja took a sip of water and sat back.

"During this third age a strict religious caste developed and sought to throw a veil of secrecy over this knowledge, fearing it was too dangerous for the common good.

"The fourth – and quite the most dangerous – phase culminated in the development of complex concepts of physics, and the desire to understand the mechanisms of the universe. It was this that led to the Tembla's destruction. They built a machine which could create colossal amounts of power: a generator so powerful that it cut into the earth's crust and went on to rip a hole in the earth's mantle..."

"Did it cause a volcanic eruption?" asked Doug.

"Oh yes. The island of Sumatra was devastated, the machine destroyed and, worse, mankind was virtually wiped out."

"But some of the Tembla must've survived? I mean, you're one."

"Before work started on the machine, a faction of the Tembla scientists, supported by the priests, foresaw its catastrophic potential and warned against building it. The population divided into two groups: those who wanted the machine and its promised benefits, and those who saw that it had the capacity to kill them all and destroy the planet.

"This faction set sail and tried to get as far away from Toba as they could, landing in what we now call Antarctica. There

were about five thousand of them. They carried all the provisions they could, dug caves deep into the rock, and took shelter. Their prediction came true; the machine did indeed rip the earth's mantle, causing an eruption of unimaginable scale. What followed was a ten-year winter."

The Duchess growled and paced forward, sniffing the air, then settled, her ears twitching.

"As conditions began to improve, the people sheltering in Antarctica left there, but they found that no other population had survived; all had starved to death. The five thousand Tembla survivors were the only humans left on the planet. As the cold winter receded, they settled in the productive and fertile valleys of Africa. So you see, we are all Tembla. We are all descended from those few survivors of the Toba eruption."

"Then what is Ur-Can? What did the Tembla build?"

"Nobody knows exactly!" laughed the maharaja. "My family believes it to be a gift to mankind, but what it actually does remains a mystery – a very powerful one."

"Yeah, well," guffawed Liberty. "I've heard some hokum in my time, but this just about takes the—"

"Does *The 99 Elements* explain it?" Becca interrupted.

The maharaja nodded. "We believe so, though the collection was split into its four parts by Alexander's men. It may be better that way."

"But do you believe we've reached a point where mankind is ready for this knowledge again?" asked Doug breathlessly.

"No," said the maharaja abruptly. He raised his index finger and looked them both in the eye. "Absolutely not."

He clapped his hands and two musicians entered the carriage. "Now we shall have some music."

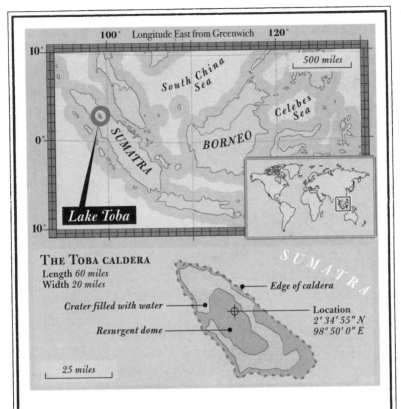

The following labels appear on the map:

100° Longitude East from Greenwich 120°

10°
0°
10°

500 miles

South China Sea

Celebes Sea

SUMATRA

BORNEO

Lake Toba

THE TOBA CALDERA
Length *60 miles*
Width *20 miles*

Crater filled with water

Resurgent dome

Edge of caldera

Location
2° 34' 55" N
98° 50' 0" E

SUMATRA

25 miles

THE TOBA ERUPTION

*Any student of early human anthropology will find many conflicting theories
on this subject, but the Toba catastrophe theory was first proposed in 1998 by
Stanley H. Ambrose of the University of Illinois at Urbana-Champaign.*

*It argues that the Toba supervolcano erupted circa 71,000 years ago in what is now
Northern Sumatra, Indonesia. The event was possibly the most powerful eruption
for the last 25 million years, and has been rated "mega-colossal", the highest
attainable scale on the Volcanic Explosivity Index. The earth was subsequently
thrown into a long, dark winter lasting several years, as debris hurled skywards
blocked out the sun and triggered massive climate change. The result was the virtual
destruction of humankind, and it therefore follows that modern humans are
descended from the few thousand survivors of this catastrophic event, as is evident in
the narrow divergence of genes found in modern humans. Mathematical calculation
suggests this genetic "population bottleneck" coincides with the eruption date.*

*Any connection between the Toba catastrophe theory and the Tembla myths has only
ever been suggested in the archives of the HGS.*

Becca had many more questions, but the maharaja had closed the subject as firmly as a bank vault door. She felt suddenly hungry after such an eventful day. As they travelled across the flat Gangetic Plain towards the holy city of Varanasi, dish after dish of fabulous food arrived. Two musicians sat cross-legged in the corner playing harmonium and tabla. Despite the European decoration of the carriage, Becca felt the familiarity of India stirring deep within her. She listened to the maharaja's stories of his eccentric family, of the many mysteries of India, and the wonder of Varanasi, nodding her head in time with the drums. She began to feel relaxed in a way she'd not felt for a long time, and not a little sleepy.

It was during one of the maharaja's tales about a baby elephant trapped in a tree that the sound of running footsteps on the coach roof made them all look up. The maharaja raised his hand to signal the musicians to stop playing.

Snave burst in, clutching a pistol. "I must insist on locking the door, sir." As he turned to shut it, the door was booted open with great force. "Capulus's men!"

"Where are my guards?" shouted the maharaja, hitting an alarm.

"It's no use ringing for them, sir. I'm afraid they're all dead."

"Oh yeah, just dandy!" yelled Liberty. "So who's drivin' the train?"

"That would be Capulus's men, madam," said Snave.

"How many are there?" asked the maharaja.

"Twenty or so." Snave paused and fired through the doorway at an attacker, who crumpled and sprawled into the carriage. He pulled the body clear and slammed the door.

Liberty jammed a chair under the handle. "That won't hold them for long."

"They want the gyrolabe," yelled Becca, grabbing the hessian sack from under her chair.

"They must have boarded when the train stopped for the cow, sir. They've been waiting for us to reach the countryside."

"Unbelievable!" spat Liberty. "Always the same with you MacKenzies. If there's trouble, y'all are sure to be slap bang in the middle of it. Metal to a magnet, cousins, metal to a darned magnet."

The maharaja opened a cupboard and pulled out a curved sword and pistol. "We will move forward to the engine and stop the train."

Liberty didn't look thrilled at the prospect. "Give me that pistol, will you, Raj? Swords ain't my style in a dust-up."

The tiger growled. She strode towards the other end of the carriage, licking her lips.

"The Duchess wants to lead the way," Becca said.

"Let her," snapped Liberty. "Snave, watch our backs; I'll follow the cat. MacKenzies, stick behind the maharaja."

Someone tried to kick the door down, but the chair held. Snave fired twice. Five shots followed in reply from the other side, splintering the finely carved woodwork around the handle. One of the bullets hit the harmonium player just above the elbow, making him cry out in pain as they hurried through the cramped kitchen. The chefs were arguing with each other as they held the door shut against someone trying to shoulder their way in. Liberty yelled for the chefs to duck, and fired two rounds blindly through the wood. A muffled scream was heard outside as the bullets found a target.

"Open it!" Liberty barked, her pistol still raised.

The Duchess's eyes glinted, her head dropping low as she readied to attack. As the door swung open, the tiger leapt onto the platform at the rear of the next carriage, scattering Capulus's men. Liberty kicked her way into the carriage, then stopped at the third compartment and carefully opened the door.

"Wait. Time to reacquaint myself with an old pal." She ducked inside her cabin, pulled her twin-barrelled blunderbuss from a suitcase, slung the ammunition belt over her shoulder, cocked the flintlocks and handed Snave the pistol.

"Maharaja, meet the Liberator," declared Liberty. "How many cars till we reach the engine?"

"Three more after this."

They heard running on the roof.

From Doug's sketchbook: The Duchess deals with Capulus's men. (DMS 7/55)

Doug
1920

"Then let's get movin'."

The Duchess's nose was barely an inch off the floor as she stalked forward. The next carriage proved empty, and they were soon outside again in the blustery night air. Liberty pulled her flying goggles down over her eyes and stealthily clambered up onto the brass railings so she could check along the top of the carriages in both directions. She bobbed down again.

"The good news is, there's four of them workin' the loco."

"The bad news?" asked Doug.

"Five more are movin' up from behind us. They're only a car away."

Snave jumped down to the carriage hitch and unhooked the connection. "We can put a stop to them immediately."

The rear of the train slowed as the front section clattered onto a low bridge spanning a river. The Duchess was already pushing her way into the next car.

"Capulus!" shouted Doug, catching a movement out of the corner of his eye.

At that moment, the Russian swung onto the platform and jumped the expanding gap between the two sections of the train. He'd been working his way along the side of the accommodation carriage using the shuttered windows as handholds. He crashed into Snave and grabbed for the hessian sack containing the gyrolabe, wrenching Becca off balance.

"Doug, help me!" she shouted, struggling to break Capulus's powerful grip.

Liberty raised the blunderbuss and squeezed the trigger, but there was just a click and a swirl of smoke, and Capulus knocked the barrels away. She brought the stock of the gun round and smashed Capulus's hand as he fumbled for the gyrolabe. Doug joined the fight by grabbing the Russian's legs below the knee, causing him to drop the bag, but Doug couldn't hold his grip. Snave finally wrestled Capulus down to the edge of the platform. The two men fought fiercely for several seconds until they crashed against the railing, which lurched and gave way. Both men hung dangerously off the platform, still struggling.

Doug grabbed Snave's jacket and the butler scrambled back to safety. Capulus clutched at the bar that had connected the railing to the roof. He pulled himself up but the damaged pole hinged outwards. He swung away from the carriage, his feet kicking wildly in the air, the pole bending until it was almost horizontal. Beneath him was the dark swirling river.

Snave aimed the pistol, but wasn't quick enough – Capulus smiled briefly, let go, and dropped into the river with a mighty splash. Becca clutched the gyrolabe closer, her hands shaking.

"Forget him," shouted Liberty. "We need to stop this train!"

They followed the Duchess, who had stalked two carriages ahead. They heard a roar and a scuffle, then two shots rang out. Liberty climbed up to check the roof.

"Well, there's no one up there that I can see."

"This is the luggage car," said the maharaja. "We are nearly at the locomotive."

They raced forward to their goal. Liberty scaled the ladder on the back of the locomotive, and crept across the heap of coal. She found the Duchess lying still, thrashing her tail angrily.

"You all right, girl?"

The Duchess gave a stifled moan. She'd been shot.

"Hang on now, d'you hear?"

Liberty's attention focused on the last four of Capulus's men, who were throwing the dead bodies of the maharaja's engine driver and fireman into the river.

From Doug's sketchbook: Capulus plunges into the river. (DMS 7/62)

"Jump!" she ordered, aiming the useless blunderbuss. The men looked at one another, then at the gun, and decided to follow their victims into the river.

Becca and Doug clambered up onto the back of the

locomotive where the tiger lay panting and licking her wound, which ran with claret-red blood.

"Duchess! Duchess, the captain will never forgive me," gasped Becca.

"It's bad," said Doug as he knelt down to examine the wound.

Liberty gestured into the empty engine cab ahead. "Y'all know someone who can drive this thing?"

"I made a bit of a study of locomotives a couple of years ago," Doug proffered tentatively.

"My father was a fireman on the Great Western Railway, madam," added Snave. "I'm sure Douglas and I can manage it between us."

Liberty raised a sceptical eyebrow.

"Tell you what," said Doug, jumping down into the cab and spotting a steaming kettle on the side. "Once we've got this loco under control and we've patched up the Duchess, we'll sit down and have a nice cup of tea."

GREAT WESTERN RAILWAY (GWR)

Railway company (1833–1948) famed for transporting British holi-daymakers from London to the seaside resorts of the south-west. Nicknamed both "God's Wonderful Railway" and "Goes When Ready" due to its informal approach to train timetabling.

Liberty sank down on her haunches by the injured tiger and stroked the animal's head. "So *he's* in charge now?"

"I hope not," replied Becca.

Liberty sighed. "Doug wearin' a tuxedo, issuin' orders and drivin' a train, a Liberator who only liberates when she's in the mood, a one-armed harmonium player, a wounded tiger, and a cup of tea. I mean, *tea*? What I need is coffee."

CHAPTER SEVEN

Becca's diary: 8th August 1920
Maharaja's palace, Varanasi

Our arrival at Varanasi caused something of a stir. The station-master almost suffered apoplexy seeing Snave and Doug driving the train. I'm forced to admit that this was a task they performed annoyingly well during the night. Doug seemed to know what all the signals meant, as well as having an unfathomable knowledge of how to make the locomotive work.

Our party hurried away from the station in a convoy of two large motor cars. The maharaja had the drivers pull the roofs over, and told us not to show our faces. I clutched the gyrolabe tightly, willing us to be somewhere safe.

We drove towards the River Ganges, weaving through the colourful, chaotic streets crowded with pilgrims either going to or coming from the water. It felt a little like our first taxi drive through Shanghai all those months ago, as curious faces peered in at us. The maharaja had told us his family had a small place here, although it was seldom used. The "small place" turned out to be a colossal river-front palace!

We had to walk the last few hundred yards through the maze of narrow streets of the old town as no car could fit down them. All about us were shrines smothered

SHRINES

Shrines like this statue of the Hindu god Ganesha are scattered throughout Varanasi, ranging from tiny niches to grand temples.

in vermilion and saffron marigold garlands, some small, others complete temples behind iron railings. All seemed built as close to one another as possible, and the air was both stifling and rich with incense and spices. It felt as if we had stepped back into some distant time, somewhere within that unbroken chain of history the maharaja had talked about.

Our course twisted and turned, until we reached a heavy door set within an ogee arch. We climbed up a steep flight of stairs that led into the palace, where we were shown to our rooms, shuttered against the heat and refreshingly cool. When I threw open the shutters, the whole of the Varanasi waterfront lay before me, the ghats[5] leading down to the Ganges overflowing with bathing pilgrims. Behind them a jumble of elegant ruins formed a backdrop of pink, red and white plasterwork, warmed by the fiery ball of the morning sun as it rose through an azure sky. It was just as Mother had once described it – pure India.

The maharaja summoned a doctor to tend to the poor old Duchess, but the doctor, on seeing his patient, fled from the room. We managed to persuade him to return, and he set to work examining the wound after assurances from us that he wouldn't be eaten alive. I held her head and calmed her while Doug assisted the doctor as he extracted the bullet. The Duchess moaned painfully, but never growled or flashed her teeth, a surprisingly model patient. The effort seemed to tire her, and once the wound was dressed she quickly fell asleep, her breathing short and laboured.

I've had to make a terrible decision. We can't wait for the Duchess to get better, so I've told Doug that we are to make our escape tonight and head north for China. The maharaja will make certain she has the best possible medical attention. I shall write him a letter explaining everything. I know the Duchess will be all right, but I can't say the same about Mother and Father.

5 Steps leading down to the River Ganges in the holy city of Varanasi.

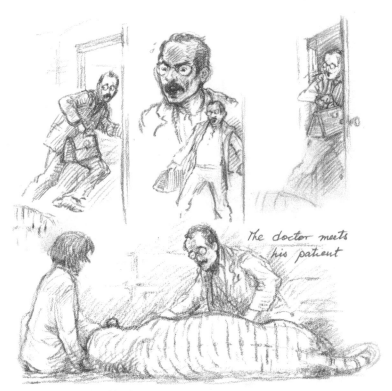

The doctor meets his patient

From Doug's sketchbook. (DMS 7/66)

In the afternoon sun, the maharaja and Doug sat on the roof
terrace of the huge palace, looking out across the silvered
expanse of the River Ganges. They drank tea silently, each
deep in thought.

Doug had assumed that the maharaja's uncle would, like
the maharaja, live in luxury. However, the man's location
was apparently unknown, although the maharaja thought
that he bathed in the Ganges every morning and night at the
Dashashwamedha Ghat. A search party had been sent out
under the command of Snave.

VARANASI

Situated on the banks of the River Ganges, or Ganga, this remarkable city is celebrated as one of India's oldest and most holy places. The riverbank has ghats leading down to the water to allow pilgrims to bathe and make offerings; some ghats are reserved for the cremation of bodies.

Doug gazed down on the ghat below. "Do you think Capulus will find us here?"

"My palace is in every guidebook; our arrival at the station was hardly discreet. I fear it is only a matter of time. We must leave tomorrow. Snave will arrange a replacement train for you to Calcutta. I will provide bodyguards for you all the way to America, if necessary. Ah, here is Snave now…"

The butler was followed by a stooped old man wearing simple Indian garb who put his hands together and returned the maharaja's bow. Becca was close behind, carrying her hessian sack.

"Uncle. It is an honour to see you."

"You have interrupted my prayers. I hope it is for some useful purpose," growled the old man.

Despite his great age he was supple, and he sat down cross-legged in the shade beneath a large silk canopy. The others followed suit as more tea arrived. Liberty, who'd been dozing on a cushion, rolled over and nodded a hello.

"Are all three of you MacKenzies?" The sage's tone was accusing.

"Two of us are," replied Doug.

"Yeah, and I'm a kinda cousin of theirs," added Liberty with a yawn.

"I sense from your faces that you are in great danger?"

"You can say that again, and so are our parents—"

"Let me tell you now," interrupted the sage. "I have met your mother; I know of your parents' reputation, and of their secret organization. I was as plain with her as I shall be with you. I will not help the Guild."

This wrong-footed Becca slightly. "Well…" Nevertheless,

she pushed on. "They have travelled to Sinkiang." She took out Doug's copy of Ezekiel Zedd's three hieroglyphs and the photograph from Ur-Can. "We think these may be the reason why. The maharaja said you are able to read the text."

The old sage's eyes flicked restlessly between the photograph and Doug's sketch of the hieroglyphs. "Your parents went to Sinkiang knowing of these symbols?"

"Yes," answered Doug. "They match some of the symbols in the photograph."

"I know they match." The old man jerked his head back angrily and stared into Becca's eyes. "I will not help you."

"But you can read the text?" insisted Doug.

The maharaja rubbed his chin nervously. "Show ... show him what else you have, Becca."

"We have this." Becca lifted out the gyrolabe. "People are trying to kill us for it."

The sage's astonishment was plain. He took the precious object and turned it in his hands, examining its markings. "The eastern gyrolabe."

"We found the southern gyrolabe a few months ago," added Doug casually, with a sniff.

The maharaja's uncle looked up slowly. "You did *what*?"

"The, er, the southern gyrolabe. We found it."

"Where? Where is it now? Do you have it here?"

"We lost it to a man called Crozier," Becca said softly. "Julius Pembleton-Crozier."

"Lost?" snapped the old man indignantly. "Is this Crozier another member of the Honourable Guild of Specialists?"

"Was. He turned bad. We understand that if you have all the gyrolabes, their combined inscriptions reveal the location of Ur-Can."

"If you can decipher them, then yes, they will. Does he know of these symbols?"

"We copied them out of an old Guild book, so it's possible."

"Has he seen the western and northern gyrolabes?"

"He's seen Guild drawings of them," said Doug meekly.

The sage seemed to freeze for a moment, and he murmured a few incomprehensible words.

The Sage of Varanasi

From Doug's sketchbook. (DMS 7/70)

Becca spoke slowly. "We think Ur-Can is where our parents were heading on their expedition."

The old man carefully put the gyrolabe down and closed his eyes.

"With all four gyrolabes discovered and these Tembla secrets loose, we have entered a new and perilous age."

"Now will you help us? Please?" begged Becca.

"No. I will take the gyrolabe for safe keeping."

"It's not yours," she protested, grabbing the gravity device.

"This was stolen from my sect centuries ago. It is mine."

"It's no more yours than theirs, Uncle," argued the maharaja. "These are my guests and I will not have them treated like this."

"You, nephew, are meddling in matters you do not understand and in which you have never truly believed... Now you want me to help you. Now, when it may be too late! You are a disgrace to the Tembla order. You expect me to translate this" – he clutched Doug's sketch in his hands – "the Tembla's most profound secret? For mere children? I will not do it."

"What about our parents?" asked Becca. "We need your help to find them."

The old man fixed her with unwavering eyes. "Your parents are nothing in comparison with the power of Ur-Can. I would never help the Guild and I will not help you either."

"But you're our last chance," she implored.

"Don't you see, Uncle? You are the last person alive, other than Elena MacKenzie, who understands this language. If she is lost and you were to die, the Tembla secrets would be gone for ever."

The old man gestured angrily. "If you had listened more when you were young, you would be able to read the symbols yourself!"

"I cannot change that. I can only offer a chance to continue this ancient connection to our past."

"It is too late," said the sage. He began to turn away. "The full weight of the Tembla secrets rests on your shoulders. You must hide this gyrolabe beyond human reach."

The maharaja stood and bowed. "Uncle..."

But the old man had gone.

Chapter Eight

The knock on Becca's door just after midnight was long and insistent. Becca, halfway through an escape attempt, climbed back in through the window. "Hide!" she hissed at her brother.

"Becca! Becca!" shouted Liberty. "Quick. Unlock this thing. The place is crawlin' with Capulus's guys. They must've got Doug; I can't find him."

Becca unlocked the door, and stood blinking in the glare of Liberty's pocket torch.

"I see you're dressed, coz. And with a bag packed too?"

"Doug's here."

Echoing footsteps along the marble hallway made Liberty push in and close the door behind her.

"Hello, Liberty," said Doug sheepishly as the beam of her torch picked him out in the gloom, holding his old kitbag.

"Not a moment too soon, hey, cousins? Plannin' a little night stroll, I see. What were y'all gonna do with poor old Duchess there?"

Becca grabbed a letter perched beside the tiger's head addressed to the maharaja. "There's no way she'd make it to Sinkiang. The best place for her is here, where she can be looked after properly."

There was a shout outside and a muffled gunshot.

"It's those darned mercenary guys back for more," said Liberty. "They came in over the roof."

"They want the gyrolabe."

"Yeah, well maybe it would be easier for all of us if you just gave them the darn thing."

"Never," vowed Becca.

Liberty opened the door a crack. A figure ran towards them and she slammed it shut, blocking it with her boot.

"It's me, Snave," said the butler, his voice muffled by the woodwork.

Liberty opened the door and let him in.

"The palace is overrun; we must get away. These men will stop at nothing. Quick, we have to reach the breakfast room."

"If it's all the same to you, I'm not that hungry right now."

"Madam, this is no time to be droll. We'll find a secret passage there. It is our best chance of escape."

Liberty swung her blunderbuss round, cocked both flint-locks, and reopened the door. The Duchess growled.

"We'll be back for you, Duchess," said Becca. "I promise."

The huge tiger gazed at Becca and Doug for a moment, then slowly closed her eyes.

They set off, following Snave, along corridors neither the MacKenzies nor Liberty had used before. They arrived at a balcony overlooking the maharaja's breakfast room, its white marble gleaming in the candlelight of the hot night. Below they saw the maharaja, surrounded by four of Capulus's men, two of them carrying what looked like a bundle of rags. Capulus himself had a pistol aimed at the maharaja. They were arguing.

"...you have no right to be in my palace."

"Where is the gyrolabe?"

"I do not have it," said the maharaja, his voice rising in anger.

"Don't lie. Those children have it – the ones I saw in

Lucknow and on your train last night. My spies saw them on the roof terrace here this afternoon; they were showing the gyrolabe to an old man."

"I don't know what you mean," bluffed the maharaja.

"Are you sure?"

Capulus gestured for his men to place the bundle on the floor, and he pulled back the rags. The maharaja gasped. It was his uncle.

Doug and Becca recoiled in horror. The maharaja rushed forward and cradled the dying man.

"You despicable, unholy murderer—"

Capulus's tone was glacial. "He told us nothing. Now I am here to find out the Tembla secrets from you. After you've given me the gyrolabe."

The maharaja lifted his uncle and carefully placed him on an ornate marble bench with elephant heads carved into both armrests.

From Doug's sketchbook: The view from the balcony. (DMS 7/75)

"The Tembla will reveal nothing to Russian mercenaries."

Capulus pushed his pistol into the maharaja's face. "I find people do what I want with a little persuasion."

In response, the maharaja reached out and pressed his hand against one of the marble elephants. "Not I, my friend."

The bench tilted back, and a section of floor opened, allowing him and his uncle to slide backwards and disappear. The floor panel slammed shut. Capulus kicked at the marble elephant head, beating it with the grip of his pistol.

"A secret panel!" exclaimed Doug. "Lethal!"

"Quickly," said Snave. "This way."

The butler led Becca, Doug and Liberty to a narrow, steeply descending staircase hidden behind a wall tapestry. They found the maharaja waiting at the bottom nursing his dying uncle.

"Is he still alive?" asked Doug.

The old man's breathing was laboured. Snave rushed forward to help.

"Have my barge prepared, there's a good fellow," said the maharaja. "Hurry now."

Snave nodded and moved off into the gloom of the passageway.

The sage called weakly for his nephew. "Amar ... listen to me..." He saw the MacKenzies and began to speak in Hindi. This was a language both Becca and Doug understood well enough from their years of living in Lucknow. "You are the last of the Tembla line. It is against my better judgement, but you must know the secret..."

"Rest, Uncle," insisted the maharaja.

The old man blinked slowly. Liberty gave him water from her flask. "No ... I am nearly dead... Listen ... the secret ... the secret..." He blinked again, more heavily this time. "It is up to you to protect Ur-Can." He was drifting in and out of consciousness. "Do not delay. Do you understand?"

"What is the secret?" asked the maharaja urgently.

"The secret is passed u..." With these last, barely audible words, the sage died.

The maharaja held his uncle and sobbed gently. For several minutes his grief overwhelmed him. Liberty, Becca and Doug sat quietly, unsure what to do.

Becca contemplated the last words the old man had spoken and wondered about their meaning. They were strangely similar to those attributed to the guildsman Ezekiel Zedd. Something was nagging at her. The sage had tried to lift his hand towards his face as he'd spoken. She'd assumed the secret was a phrase or sentence passed on verbally from one generation to the next, but now she began to wonder.

"I'm sorry about your uncle." Doug tried to find some words of comfort, but lapsed into silence.

"Pity he didn't tell y'all that secret he was trying to get out," Liberty mused.

"Now we will never know," answered the maharaja. "He drew his last breath before he could reveal it."

"Actually, I'm not so sure about that," said Becca. "I think he did tell you."

"What do you mean, Rebecca?"

"May I be permitted?" she asked, reaching a finger towards the old man's mouth. She gently pulled down his lower lip to reveal hieroglyphs tattooed on the reverse side, hidden from view on the inside of his mouth. *"Secrets passed upon the lips…* It was the phrase quoted in the Guild book."

Liberty recoiled. "Mercy me. If we ever do catch up with your parents, don't let on you've been pokin' around in dead people's mouths, you hear?"

The maharaja looked surprised at first, then carefully lifted the sage's upper lip. There, hidden from sight, were another three hieroglyphs.

"Three upper symbols, and three lower – each with a blank space," said Doug.

Becca pulled her brother's sketch of Zedd's hieroglyphs from her bag. "Look, Ezekiel's symbols match those on your uncle's upper lip exactly."

"No wonder he was so angry when he saw them," said the maharaja, gently closing his uncle's mouth.

Snave returned, slightly out of breath. "Everything is prepared, sir. The boat is waiting."

"We must delay no longer. We follow this tunnel to safety. Snave, you and I will carry my uncle. We must find priests to tend to his body."

Ten minutes later, they emerged from narrow, fetid tunnels into a silk shop some distance from the palace. A young shopkeeper helped them out of the trapdoor, bowing to the maharaja, then opened his front door to let them out onto the Ram Ghat.

Doug was fascinated by the maharaja's escape route. "How did your trick bench work?"

"Did you like it?" The maharaja was still tearful, but gulped

THE MAHARAJA'S TRICK BENCH

A simple balance mechanism activated by pressing a button on the elephant's head, releasing a catch on the tilting floor (fig. 2). The weight of the bench caused the floor to pivot backwards (fig. 3). The floor hit a buffer stop, whereupon the sitter could roll away onto a cushioned bed. Simultaneously, the counterweight mechanism was activated (fig. 4). The four lead counterweights pulled the bench back to its original position. The system could not be used again until the counterweights were reset (fig. 5).

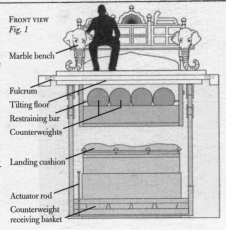

FRONT VIEW
Fig. 1

Marble bench

Fulcrum

Tilting floor

Restraining bar

Counterweights

Landing cushion

Actuator rod

Counterweight receiving basket

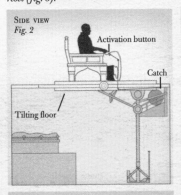

SIDE VIEW
Fig. 2

Activation button

Catch

Tilting floor

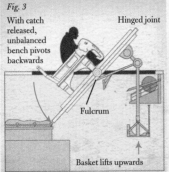

Fig. 3

With catch released, unbalanced bench pivots backwards

Hinged joint

Fulcrum

Basket lifts upwards

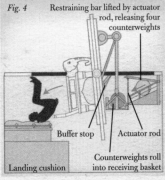

Fig. 4

Restraining bar lifted by actuator rod, releasing four counterweights

Buffer stop

Actuator rod

Counterweights roll into receiving basket

Landing cushion

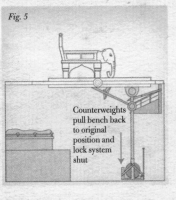

Fig. 5

Counterweights pull bench back to original position and lock system shut

and smiled, glad of Doug's distraction. "I have wanted to use it all my life. It was installed by my father for the amusement of his guests. He was a great practical joker."

After some minutes, priests were summoned by Snave, and they carried the body of the sage onto the foredeck of a forty foot long riverboat waiting at a small jetty. Silently they all stepped aboard, and the crew cast off. The spoons of the blades disturbed the moonlight shimmering on the smooth surface of the Ganges. Their escape appeared to have worked.

"We're meant to be catchin' a train out of Varanasi to get these kids to safety," said Liberty once they were all settled on the deck.

"Only a slight diversion," the maharaja reassured her. "Tomorrow we will find you a railway station further downstream."

"Won't those guys have caught us up by then?" Liberty pointed astern, where two rowing boats were pushing off from the ghats.

"Oh, I very much doubt it. We have a team of twelve of the finest oarsmen working the Ganges. And even if they do, we are safe for the time being."

"How do you know?"

"They may be mercenaries, Rebecca, but they are Indian," he said. "They would never kill a man here in Varanasi, no matter how much they were paid. It is our holiest city; and this is India's holiest river."

Becca thought of the tattoos – of how tantalizing yet useless they were. "Your uncle may have given you a Tembla secret, but he didn't translate it."

"The only person who can unravel it all now is your

mother, and she's in the Sinkiang. I have a friend who will help me get there; I have arranged to meet him tomorrow."

"I think Ur-Can may be situated at a place called Daotang somewhere in the desert near Korla, if that's any help," offered Becca.

"Then that is where I shall go. I will send communication as soon as I have located your parents, Rebecca and Douglas. Now I must go and pray beside my uncle. Tomorrow the priests will return to Varanasi with his body for cremation."

The oarsmen pulled away, propelling the boat forward, and the boats chasing them fell behind. Becca pulled the

From Doug's sketchbook: Setting off by moonlight. (DMS 7/84)

gyrolabe closer to her as they settled on rugs laid over the poop deck. Insects flitted and buzzed tirelessly around the lantern beside her. Guarded by Liberty, and lulled by the swish of the oars, Doug and Becca were soon asleep.

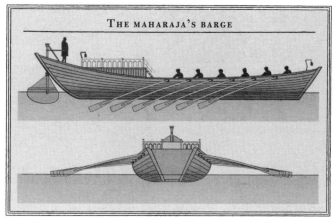

THE MAHARAJA'S BARGE

(MA 263.24 VARA)

CHAPTER NINE

From Doug's sketchbook: Villagers on the riverbank. (DMS 7/87)

As the boat nudged into the bank, a group of curious villagers took hold of the bowline and tied it to a tree.

"Does this look like a port to you?" Liberty asked Doug, who merely shrugged.

"The road runs beside here," said the maharaja. "This will suit us very well."

Snave was first off the barge. "I'll get up to the road and see what transport I can find, sir."

A mud track led up the bank to a few simple houses.

"There'd better be a train here," grumbled Liberty.

Snave returned a few minutes later. "I have sent word on to the next village. A motor car should be with us in the next half-hour."

The maharaja beamed. "Good."

Liberty's sharp pilot's eyes picked out a flash of light reflecting off a car driving at speed along the opposite bank.

"I hate to worry y'all, but what's that automobile doin' over there?"

Doug took out his binoculars and focused on the vehicle. A long cloud of dust trailed behind it.

"Capulus?" asked Becca.

Liberty shouldered her blunderbuss. "How long d'you say this motor car's gonna be, Your Highness?"

"We shall go ashore," urged the maharaja, ignoring her question. "Quickly. My friend is waiting not two miles away."

"Would you say Capulus has done the smart thing and put a car on each bank, and driven like stink out of Varanasi after us?"

"Perhaps, Miss Liberty."

"There's no *perhaps* about it. Boats, darn them! If we'd flown, we'd've been hundreds of miles away by now! I suggest we get up to that road and hitch a ride."

Doug felt drowsy and half asleep. He splashed some water on his face, gathered up his meagre belongings and filed down the gangplank behind the others. The road lay up a short track in open arable country, the flood plain of the river undulating to a rise with little cover. A truck drove by but ignored Liberty's wild attempt to flag it down with her blunderbuss.

"Snave, get everyone behind that wall. Doug? See anythin'?"

Doug had his binoculars trained on the road. "There's a red truck coming, but it's not going very fast. There's another vehicle about half a mile behind it, I'd say. And that one *is* moving fast."

"That's them. We need that truck."

"Miss Liberty," said the maharaja, "if our best chance of escape is to hitch a lift, may I suggest you hide the gun? It puts people off rather, don't you think? We're not highway robbers, after all."

As the red truck approached, the maharaja, all beaming smile and flowing robes, stepped out and waved courteously for the driver to stop. The truck slowed and pulled over.

"Beginner's luck," muttered Liberty as the maharaja fell into conversation with the driver. "Come on, come on! This ain't afternoon tea!"

"I hate to say it, Liberty, but I can see more than one car approaching. It's definitely Capulus's men," said Doug.

"This way." The maharaja smiled, waving to his waiting party. "Everyone hurry aboard."

The truck only had room for three in the driver's cab so Liberty and the young MacKenzies climbed into a wooden cargo box on the back. It was dusty and hideously hot inside; crates of mangoes were stacked on the right-hand side, while a consignment of straw mats occupied the left.

Snave, the maharaja and the driver hurried to the cab.

"I hope they pick up the pace," barked Becca, slamming the rear doors shut.

"Snave's driving," replied Doug. "I saw him take the wheel."

"What, that fusty ol—"

Liberty was cut short as the engine screeched and they all lurched backwards. The wheels bounced over the potholed road so hard that they had to cling to the mats for support.

The maharaja turned and called through the slats, "Is everyone comfortable back there?"

"Yep!" shouted Liberty. "It's like the Ritz. Is the driver givin' you trouble?"

"Not any more. I have just bought his truck for four times its value. Now he is happy for us to ruin it!"

"So you won't mind if I kick a hole in the rear doors?"

"Be my guest!" laughed the maharaja.

With a firm kick Liberty dislodged a plank of wood, allowing a limited view of the road behind. Despite Snave's efforts to coax maximum speed from the engine, the cars behind had almost caught them.

"Right, my old pal," said Liberty to the blunderbuss, sighting the barrels on the first car. "You'd better work this time, or you and me are gonna have a fallin'-out."

Their pursuers' first bullet ripped into the bodywork. Snave swerved the truck to throw their aim, bouncing Liberty into the mangoes. She recovered, braced herself against the stock of the gun, and squeezed the trigger. Nothing happened.

"Come on! Fire, darn it!" She shook the weapon and examined the flintlocks. "You're as reliable as a politician's promise."

She fired again. The hammers on the flintlocks dropped but the charge failed a second time. Outside, they could hear pistol shots at close range. The truck veered violently to the right. Becca and Doug crouched as low to the floor as they could. Through the cracks in the planks Doug could see the cars trying to overtake, horns blaring.

The truck turned off the road, and the ride became even worse as they flew this way and that. They could hear the rushing sound of crops brushing the underside of the truck.

"We're in a field. They're sure to catch us now!" yelled Doug.

The sound of machine-gun fire cracked out, fast and heavy.

"We're done for!" yelled Liberty.

At almost the same moment, a bullet ricocheted off the metal hinge of a crate, sending out a spark that ignited one of the straw mats.

From Doug's sketchbook: The chase. (DMS 7/90)

Dm. 1920

But the maharaja was calling out triumphantly, "You see, I told you my friend would be here."

"See? *See?* We're suffocatin' in here," coughed Liberty as smoke filled the cargo box.

They slewed to a stop and lurched into reverse, sending the mangoes flying. Snave hit the brakes. The gunfire was reaching a crescendo outside. Liberty kicked the doors open, and dragged Becca and Doug out.

"Keep your heads down!" she ordered.

Snave had backed the truck up to a rope ladder. The maharaja shouted that they should climb it, and fast. In the confusion they followed his order without question. Only as Becca reached a patch of clear air did she consider where the ladder led. She looked up, and saw with a shock the hull of a vast silver airship. It was the airship they'd last seen at Sulphur Island. The airship that had transported the Coterie of St Petersburg.

"Liberty, no! We have to go back."

But they were already twenty rungs up. The mighty petrol

Trapped !

From Doug's sketchbook. (DMS 7/93)

engines rumbled into life above them. A deluge of water fell from the ballast tanks and extinguished the burning truck. Becca saw the ground falling away as the ship immediately gained height. For a moment, she considered jumping, but they were already too high.

Snave, on the bottom rung, bellowed up, "Move, Miss Rebecca. Climb up to the gondola. We're hanging up like Mother's washing – they're sure to shoot."

With no other choice, Becca and Doug clambered higher. Becca thought of throwing the gyrolabe to the ground to keep it away from the Coterie; then through the smoke she saw Capulus standing beside his car, gazing up grimly at the immense machine.

The door to the airship gondola slammed shut behind them. Liberty whooped and caught her breath. "That was close."

"We trusted you," Becca shouted angrily at the maharaja. "Bergstrom trusted you! But you're Coterie after all."

The maharaja looked puzzled. "I am not a member of the Coterie, Rebecca. Nor am I a member of the Guild."

"But this airship carried the Coterie to Sulphur Island."

"No, no, no. This belongs to my friend, Baron Vanvort. He is a fine, upstanding member of the Guild. An honourable man. Bergstrom trusts him and so did your parents," said the maharaja firmly.

"Then they were duped. Vanvort's Coterie. We saw him."

The door from the next compartment opened. It was Baron Vanvort himself, his eyes as piercing as Doug remembered.

"The child is right, Maharaja. I'm afraid Bergstrom has no idea I'm a member of the Coterie of St Petersburg."

The maharaja stumbled back, his mouth agape. "I never knew, I swear it to you!"

Liberty raised the barrels of her gun.

Baron Vanvort gave a dry laugh. "To fire that aboard this ship would be almost certain suicide. We are being carried aloft by explosive hydrogen. When we saw your truck was alight we were only too keen to launch. Your weapon, madam." Liberty surrendered the blunderbuss to a crewman with a look of defeat. "This way, if you please."

They followed him into a broad saloon car, well appointed with sofas and wing-backed chairs, one of which was occupied by a man reading the *Indian Times*. He dipped the edge of the page with his index finger, but Becca, Doug and Liberty had already recognized the cut of his linen suit.

"Where's my plane, you Limey thief?" roared Liberty.

"Ah, Miss da Vine. How charming. *Lola*'s a very beautiful plane," sighed Pembleton-Crozier. "The engine's running as sweet as a nut now."

"Nut? You're the only nut around here."

Crozier's voice was suddenly languorous and detached. "I think I'll take that gyrolabe, Rebecca my dear."

The baron came close and pulled a dagger from his inside pocket. She had no choice. She took the gyrolabe from its bag and handed it to the Englishman with a look of furious defiance.

Crozier inspected it closely, turning the glittering object in his hands. He got up and opened a cabinet beside him

 and took out the southern gyrolabe to compare the two.

"Thank you, children," said Crozier smugly. "Now the Coterie has both gyrolabes again."

The white linen suit
- again

From Doug's sketchbook. (DMS 7/96)

CHAPTER TEN

Becca's diary: 9th August 1920
Over the Himalayas

Despite the heat of India thousands of feet below, we're high enough for our breath to condense in the icy-cool thin air. The light falling on my diary is crisp and harsh, casting sharp shadows where my pencil touches the weave of the paper. Outside, the sky is an unblemished blue. Liberty is sitting at the other end of this tiny bunk here in the accommodation gondola, scowling, her arms crossed. She is deep in thought, her foot tapping against the bulkhead in time to the slight oscillations of the engines' growl. Neither Doug nor I dare speak.

We've been given fleece-lined flying suits, gloves and helmets, and a bottle marked LIQUID AIR *– all to limit the crippling effects of altitude. Doug and I put these bulky outfits on over our clothes, but Liberty, used to high altitude, merely buttoned her flying jacket tighter and continued with her silent meditation.*

Doug is staring out of the window holding his compass. He's keeping a

High-altitude flying gear.

proper log, using his chronometer and one of Father's maps and marking the course. He has charted our progress over northern India and calculated our speed at an average of sixty miles an hour. The ride is so smooth it feels as if we are stationary.

We are skirting the foothills of the Himalayas now. I can see the primitive beauty of the jagged peaks rising up like an impenetrable city wall. Away to the north, guarded by the saw-toothed mountain range, lies China and the mysterious, fateful Sinkiang region. We are climbing, the air thinning so that every breath takes a little more effort.

As we ascend, our chances of escape seem to fall away behind us.

Liberty pulled up her jacket collar a little further. "We need to ground this gas bag or find a way off it. What'd happen if I burst the hydrogen cells, Doug? Any chance it would land safe?"

"We'd land all right," Doug answered thoughtfully, "but hydrogen is explosive stuff. One spark and this thing'd go off like a bomb. When we hit the ground, it'd be a toss-up between dying from the impact or being burnt alive by the explosion."

"Oh, that sounds just peachy," retorted Liberty bitterly. She jumped up from the bunk and put her hands on her hips, staring down intently at the deck. Suddenly she looked up, a grin breaking out across her face. "D'y'all know I saw parachutes in the other gondola?"

"We'd never get there undetected. I suggest we hang on tight," cautioned Doug.

"Has this thing got the range to get to China?"

Doug thought. "Don't see why not. The *Afrikaschiff* had a range of over four thousand miles. This must be a hundred feet longer at least, and probably carries more fuel... Wait a minute!" It was Doug's turn to grin. "I think I know where there'll be some more parachutes. Chances are they won't be guarded."

THE AFRIKASCHIFF

Flying from Bulgaria to East Africa in November 1917, the German airship L59 (later called the Afrikaschiff*) set an endurance record for flying 4,199 miles (6,757 kilometres) in 95 hours.*

"Y'all think we can break out of here and find them?"

"Should be able to." He sniffed and pulled up the left leg of his flying suit so he could adjust his lucky sock.

"There's a guard outside," said Becca sternly.

"We can climb out of the window – look, there's just a catch." A rush of icy air filled the cabin as he opened the window. "We'll have to wait till it's dark or we'll be seen from the engine gondola."

"So where are these chutes, then?"

Doug grinned. "You're going to need a head for heights..."

"My head ain't good for nothin' else," said Liberty. "World's greatest wing-walker at your service."

With time to kill, Becca took out the Guild history and the Ur-Can photograph. She turned the picture over and looked at the white reverse side. There was nothing apart from the pencil caption, not even a photographer's stamp. She turned it back and saw the faintest of shadows – an imprint of writing could just be made out. Rotating it slowly, she angled the brilliant glare of sunlight so the indents were just in shadow. It was her mother's hand. Becca could see outlines of the hieroglyphs, as if she had been copying them onto another sheet of paper while resting on the photograph.

"Doug. Got a pencil?" she asked anxiously.

He nodded.

"Write this down: *(a) To begin/start... (b) Blank... (c) Four gyrolabes (in this context, poss. dual meaning – a symbol for absolute caution)... (d) Daughter of the Sun.*"

"Is that the translation?" he asked.

"It's possible."

Doug and Liberty examined it for themselves.

"There's another line here at the bottom," added Liberty.

"*Act... Act...*" tried Becca. "I can't read it. It's too faint."

Doug flinched as he read his mother's words. "*Activation sequence.*"

"So this panel must start the machine at Ur-Can using that sequence," exclaimed Becca. "No wonder the maharaja's uncle was so jumpy."

"I suddenly wish we hadn't found the southern gyrolabe." Doug examined the photograph again. "*Second sequence unintelligible due to loss of...*" The indent ran off the end of the photo. "The loss of what?"

"The southern gyrolabe? The southern quarter of *The 99 Elements*?" suggested Becca.

"We're just guessing, sis. It could be anything."

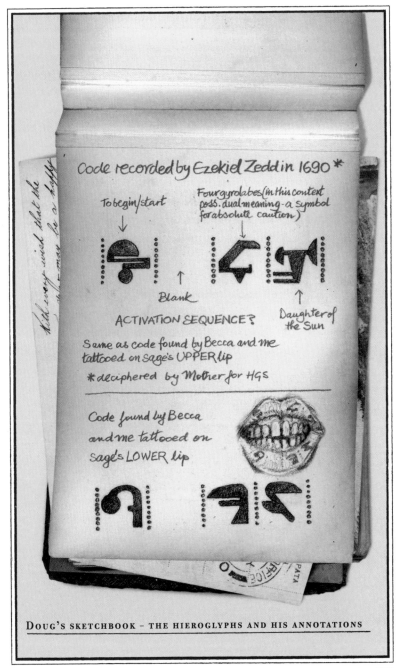

Code recorded by Ezekiel Zedd in 1690 *

To begin/start

Four gyrolabes (in this context poss. dual meaning - a symbol for absolute caution)

↓ Blank

ACTIVATION SEQUENCE?

↑ Daughter of the Sun

Same as code found by Becca and me tattooed on Sage's UPPER lip

* deciphered by Mother for HGS

Code found by Becca and me tattooed on Sage's LOWER lip

With every wind that the ... may be a ...

The escape through the gondola window was not difficult,
but they were flying at about fourteen thousand feet and one
slip would be fatal. In the dark Doug clutched one of the
Duralumin supports, slippery with a thin film of ice, and
braced himself against the slipstream. He was thankful for the
bulky flying suit which bore the brunt of the cold, but he
could feel his face tightening in the bone-chilling rush of air.

Becca climbed up next, then Liberty, with her trusty flying
goggles pulled down to protect her eyes. Once they were all
on the roof of the gondola, Doug nodded and edged gently
towards the ladder leading upwards into the main body of the
airship.

The twenty-five rungs took Doug from the roaring slipstream to the tranquil interior of the vast airship hull. Dim
lighting revealed the angular internal skeleton of the colossal
machine. He stood for a moment on the inverted V keel – the

From Doug's sketchbook: Inside the airship hull. (DMS 8/06)

backbone of the ship. Above him were the bulging gas cells containing hydrogen. Liberty and Becca clambered up and joined him on the narrow walkway lined with fuel and oil tanks for the engines.

"Which way, Doug?" whispered Liberty.

"Forward ... and up."

The walkway was slightly curved so it was impossible to see from one end of the ship to the other. A series of faint bulbs running down the spine illuminated the spider's web of wire bracing and honeycombed girders holding the ship together. Liberty took the lead, and almost immediately slowed as she saw eight hammocks slung from the girders occupied by sleeping crewmen.

Doug's elation at having escaped the gondola was replaced with a vice-like fear. "Off-duty crew," he whispered, watching their breath rise in the half-light.

Liberty stopped and crouched down, uncertain whether to turn back. "The chutes are definitely this way?"

Doug nodded.

Liberty seemed to waver, looking aft towards the cargo compartment. "What d'y'all think Crozier's got in the hold back there? Whaddya say we take a little look around?"

"No, Liberty," said Doug. "There should be a ladder leading up to the forward machine-gun post on top of the ship. There'll be parachutes up there, I'm certain of it. They carried them in the war."

"I'm with Doug," agreed Becca. "We should stick to our plan."

But Liberty was not to be deterred. "I saw cargo hatches on the belly of this thing. Let's see what she's carryin'." She moved off at a run towards a narrow door leading into the mysterious hold.

Reluctantly they followed.

"The chutes will be where I say," grumbled Doug. "We're going the wrong way."

Liberty cautiously turned the handle and stepped into the hold, then beckoned to them, smiling broadly. Below was a Vimy aircraft hanging from a wire-braced launching mechanism.

"Lethal! They experimented with launching aircraft from airships during the war," said Doug.

"Successfully?"

"Yes, I think so, but nothing as elaborate as this."

"Oh, would you look at this – it's *Lola*!" exclaimed Liberty, seeing her own plane, which Crozier had stolen from her many months before. She raced down and climbed up into the cockpit in one graceful, easy movement. The craft swung silently on its launching mechanism, looking poised for take-off.

"Well, I'll be darned! Our run of bad luck is at an end, cousins."

"Er, not quite," replied Becca as she felt the point of a sword jab into her back.

"Whaddya mean?" Liberty's head bobbed up from the cockpit to see Vanvort holding Becca, flanked by five crewmen. She slowly raised one hand, reaching for the release mechanism with the other as she did so.

"Launch that plane and I'll kill these two before you've left the hull of the ship."

Liberty gave a defeated smile, and raised her other hand.

"Tie up the American and put her in the rear machine-gun post. Make sure the hatch is locked. MacKenzies, follow me."

Becca and Doug were hustled into the stateroom, where Pembleton-Crozier, wearing his flying suit, was holding a brandy glass in one hand and a radio message in the other. With a shock they saw that Snave and the maharaja had been gagged and were sitting on the floor with their hands tied behind their backs.

"Good news, Baron." Crozier waved the message. "I've had word from Lucretia. She's about to board a ship bound for Naples. Borelli is in Italy and has been set free from the

From Doug's sketchbook: Crozier and his captives. (DMS 8/10)

of the gondola, letting in a rush of freezing air, and held Doug in the slipstream. "I told you not to fool with me, MacKenzie. Understand?"

Doug went white with fear. He flailed his arms, trying to find a hold.

Becca looked at her brother in terror. Crozier shoved him further out of the gondola to a point where he was about to fall.

"Dante!" she shouted. "Find Dante. He'll lead you to Pugachev."

Doug twisted slightly as he edged his feet apart. He looked down and saw that there was nothing but mountains below.

Crozier turned to Becca. "That's better. Now keep going. I want to know everything you've discovered."

"There's not much," said Becca, rapidly weighing up her options. She had to tell Crozier something, but she must keep the location of Ur-Can safe if she could. "I believe the Russians have found Ur-Can. Capulus said as much in Lucknow. Remember? You were there."

"I recall. Go on."

Becca pulled *Imperial Expeditions in Sinkiang* from her pocket. It was the slim volume Mr Rampal had given her when they'd parted. "This lists all the Russian archaeological expeditions to China. *Imperial* expeditions, which means they must have been backed by money from the tsar. Here's a list of the expedition members in 1912. Look who was chief scientist – an expert in physics."

Becca pointed to a name with a shaking finger, her eyes wide as she looked out at her brother's terrified face.

"Zorid?" exclaimed Crozier.

"Exactly. Why would you need a physicist on an archaeo-logical expedition? They were chasing after the secrets mentioned in the Coterie's papers confiscated by the tsar. The Russian army needed new equipment to fight the coming war." Becca moved her finger down the column and thrust the book in Crozier's face again. "Expedition director was a certain General Pugachev. They employed a local guide nicknamed Dante. Pugachev's deputy was a man called—"

"Capulus," breathed Crozier. He dragged Doug back inside and dropped him to the floor, where Doug collapsed trembling and unable to stand.

"We don't know where Ur-Can is, but if Pugachev has found it ... if they have managed to decipher what the machine is or what it does, it can mean only one thing: Ur-Can must be useful to Pugachev. Why would he be there otherwise? Face it – he's years ahead of you, and the Coterie."

Crozier's face hardened with rage. "Get them out of here. All of them."

Vanvort attempted a smile. "I think our guests will enjoy a night under the stars. Put them all outside on the rear observation platform with that ridiculous American."

Baron Vanvort

DM .

From Doug's sketchbook. (DMS 8/12)

CHAPTER ELEVEN

The rear observation platform and machine-gun post was little more than a cramped niche behind the vast fins at the stern of the airship. As the captives squeezed through the narrow hatchway, they found Liberty sitting on a sand ballast bag, her feet propped against a telescopic machine-gun stand.

"Where've y'all been?" she said. "The million-dollar view on this fairground ride comes for free."

The maharaja, Snave and the MacKenzies huddled down, sheltering from the slipstream. Liberty budged over as the hatch was slammed shut and locked from the inside. There was no escape.

Doug was still shaky after his interview with Crozier. Fear and adrenalin pumped through his system.

"You all right, coz?" said Liberty with a sideways glance.

"I ... I think so. Crozier decided to show me the outside of the gondola."

"Yeah? Sounds dangerous."

"I couldn't have fallen, though."

"How's that?"

"He was holding me by the throat the whole time."

Liberty grinned with something like respect. "Well, you're still in one piece. Take a few deep breaths. That's the way. Hey, I need to know somethin', Doug."

He nodded, his teeth chattering. "Go on."

"Where in hell are we?"

Doug looked about. The buckled landscape of ice-capped

peaks glimmered an iridescent blue-white in the moonlight as the airship climbed higher. It was astonishingly cold, yet eerily tranquil. The scale of the panorama was epic, and they gazed down like classical gods on the towering mountain range. The dark vista of the Karakoram Mountains glided silently by on either side, snow blasting from their fiercely silhouetted pinnacles like smoke billowing from the roof of the world.

"Doug, where's the map?" Becca prompted.

As he took it from his pocket and held it out, she saw the way his hand trembled. She gave him a rare smile and rubbed his shoulder. "Xi would say 'Sujing Cha!'"

Doug pulled himself together. "Xi's a brave fellow, but let's face it – he's never been dangled outside an airship at fifteen thousand feet." He grimaced, and turned to Liberty. "We're approaching the Mintaka Pass."

"Sure?"

Doug nodded. He felt his nerves settle a little as he returned to the world of facts and figures. "I'm certain. Becca and I have been here before on a walking holiday. The first time I wore my lucky socks. It's the best way into China through the mountains. Has been for centuries." He looked at the map and made some calculations. "There's another hundred miles of high mountains to cross, then it's downhill all the way to the desert."

"If we're gonna get off this overgrown balloon, we'd better start makin' some plans," said Liberty. "My vote is we get that plane flyin'. Any ideas how we can sabotage this thing, and give me enough time to launch the Vimy without interruptions from the crew? We need the airship to carry us through the mountains first, so we've got some thinkin' time."

"Why wait, Miss Liberty?" asked Snave.

"Hmm, let me see now. I've never been one for figures, but

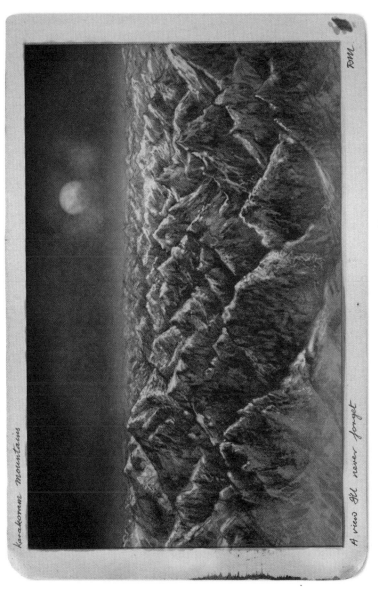

Karakoram Mountains

A view I'll never forget

BM

MOONLIGHT OVER THE KARAKORAM MOUNTAINS

I'll bet my boots that the Vimy doesn't fly much over eight thousand feet and we're cruisin' at over fifteen thousand right now. That right, Doug?"

"Yep, something like that. We're approaching the highest peaks now. It'll be another couple of hours before Vanvort can descend."

"The time to strike is when we've reached the foothills," said Liberty, a daredevil glint in her eye.

Almost as she said it the elevators levelled off, and the airship stopped climbing. In the moonlight, Doug looked down and quite clearly saw the top of the Mintaka Pass a thousand feet below.

Airships, considered Doug, were not the safest form of transport. There were many scenarios for sabotaging such a craft, all of which were likely to end in a huge and lethal hydrogen explosion. He half listened to Liberty working up an elaborate scheme that involved capturing a guard, taking his gun and storming the control gondola. That would never do, thought Doug, just as the maharaja voiced his thoughts.

"But one spark from a gun could destroy the whole ship, Liberty, then we'd all die."

However, if *they* were all frightened of the hydrogen, then so were the crew. Doug began to think the solution might well lie in using the hydrogen to their advantage. The crew would be fearful of explosion, certainly, but in a remote area such as this, they'd also be terrified of a sudden loss of gas and crucial buoyancy. The spark of an idea flared in the recesses of Doug's brain.

"We change the ship's trim," he announced suddenly.

"What?" snapped Liberty.

"We burst one of the cells."

"That was my idea this afternoon. You said it was too risky."

"You wanted to land the airship by bursting *all* the bags. My plan means we only burst one – enough to cause panic. The ship will still fly."

"So how's that gonna help?"

"We burst one of the gas cells at the stern of the ship. The tail will then become heavy, less buoyant. The nose will rise, or the stern will sink – depending on how you look at it. It's a precarious position for an airship."

"So what? Vanvort keeps flyin', nose in the air, just like our pal Snave here."

Snave winced and lowered his nose slightly.

"But he can't fly like that for long. These things need to be level or they burn too much fuel. What's Vanvort going to do?" continued Doug, working through his plan. "It's an emergency situation. It'll cause pandemonium. He'll drop his stern water ballast, pump fuel forward, but that'll take time. In those first few minutes, he'll bring forward the most mobile, most concentrated weight."

Liberty looked puzzled.

"The crew! He'll send his men to the nose to balance out the ship. That's

BALANCING THE AIRSHIP

Most of the airship's interior was occupied by huge gas cells filled with hydrogen. This gas is lighter than air, and so supplied the lift needed to make the ship fly.

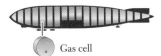

Gas cell

Water was carried as ballast. This was released to adjust the ship's balance and trim.

Stern rises

Water ballast being released

As the airship ascended, the hydrogen naturally expanded; gas had to be released through control vents or the cells would split. These vents were also used to trim the ship so it could fly straight and level.

Gas released ——— Stern sinks

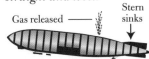

what they did in the war. And to get out of here we can climb over the top of the envelope, find the ladder I was looking for earlier and get down into the ship from there."

Everyone looked at Liberty, who turned to look at the smooth sloping stern of the airship, open-mouthed. "Y'all expect me to climb up there? With no handholds?"

Doug stood and pushed his finger through the thin outer fabric and tore a strip off to reveal the metal skeleton beneath. "We can make handholds."

Liberty nodded slowly a couple of times as she thought through the plan.

"With the cell breached, and the crew in the nose, if we find the ladder down we should have a clear run to the aircraft," added Doug, knowing the word "aircraft" would be music to Liberty's ears.

"Just a minute, though," said Becca thoughtfully. "If it looks like sabotage they'll suspect us straight away. Why not use one of the valves that vent hydrogen from the cells? It'll simply look as if one of them has broken or failed."

Doug silently chided himself for not remembering the valves. It was an obvious refinement to his plan.

"How do you know about the manoeuvring valves?" he asked.

"Well, even my grasp of physics tells me these gas cells have to conform to the laws of Boyle, Mariotte and Gay-Lussac. If they didn't they'd burst. You don't have the monopoly on science, brother."

BOYLE, MARIOTTE AND GAY-LUSSAC

The Boyle–Mariotte law and Gay-Lussac's law form two parts of the combined gas law, relating to the properties of gases and the relationship between pressure and volume of gas.

Robert Boyle (1627–91) is regarded as one of the first modern chemists; French physicist Edme Mariotte (1620–84) also discovered the eye's blind spot; and Joseph Louis Gay-Lussac (1778–1850) pioneered research into the earth's atmosphere by ascending in a hot-air balloon.

Doug rocked back in surprise. Liberty looked amused and grinned excitedly.

"Y'all in?"

They each nodded in turn.

"I've another idea for slowing this thing down," added Doug enigmatically. "I'll need the contents of that ballast bag you're sitting on, Liberty."

"Be my guest," she said, standing up.

He opened the two sand-filled bags and began to stuff their contents into his pockets.

Now he's back to normal, thought Becca with relief.

Peering over the side, Liberty and Doug carefully plotted their course on the map. They'd flown for more than two hours and the lofty peaks had subsided; they were in rugged terrain now, and low enough for the Vimy to fly.

Liberty looked at her friends and nodded. "This is it. Y'all stay here, and keep your heads down."

She carefully climbed onto the thin outer skin of the airship and slid along the surface, hand outstretched for the tubular bar on which the rudder pivoted. She grabbed at the metal and pulled herself into a sitting position, then set about ripping a small panel of material from the vertical fin in front of the rudder. Beneath this was the solid metal structure of the ship's skeleton. She locked into the handhold and edged further forward, making another handhold, and then another…

They watched, holding their breath, as she disappeared from sight, their view of her blocked by the curve of the airship's fat body.

From Doug's sketchbook: Liberty climbs up the airship. (DMS 8/14)

Ten long minutes later the airship's nose began to rise noticeably. The engines revved in response.

"It's working," Doug remarked with satisfaction.

The shadowy figure of Liberty was seen again. She stopped near one of her last handholds and ducked down, then flattened herself to the surface of the airship.

"The crew must be investigating the cell already," whispered Snave.

Becca willed her not to be caught.

After several anxious minutes, Liberty arrived back at the rear machine-gun post, gasping for breath.

"You did it! The nose is lifting," Doug enthused.

"It sure is. You were right, Becca," Liberty breathed. "A couple of the crew took a look at the valve. Darn nearly saw me. They searched about but didn't find nothin'. It's all clear. Let's get movin'."

Liberty slid back out and found her first handhold again,

drawing herself up against the fin. Snave, who seemed to have nerves of steel, went second, overtaking her as he swiftly worked his way forward into the darkness.

Doug was next up. He tried to banish all thoughts of the thousand-foot drop, but couldn't block out the sharp crevasses and jagged outcrops far below, silent and menacing, like the jaws of some prehistoric monster waiting for its prey to fall from the sky. "Sujing Cha-a," he whispered feebly, and reached out shakily for the rudder bar. Liberty gripped his wrist and pulled him up. He found the first handhold and froze, waiting for his sister. Becca managed the manoeuvre with little difficulty, but as he held out his hand for her, he saw the same hollow terror reflected in her eyes.

The maharaja was last, but Doug, on Liberty's signalled instructions, was already moving along the line of handholds, his limbs fuelled by pure adrenalin. He kept going until he found Snave waiting patiently, stooped low against the slipstream.

"Everyone clear, Douglas?" he asked, his cool Englishness untouched by their bizarre circumstances.

"Er... Yes, I th-think so."

"Righty-ho. Hold on to this safety wire and keep as low as you can now."

The nose was tilting upwards by about fifteen degrees now, and the slipstream was much less severe. Snave led the party up the shallow incline to the flat top of the structure.

To Doug's relief, the front machine-gun position was exactly where he'd said it would be. What was more he could see four parachutes lashed to the plough-shaped canvas dodger designed to deflect the slipstream away from the gunners.

"Shall we bring the chutes, Miss Liberty?" asked Snave.

"Don't you trust my flyin'?" She didn't give him a chance to answer. "Too bulky. They'll slow us down."

Once the hatch was open, they climbed down the flimsy ladder into the quiet of the airship. Liberty paused at the bottom rung, ducked down and checked the walkway, the angle of the airship increasing by the second.

Doug gripped the ladder tighter. He could hear shouts and a bell ringing. Someone was issuing the order he had hoped to hear: "All hands forward to the bow." A figure rushed by below them, then another. More men ran past. Still the nose lifted, as if guided by some invisible hand.

"Time to make for the plane," Liberty whispered.

"Go and prepare for the launch," said the maharaja. "Snave and I will guard the walkway. We will ambush any crew who approach."

"As you like. But when y'all hear me fire up those big Rolls-Royce engines, I'll be all set and ready for take-off."

The maharaja nodded. "Good luck."

"Luck's for amateurs, Raj. See y'all in five."

Doug looked ahead. The hammocks of the off-duty crew now hung limply, and all seemed clear as far as the hold. Thanks to Liberty's sabotage, the airship's nose had achieved such an angle that the walkway was like a steep hillside path. Becca clutched the girders for support.

They soon reached the ladder leading down to their old accommodation gondola.

"Our stuff – the drawings and maps," said Becca suddenly. "We'll need them in the desert."

Liberty shook her head. "I need you to help me start the plane, Becca. We don't have much time."

"I'll get them." Doug shinned down the ladder and stepped blindly into their old cabin with the words *This is a very dangerous enterprise* revolving in his head like a mantra. He grabbed the two bags and retraced his steps.

Three rungs up the ladder he paused and looked back at the engine room. He dropped down again into the corridor and cautiously stepped inside. It was deserted. The Maybach engine made an incredible din. He pulled a handful of sand from his pocket and held it beside the air intakes to the carburettor. The grains were sucked in, causing an immediate change in the engine note. Then he found the oil reservoir, added sand to it and left swiftly, climbing the ladder back up into the hull of the ship.

On the walkway he undid the caps of the aluminium fuel tanks lining the keel, dropped a handful of sand in each and patted his now empty pockets with a satisfied smile.

Meanwhile in the cargo hold, Liberty's reaction to the Vimy was far from encouraging. "That plane's the size of a darn ocean liner! We've gotta hope the launch works at this crazy angle. Climb aboard, coz. Let's see what we can do."

Becca stepped forward and clambered up. The cockpit was so large it had the pilot's and co-pilot's seats side by side. She swung down and settled in nervously. Liberty ducked her head into the cockpit and checked the controls.

"Right – fuel, power, throttle for both engines … remember all this, Becca?"

"Yes, but it looks different."

"There's just two of everything. Here – I'll set it up. Electrics on. Throttle set, should be fine. Now this launch system. How in the name of—" This was the moment Doug appeared, brushing sand from his hands. "Get aboard with your sister. There's a navigator's seat up there. See if y'all can find us a map and plot a course out of this mess."

Liberty climbed along the narrow walkway in front of the aircraft and looked about her. The lever to open the cargo hatch was on the starboard side. She kicked it open, and prepared to swing the propeller. A rush of night air rocked the plane. Becca looked at the launch mechanism and prayed it wouldn't activate before Liberty was back on board.

"Contact!"

"Contact!" called out Becca, frantically trying to remember what Liberty had taught her at Sulphur Island.

Liberty swung the starboard prop, and with a belch of smoke the engine fired into life. She gave a thumbs up and moved to the port engine to do the same. With both Rolls-Royce engines running, the plane rocked violently as Becca found the throttle and gunned the engines. Liberty bounded up the ladder, dropped into the cockpit and pulled on her flying goggles.

The maharaja and Snave burst through the door. It was clear Snave had been injured; Becca was shocked to see him clutching a bloody wound on his right forearm. Liberty leapt up on her seat and waved at them to board, yelling over the din. The maharaja stepped two paces back, and for the first time their attackers could be seen. Five crewmen were grappling to overpower them in the confined space.

"Come on!" yelled Liberty.

Snave was tackled to the floor. The maharaja tried to force back three assailants, but the battle was unequal. His last action before being overwhelmed was to wave Liberty away.

From Doug's sketchbook: The crew overpower Snave and the maharaja. (DMS 8/21)

She jumped down into the pilot's seat and gunned the engines.

"No – we can't leave them!" yelled Becca.

"If you wanna get out and fight those guys, don't let me stop you."

Becca glanced at the crew, who were surging forward to storm the plane. There was no choice.

"Sinkiang, here we come!" cried Liberty, releasing the first handle on the launch mechanism. The plane swung down into the slipstream with a spine-jarring bang, bucking and twisting in the airflow. Suddenly they were dangling under the hull just a few feet below the airship's underbelly.

"Hang on," shouted Liberty. "This rodeo ride's gonna be bumpy."

She grabbed the second handle and pulled, releasing the aircraft into a steep dive. She slammed the throttles forward to full power as the plane dropped like a stone. Becca watched through her terror as the airspeed indicator climbed, and noticed Liberty was turning to starboard. The air began to scream through the rigging wires and propellers. They continued to dive, losing height, the airframe juddering and shaking with the strain. Doug wedged himself further down into the navigator's seat, braced himself against the map table and shut his eyes.

Liberty yanked the joystick back with all her might, screaming for Becca to help. Together they battled to level the plane, until finally their efforts began to have an effect. They pulled out of the dive and descended into a river valley.

From Doug's sketchbook: Escape from the airship. (DMS 8/24)

The situation stabilized. Doug unscrewed his eyes and Becca started to breathe again.

"Yeehah!" shouted Liberty, throttling back and slapping Becca on the shoulder. "We can't fly back over the mountains in this old boat. We're trapped in China. So y'all got what you wanted, cousins. Which way now?"

"Khotan! East!" shouted Doug. "We follow the only road there is. The old Silk Road. Do we have enough fuel?"

Liberty grinned and wobbled the plane's wings. "Plenty!"

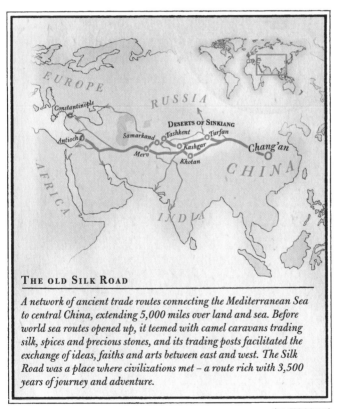

THE OLD SILK ROAD

A network of ancient trade routes connecting the Mediterranean Sea to central China, extending 5,000 miles over land and sea. Before world sea routes opened up, it teemed with camel caravans trading silk, spices and precious stones, and its trading posts facilitated the exchange of ideas, faiths and arts between east and west. The Silk Road was a place where civilizations met – a route rich with 3,500 years of journey and adventure.

The dawn sun burst over the horizon ahead, revealing the aching emptiness of the Takla Makan Desert off their port side. The immense duned surface stretched away to the far horizon, untouched by any road or sign of human habitation. It was breathtaking.

"Say hello to Sinkiang!" said Liberty. "Lots of fresh air and big open spaces. Looks charmin', don't it just?" She reached down and pulled out two pairs of flying goggles from a locker. "Here. You'll need these."

Becca laughed aloud. "Real pilot's goggles! It's good to have you back on our side, Liberty."

Doug wiped the dust off the lenses and put on his pair, gazing at the empty folds of the Takla Makan. It looked impossibly vast – and impossibly hostile. He leant close to his sister's ear and shouted, "Well, sis, this is it. Welcome to the Sinkiang."

Becca's thoughts turned to her missing parents. "Welcome to the Desert of Death, you mean."

CHAPTER TWELVE

From Doug's sketchbook: The oasis seen from the air. (DMS 8/27)

Liberty circled the Khotan oasis for a third time.

"It's gonna have to be that stretch of riverbank down there. Brace yourselves – this could hurt."

They lost height and turned to make the landing run. The ground seemed to rush up to meet them. Liberty straightened up, aiming for what seemed a very small landing strip for such a huge aircraft. The wheels touched down, making the airframe rumble and shake. She cut the engine revs, and the plane screeched to a sudden stop just short of an outcrop of rocks.

Four children ran to greet them, heralding the arrival of an elderly farmer riding on a donkey cart. The children squealed and chattered with delight at the aircraft, running up to touch its wing then racing back to the safety of the cart.

Doug climbed down onto the wing and jumped to the

ground. He made straight for the river, where he scooped lux-
uriant handfuls of water over his hair and face. Liberty began
pacing around the plane, checking for damage and testing
the firmness of the ground. Becca tried talking to the man on
the donkey cart. He looked bewildered.

"Sujing Quantou?" she kept asking, her words carrying on
the faintest of breezes.

Liberty strolled over and sat on a rock beside Doug.

"A river in the desert. Who'd have thought it. Great landing
by the way, Liberty."

"Why, thank you, cousin," she said with a smile. "If we're
dishin' out compliments, your navigation is deadly accurate."

"Is Becca having any luck?"

**THE SIGN OF THE
SUJING QUANTOU**

*The ram's head with
downturned horns – often
simplified to a stylized
single ram's horn – was
recognized throughout
China as the symbol
of the Sujing Quantou.
It indicated the Sujing's
Alexandrian heritage;
Alexander the Great was
often depicted wearing a
ram's horn, symbolic of
the Greek god Zeus.*

They watched as she acted out sword
strokes, but the confused farmer started
to back off in alarm. In frustration Becca
grabbed a stick and began scratching in
the sand.

"Helluva long way to come to play
hopscotch," said Liberty.

They continued to observe for a few
moments, wondering what she was trying
to draw.

"More likely a ram's horn, I think,"
said Doug.

"Ah," said Liberty, closing her eyes and
tilting her head back to catch the sun.
"The sign of the Sujing Quantou."

One of the children recognized
Becca's drawing and started to jump up
and down, pointing to the north. All the

children began to gabble at once until, with a look of surprise, the farmer nodded his head. Becca launched into
another series of mimes, pointing at Doug and Liberty, and
the ground again. The man smiled and nodded.

"I think," said Doug hesitantly, "he's going to take us there."

They followed the farmer and his cart through cultivated
fields for half a mile or so, then the track turned in the direction of the desert and they arrived at a dune field, where great
banks of sand reared up at steep angles.

After about fifteen minutes the farmer stopped at a
stumpy, weather-worn statue of a ram's head. The children
fell silent. Becca nervously shook the farmer's hand in thanks.
He muttered something and the children leapt onto the back
of the cart. With a sharp exclamation, he urged his donkey
to a fast trot, wheeled round and turned back for the river.
Suddenly the three aviators were alone.

Doug caught the anxious look in Liberty's eye. "If only I had
the Liberator with me, I'd feel so much easier," she mumbled.

"Why are you worried?" asked Becca. "The Sujing Quantou
are our friends."

"The eastern chapter are our friends; we've never met this
lot before," muttered Doug.

The sound of charging hooves silenced them. Ahead the
path curved round a tapering spur of sand.

"Quick. Take cover," ordered Liberty.

Two horsemen approached, swords drawn, their armour
and helmets glinting darkly in the sunlight. In a great flurry
of sand the warriors leapt over the spur with a fierce cry

From Doug's sketchbook: The mysterious horsemen. (DMS 8/33)

and turned, drawing up beside the hideaways, blades levelled. The horses snorted and whinnied, stamping their hooves impatiently.

"I thought you said they were friendly," whispered Liberty.

The first horseman broke into giggles.

The second pushed him, and began to chide in a whisper, "You are Sujing Quantou! You do not laugh at strangers when they approach the temple."

The other horseman pushed his eye guard up, his face scornful. "These are not strangers. I would never have laughed otherwise. What do you think I am? A fool?"

Becca recognized the voice. "Xi?"

"Xu, actually."

Xi removed his helmet. "Douglas! Rebecca! You see. You got here in the end. It's good to see you – things were getting boring."

The twins dismounted simultaneously with an effortless jump. Doug patted Xi's horse, making him whinny again.

Xu sheathed his sword and shook their hands. He was serious now, and seemed less welcoming. "We were not expecting you."

"We need the help of the western Sujing. Can you introduce us to them?" asked Becca, pleased to see her old friends. "And we need your help too."

Xi's eyes lit up. "Again?"

But Xu looked troubled. "Much has happened. Come. You look tired. The temple is this way."

The path meandered to the magnificent stone frontage of a building jutting out of a dune.

"Is it sinking?" asked Doug, looking at the temple. The drifting sand had swamped the structure so that the sturdy columns supporting the triangular portico were barely visible.

"The desert is unstoppable," lamented Xi. "Over two thousand years of war with the desert winds, and the desert is winning. Every year it covers a little more. It is now quite a climb down to the entrance. Welcome to Khotan, the temple of the Sujing Quantou."

A nagging thought had crept into Doug's head: if this was the headquarters of the Sujing Quantou, where was everyone? The place seemed abandoned.

A set of wooden steps built over the brimming sand led downwards into the gloom. It took a few moments for their eyes to adjust as Xi picked up an oil lantern and led the way.

"How big is this place?" asked Doug.

"Oh, there are many wings. We are staying in what used to be the stable block."

Their footsteps echoed through the great halls of the temple. The ceiling was over fifty feet high, supported by lines of Doric columns. Their dancing shadows, elongated by the lamp, flickered against walls carved with bas-relief scenes of battle. The air was cool, and the sweat quickly dried on Doug's skin. Further chambers could be glimpsed through tall doorways, but much of the furniture and silk wall hangings had been damaged, and it was apparent that the building had been looted.

"This way," urged Xu.

They turned into a long corridor lined with terrifying life-size statues of Sujing warriors, some of them adorned with fresh garlands of flowers. Doug could see that the craftsmanship was exquisite, and every fine detail of costume and weaponry was exact. The first figure held a sword in one hand and discus in the other, frozen in a battle stance he'd seen many times at Wenzi Island and the Sulphur Archipelago. But the statue's face had been smashed. Doug looked down the hall of warriors. All of them had been defaced.

"Our ancestors," remarked Xi. "These are all Sujing masters. One day my likeness will stand here." He made no mention of the damage, and Doug was too in awe to ask.

They reached a vestibule dominated by a monstrous thirty-foot bronze statue of a solitary warrior, standing with a sword raised in his left hand. The statue was lit from above by a shaft of sunlight, and at first appeared to be undamaged. Then Doug saw the telltale line of machine-gun bullets, slashed across the fighter's chest.

An elderly woman chanted as she placed fresh incense

sticks into a massive three-legged offertory bowl. The rising smoke created a mystical aura around the warrior, as if he might be alive – an outraged giant guarding this desecrated desert temple.

Soon they were in an open courtyard, where the desert heat blazed.

"These are the stables," said Xu, seeming ashamed. "The accommodation wing was completely destroyed. Watch out for scorpions; they are everywhere."

"Joker," scoffed Doug.

"I do not joke. And spiders as big as your hand."

From Doug's sketchbook:
The bronze warrior. (DMS 8/39)

Doug stopped smirking. They entered a stable that had been converted into a kitchen. A feeble fire warmed a steaming kettle. Xu poured them each a small cup of tea.

"For the love of caffeine!" grumbled Liberty. "Doesn't anybody drink coffee out here? My last fix was in India."

"You came here from India?"

"Yes," said Becca. "How did you get here?"

"We left the submarine at Calcutta," said Xu. "We travelled across India and over the passes. It was a terrible journey on foot over the Mintaka Pass. Captain MacKenzie and a team from the *Expedient* were our companions."

"And Chambois. Don't forget the Frenchman," added Xi.

"Chambois?" Liberty looked amazed. "*Out here?* Who else?"

"Ives, Slippery Sam, Sparkie, Fast Frankie, Ten Dinners," rattled off Xi.

Doug smiled. "What about Mrs Ives?"

"She stayed in Calcutta to look after Charlie. He is better, by the way. Still weak, but he will recover in time."

Xu's eyes welled with tears. He couldn't keep up the pretence any longer. "Friends. Terrible things have happened. When we arrived here a month ago we found the temple had been sacked, and all the supplies of Daughter of the Sun looted. The guardians of the building, our Sujing Quantou brothers, had been slaughtered. Shot with machine guns, and suffocated with yellow gas."

MUSTARD GAS

A yellow-brown gas which causes blisters, burns, blindness and damage to the respiratory system. A chemical weapon first used for mass warfare in the First World War, it was responsible for many thousands of deaths in the trenches.

"Mustard gas?" Doug said incredulously. "Who would use mustard gas? That stuff's toxic! Do you have a shell case from the machine guns?"

"Here," said Xi, taking a brass case from his pocket and throwing it to him.

"Russian," said Doug. "Pugachev."

Xu continued in a tired voice, staring at the floor. "This temple has never been successfully attacked in all our history – but the Sujing have no answer to yellow gas and machine guns. The temple lies in ruins. The western gyrolabe has been stolen. The only survivor is the old woman you saw. It is she who told us what happened."

"The gyrolabe's gone?" said Becca.

"Yes. And the western quarter of *The 99 Elements.*"

"You say the guardians of the temple were killed. What about the rest of the western chapter?"

"The old woman told us that a western couple had employed them as guides for an expedition into the desert. The commission was for two months. But that was a year and a half ago. Master Aa fears that the rest of the western chapter has been lost with your parents in the desert hunting for Ur-Can."

Xu prodded the fire into life, sending embers flying upwards. "Master Aa is out there now, searching for our brothers and sisters, your parents and the Russians who stole our gyrolabe."

Becca's mind was working overtime. "Then there are three gyrolabes heading towards Ur-Can."

"What do you mean?" asked Xu.

"Pembleton-Crozier and Baron Vanvort have two aboard the airship that brought us here. And from what you've just told us, the western gyrolabe is somewhere out in the desert in the hands of General Pugachev."

Xi looked at his brother and shook his head. "The situation is much worse. This means there are not three gyrolabes in China, but four."

"All of them?" gasped Becca.

"The last message Master Aa received before leaving India was from a contact in Macao. Kuibyshev and some of the Kalaxx survived the volcanic eruption and escaped from the Sulphur Archipelago. They had been asking about Ur-Can and were bound for Korla to meet with a man called Dante. They will have their gyrolabe with them."

MASTER KUIBYSHEV AND THE KALAXX (NORTHERN SUJING)

The corrupt northern chapter of the Sujing Quantou fled to Russia after the Ha-Mi Wars, where they became tsarist mercenaries and founded the notorious Kalaxx Mining Company. Commanded by Master Kuibyshev, they battled with the Guild and eastern Sujing at Sulphur Island.

(See also Book II.)

Decorative elements

Statue

Marble relief

Front elevation :
Of note is the unique combination of
Greco-Chinese style. The temple is
framed by wind chimes from behind.

Main entrance is set within
a Doric portico.

0 5 10   20   30 ft

IMAGES FROM THE HGS SURVEY OF THE TEMPLE AT KHOTAN

These illustrations of the Sujing temple were drawn during the Guild's expedition to Khotan in 1870. They had been invited there by the Sujing Quantou to celebrate and renew the old Treaty of Khotan on its one hundred and fiftieth anniversary. This agreement had the mutual aim of protecting ancient Tembla secrets.

The temple's many architectural influences, both eastern and western, reflected the diverse history of the fighting order.

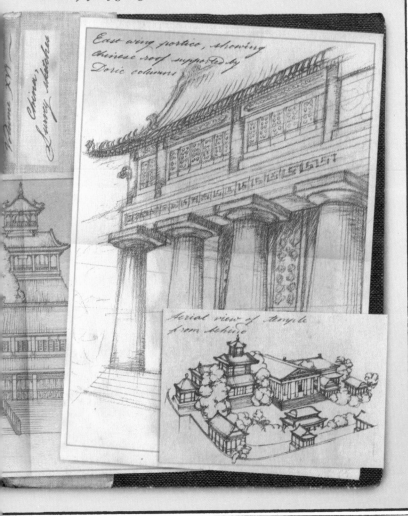

East wing portico, showing chinese roof supported by Doric columns

Aerial view of temple from below

"And Dante will lead them to Pugachev," said Becca. "It seems all four gyrolabes will soon be reunited."

Xi leapt up and began to pace the stable. "We should be out there now with Master Aa."

"Why aren't you?" asked Doug.

"We are guarding the southern chapters of *The 99 Elements* – the texts you pulled out of the trireme! When we got here we were so excited. We thought we would be able to take the Khotan challenges and set out across the desert as full Sujing Quantou warriors. But Master Aa said there was no time. We have been left here to sit and await their return like a pair of donkeys!"

"We must catch up with Master Aa and the captain as soon as possible," stated Becca. "We've got to find our parents and Ur-Can before it's too late."

Xu shook his head. "Our orders are to stay here and guard *The 99 Elements*."

"Why not hide it and come with us?" suggested Doug.

"Hide it?" Xu and Xi looked at each other nervously.

"What do you think, Liberty?" asked Xu.

"Heck, events have certainly outpaced Master Aa and the captain. They could be walkin' into a trap out there in the desert. Leavin' this ol' place would be going against your orders, but if those orders are out of date, it would be your duty to tell Master Aa."

Xu's frustration boiled over. "But how are we ever going to discover the true location of Ur-Can, when it has remained hidden for thousands of years?"

"Er, well, we have a message written by our parents," offered Doug. "They mention a place called Daotang. Could that be it?"

"No. It cannot be," protested Xi with a knowing expression. He spoke to his brother in a low voice. They argued back and forth for nearly a minute.

Finally Xi turned to their friends. "We will show you the Sujing Quantou Chambers of Knowledge. They will prove to you that Ur-Can cannot be located at Daotang."

Xi pushed open one of the largest doors Doug had ever seen and led them into a chamber deep within the temple complex. The shuttered windows were braced with huge beams of wood to hold back the weight of the encroaching sand outside.

"This is the map room. Xu, draw back the curtain so our guests can see."

With the pull of a rope, sunlight flooded through the dusty atmosphere from a window high in the wall and fell onto a scale model of great antiquity depicting the bowl of the Sinkiang deserts. The extraordinary map was constructed on a raised platform sixty feet by thirty, its base carved with Sujing Quantou guardian warriors in contemplative poses, all of them defaced.

As Doug's eyes adjusted to the gloom, he noticed the walls of the room were decorated with many trophies of war.

"They left most of our mementoes," said Xu, gazing upwards. "Weapons taken in battle from the armies of the great khans – Genghis and Kublai. There" – he pointed – "is a saddle used by Tamerlane himself. The flag beside it belonged to the Tang army…"

Doug's attention turned to the map. The northern boundary was described by the Tien Shan, or the Celestial Mountains; the southern boundary was defined by the Himalayas. Each trade route, oasis and town was marked as far as Kashgar in the west and Anxi in the east. Doug quickly found the Mintaka Pass, and the desert they had flown across to reach Khotan. The spot was marked by a miniature temple made of solid gold.

Becca recalled maps she'd seen of this area, one of the world's wildest regions, drawn by recent explorers and archaeologists. "But there are many more cities marked here than on modern maps. What's happened to them?"

"The desert is restless," said Xu. "You say that Ur-Can is lost in the desert, but we, the Sujing Quantou, could show you the sites of a hundred lost cities. Nearly all are buried now, just as this temple will be buried in the next fifty years."

"But archaeologists have found some of them."

"Those grave robbers!" raged Xi. "The cities should be left to their rest. To disturb them is to cause grievance to the djinn who live in them."

"Djinn?"

"The spirits of the desert."

"Ghouls now?" sneered Liberty. "Well, I guess it was only a matter of time…"

"So Ur-Can's not marked on here, then?" asked Doug, admiring the elaborate detail. Each city was carved in jade and marked with a bright blue gemstone.

"What about Daotang?" asked Becca.

"Take your shoes off and join me. It is easier to see." Xi jumped up onto the map and strolled north. "This is Daotang. It was one of the most important of all the northern oasis cities. Ur-Can could not be located here. It is a ruin now, but the place was built on and lived in for too long for such a secret to remain hidden."

KHOTAN MAP ROOM

The vast and empty Takla Makan Desert is encircled by high mountain ranges to the north, south and west. The extremes of temperature and steep dune fields present a natural barrier of exceptional harshness. The heart of the desert is impenetrable to all but the most skilled and hardy travellers.

Ancient traders exporting rare and valuable goods westwards on camel caravans from central China were forced to cross this hostile territory to reach the profitable markets of the Middle East, Europe, India and southern Russia.

As the desert was impassable, routes were forged north and south to skirt the desert's periphery. Over time, oasis towns and trading centres developed between Kashgar and Anxi. Sinkiang was a lawless region and the caravans with their precious cargoes of silks, spices and gemstones were vulnerable to attack from bandits.

Mercenaries such as the Sujing Quantou could be hired to protect the caravans. The Sujing relief map constructed at Khotan was used to calculate scales of pay for such commissions. It marked every known well, spring, watercourse, city, town and village. It was also used in times of war to plan attacks and strategies against Sujing enemies. For this purpose it also displayed military information, noting forts and watchtowers and known hideouts of enemies, bandits and warlords.

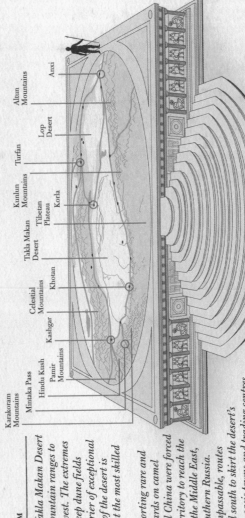

Karakoram Mountains

Mintaka Pass
Hindu Kush
Pamir Mountains

Kashgar

Celestial Mountains

Khotan

Takla Makan Desert

Tibetan Plateau

Kunlun Mountains

Korla

Turfan

Lop Desert

Altun Mountains

Anxi

"What about Karez then?" pressed Becca.

Xu laughed. "Karez is not a place; it is an irrigation tunnel. There are thousands of them in the Sinkiang. Tunnelled by hand, long ago. They are marked with these blue lines. Water from the mountains is channelled underground to irrigate the crops and provide drinking water. Some of the karez are over fifty miles long."

Doug was thinking hard. Something was nagging him about the shape of the lines. "I've seen these lines before." He crouched down and looked at Daotang's jade marker. "Why is it covered with red paint?"

"Because it was a Ha-Mi city destroyed by the Sujing Quantou," Xi stated with pride.

From Doug's sketchbook: Walking on the map. (DMS 8/42)

"When?"

"In your calendar, about 300 AD."

"What does this other stuff mean?" Doug was looking at some text carved into a darker stone a little way out into the desert.

"Dark stones warn of djinn. Let me see." Xi's voice dropped as he read the faint text. "This is the abode of Qui'l'bharat."

"Qui'l what?" asked Liberty.

"Qui'l'bharat. The most powerful djinn in the desert. Master Aa once told us that Qui'l'bharat is the djinn of all djinn. Qui'l'bharat watches you, listens to you, makes your throat burn with an unquenchable thirst to speed your death. He will appear as a storm when angry, raining death by throwing rocks and stones, and blocking out the sunlight so day becomes night."

"More darned hokum," sighed Liberty.

"The ancient Sujing gave Daotang another name," said Xu. "Because of Qui'l'bharat, Daotang was also known as Storm City."

Doug turned to his sister. "Have you got Father's sketch map?" Becca swiftly pulled it out of her bag. "Daotang is, say … thirty or forty miles south-west of Korla?" guessed Doug.

"Yes … about that."

"This karez." Doug traced one of the blue lines on the Sujing map with his foot from the Tien Shan passing Daotang and out into the desert. "This must have supplied water to Daotang?"

"Yes."

"I think Father's sketch shows these karez. It matches the lines on this Sujing model precisely. Father has circled this karez here. It's the one leading to Daotang. Are you sure Daotang can't be Ur-Can?"

Xi shook his head. "No, as I said, the Sujing sacked the city. We would have found it."

Doug looked again at his father's overlay. He traced the thin blue line on the Sujing model from Daotang northwards. He glanced back at his father's neat line. But there was a difference – he'd marked a branch in the karez that led some way into the desert that wasn't on the Sujing map.

"Say the Ha-Mi found Ur-Can when they were tunnelling the karez to supply water to their city," he suggested. "Say they knew where it was, but not its true purpose?"

Becca saw what her brother was getting at. "The Ha-Mi never had the gyrolabes. Even if they found Ur-Can, even if they translated the hieroglyphics, they could never have unlocked all its secrets."

"And the reason the Sujing didn't find Ur-Can when they sacked Daotang is that it's stuck out in the desert somewhere along this karez," Doug continued.

Becca saw an obvious flaw in Doug's hypothesis. "Surely the Sujing map makers must have walked through the tunnel to map it. If Ur-Can was somewhere off the karez they would have found it."

Xu looked at Becca strangely. "You've never seen a karez, have you?"

Becca shook her head.

"There is no need to go underground to map them. Every few hundred feet there is a hole where the tunnellers removed the spoil. A karez looks like a line of molehills across the desert. It would be far easier to map it from above."

"So Ur-Can could lie somewhere along the karez," suggested Becca, "unknown to the Sujing."

Xi nodded. "I suppose it's possible."

"The problem is, Pugachev and his army must be sitting right on top of it," murmured Doug gloomily. "And if Pugachev defeated the western chapter of the Sujing, what chance do Master Aa and the captain have?"

"They were heading for Korla. If they have crossed the desert at Sujing marching speed, they will be there by now," said Xu. He turned to Xi and they argued for a couple of minutes, Xu pointing repeatedly at the area around Daotang.

Xi finally seemed to relent with a hesitant nod. "We must set out immediately and find Master Aa. He must be told of the possible location of Ur-Can. As my brother reminds me, Sujing law dictates this. We will hide the southern quarter of *The 99 Elements* in a place known only to us."

"Can you fly us?" Becca appealed to Liberty. "That way we get there before Crozier and Vanvort."

"We saw how fast you flew as you circled around in the sky like a bird," enthused Xi.

Liberty pushed a hand through her tangled hair. "Wait a darned minute – I know I've been sucked into this crazy scheme but there are limits." She pointed at the vast blank void on the map. "This Storm City place must be close on four hundred miles away. We don't have enough fuel."

"We'll walk then," said Becca.

"Whoa. Hold on there. We'll just need to take a little detour first. Da Vine Oil has a camp out here, at Maralbeshi, on the other side of the Takla Makan. It's about a hundred and eighty miles away, only a couple of hours flyin'. We oughta make it with what we've got left in the tanks. They're not meant to be out there, so it's all hush-hush. But they'll have fuel. I'll bet my goggles on it."

That evening, in the yellow light of an animal-fat lamp, Doug and Becca examined the ancient texts of the southern quarter of *The 99 Elements*. Each sliver of wood on which the Tembla scribe had written was as delicate as a dried autumn leaf. The minute hieroglyphs were perfectly regular yet totally incomprehensible.

Xu and Xi had been reluctant to show them the texts, but had finally relented on two conditions: they could only view them in the feeblest of light, and only for as long as the sand lasted in an hourglass. These were strict Sujing rules to ensure the fragile texts didn't fade.

Doug replaced the last strip in the wooden chest and rubbed his chin. "I've never really grasped all this *99 Elements* stuff, Xu. I mean, can the Sujing Quantou understand what it says on these codexes or not?"

"Codices," corrected Becca. "It's the plural of 'codex'."

Doug pulled a face. "All right. Do you understand what these *codices* mean?"

"We understand their general meaning." Xu carefully pulled out one of the strips. It was a slightly different colour and had a different script which Doug recognized.

"That's ancient Greek."

Xu nodded. "The Sujing's limited understanding of *The 99 Elements* goes back to the River Hyphasis in 326 BC, when the gyrolabes and *The 99 Elements* were looted by the troops of Alexander the Great's army from a caravan of Tembla priests fleeing the war."

"Many of the Tembla sect were killed, and the survivors

scattered into the night – but not everyone got away," continued Xi. "Sujing history tells us of a Tembla servant who was found hiding in the shallows of the river. This man had no love for his masters and he revealed to the Greeks how the gyrolabes worked and explained *The 99 Elements*. He had attended many of the Tembla's secret ceremonies, and understood much of the Tembla beliefs."

From Doug's sketchbook: Becca examines The 99 Elements. (DMS 8/46)

"These few Greek texts" – Xu held up the codex – "were written by the prodromoi. They are notes, taken in haste from this servant. Notes, alas, containing inaccuracies due to gaps in the servant's knowledge. Each of the other three boxes – the north, the east, and the west – has these accompanying Greek notes roughly explaining its contents. These are what the Sujing and the Guild have been using for centuries to try to understand the Indus script in which *The 99 Elements* is written."

The teachings of The 99 Elements *originated circa 4,000 BC and were handed down by word of mouth within the Tembla cult. The texts were eventually copied onto wooden codices approximately a thousand years later. Over the following two millennia language and writing evolved and newer versions were written. One HGS source suggests that with each new incarnation, the old versions were burnt to ensure secrecy. This process inevitably introduced inaccuracies into the texts. The last surviving copies were written circa 1,000 BC; it was these that were discovered by Alexander the Great's army in 326 BC.*

The two strips pictured here are taken from a set of 26 creeds which make up the complete southern quarter of The 99 Elements. *When compared with original*

Tembla hieroglyphic script as seen in both Elena MacKenzie's photograph taken at Ur-Can (page 28) and Ezekiel Zedd's drawings of the Tembla death ritual hieroglyphs (page 41), it should be noted that the styles of the letter forms are quite different due to developments in writing and language.

The inherent inaccuracies within the northern, eastern and western texts would later cause HGS researchers almost insurmountable difficulty in perfecting any modern translation of the Tembla teachings. These southern creeds had, of course, never been seen by the Guild because they had been lost aboard one of Alexander's shipwrecked triremes until their rediscovery by Becca and Doug during their stay on Sulphur Island.

Becca thought about the complicated history of the texts on the table in front of her. "So the Greek translation codex you have in your hand contains simplified notes taken from a servant about the other, even older Indus codices in this box ... and from what our uncle has told us, the Indus codices are, in themselves, just corruptions of even older Tembla texts now lost to history?"

"Mercy me, it's the all original Chinese whisper!" laughed Liberty.

"Graeco-Indian whisper, if you want to be accurate, Liberty." Doug grinned.

"That's why the Tembla secrets have been hidden for so long. What is contained in these chests is but an echo of that great people's original work."

"So what do you actually know?" asked Doug, his face fixed in concentration.

"*The 99 Elements* is a collection of creeds ... beliefs and learnings. These creeds are separated into four disciplines, each linked to particular aspects of human nature and knowledge."

Xu and Xi spoke passionately, one following the other. "Each of the four disciplines is broken down into smaller, elemental creeds. There are ninety-nine in total."

"The eastern quarter is the one we eastern Sujing know best. It contains twenty-four elemental creeds and concerns itself with mankind's mastery of science. These explain the Tembla's highest level of achievement – the manipulation of gravity using Daughter of the Sun."

"The northern quarter relates to man's intellect."

"The western quarter concentrates on man's innate desire for survival. The Tembla's science is interwoven with all of these creeds and constant reference is made to the Toba catastrophe to caution against what can go wrong. Do you know about Toba?"

"Of course," sniffed Doug.

"So what's the southern quarter about?" asked Becca, pointing towards the simple wooden box.

Xu and Xi paused, looking anxious. "These creeds are not teachings like the other sections of *The 99 Elements*," Xi confided. "These are warnings. These chapters have been lost for so long that what little knowledge we had about them was passed down by word of mouth through generations of Sujing Quantou."

"This box contains twenty-six elemental creeds. They deal with the destructive tendencies of man," continued Xu. "They are the sum of all the Tembla's fears for the future of mankind. The first ten creeds warn of the destructive potential of Daughter of the Sun, and the dangers of misusing gravity manipulation. They warn again and again that the substance can as easily be used for evil as for good."

Xi took over. "The next ten creeds discuss those aspects of human behaviour most feared by the Tembla survivors, in particular the scientific ambition which had led their ancestors to almost destroy the human race with the generator at Toba."

"What about the last few creeds?"

"Five deal with the science of war," Xi replied. "And the final creed – the ninety-ninth – tells of the Tembla's city refuge in Antarctica, where it is said that there is a library containing all their collected knowledge. But you surely know of this? Your uncle has searched for it using the Sujing myths concerning the southern quarter of the texts. Many of his men were lost to the cold, I believe."

Doug recalled the captain telling them the *Expedient* had

been *trapped in a southern ice pack* during their first interview aboard ship. At last this made sense. The crew had never mentioned the deaths of fellow shipmates, but this could have been a secret HGS operation. And the crew were very good at keeping secrets.

"Time we all got some shut-eye," said Liberty, yawning. "We've got a long way to fly tomorrow."

"One last question," said Becca. "What about Ur-Can? What does *The 99 Elements* say about that?"

"Ur-Can is heavily connected to the western quarter. Elemental creed seven states that the Tembla built Ur-Can as a gift. And yet the warnings about using it are many. The Tembla servant was unable to locate it on any map or give the Greeks any idea as to what it actually was."

"Why?" asked Doug.

"Because these were the deepest secrets of the sect and he was just a servant."

"The western chapters speak much of nature itself as a threat to mankind's survival," added Xu. "They tell of volcanoes, earthquakes and comets as dangerous to us as mankind's misuse of science—"

"Nice story, twins, but hey, we've got a desert to cross tomorrow. Time we all got some sleep. Now."

"Yes, Liberty. But first we must hide the southern quarter of *The 99 Elements*," said Xi solemnly. "Three days ago we found a secret cache of western Sujing battle equipment missed by the raiders; we will conceal *The 99 Elements* there and take the equipment. It may be useful when we meet the Russians."

CHAPTER THIRTEEN

After loading Xu and Xi's special battle equipment into the plane we took off, flying a little west of north at first light. We caught a last glimpse of the green of the Khotan oasis, then turned and flew towards the undulating sand dunes of the desert. Two colours stretched ahead of us: the tan of the sand and the azure blue of the sky.

We climbed slowly to ten thousand feet, where the air was cooler. The aching vastness of the desert was mesmerizing. Once we reached our cruising height Liberty put me in charge of the plane. Xu and Xi looked on anxiously as I took the controls. "Sujing Cha!" shouted Xi, his face a picture of concern – this was their first ever flight. Memories of my last flight flooded back, but this plane, although larger, seemed easier to handle. Liberty encouraged me with simple advice: "Straight an' level and watch the compass bearin', coz." My nervousness was quickly overwhelmed by the sheer exhilaration of flying again. How I love to be in the air!

The first hour shot by – I was concentrating so hard. For much of the second hour, I kept looking at the fuel gauge. The flickering needle seemed to move more quickly after half full. Liberty dozed, arms crossed behind her head. A distant range of mountains came into view on the horizon, defining the edge of the desert. Doug identified them as the Tien Shan, which made navigation simpler as I chose a peak that was on course, and aimed for it. This gave me more time

DA VINE OIL

Giovanni da Vine, recuperating from wounds suffered in the American Civil War (1861–5), bought a share in his brother Marcello's Angry Bear Salt Works Company, West Virginia. Giovanni saw the future was in oil, at that time being discovered in large quantities in close proximity to their manufactory. He bought a plot of land in Four Oak Valley, Webster County, and began drilling, striking oil 80 feet down on his first attempt. This "shallow gusher" was just the beginning. In 1866 he and his brother founded da Vine Oil, rapidly expanded to thirty wells, and within two years had made their fortune. By 1910 the company was extracting oil in Pennsylvania, Oklahoma, Ohio and finally Texas. Giovanni's son Theodore (Liberty's father) moved the company's headquarters to Texas in 1912.

to worry about the fuel gauge, which was now hovering under quarter full.

Finally the dune field broke and we were out of the desert. I woke Liberty as we passed over the tangled bed of the River Yarkan He. Maralbeshi was almost exactly on our compass bearing, a straggle of buildings surrounded by fields. Doug grinned. "Lethal! Right on target."

I lost height as Liberty hunted for the da Vine Oil outpost with Doug's binoculars. With a shout she pointed down at a ramshackle-looking farmhouse, with a truck and an ancient biplane parked outside. Liberty took control and wheeled us round. As we roared overhead, a man ran out waving his arms frantically. Liberty landed in a swirl of dust beside the parked plane, and jumped out looking very excited.

"Uncle Pete! What are you doin' here?"

"Are you here to collect me?" pleaded Pete.

"No, just visitin'!"

"No? *No?*" The tone of Uncle Pete's voice twisted maniacally upwards. His face was contorted with anxiety and he was close to crying. Despite the heat,

Uncle Pete -
quite an unusual
chap

he wore a three-piece suit and bow tie. Doug had heard tales of company agents who went mad working for years away from home in isolated parts of the world. Uncle Pete was clearly one of them. He was standing outside the farmhouse with a hastily packed suitcase waiting for them to take him away.

"What are you doin' here, Uncle Pete? I had no idea."

"Sent out here by your daddy. 'Spend some time in the field; get some experience,' he said. 'After that I'll put you on the board of da Vine Oil.' I've had experiences, all right. I've been stuck here for two years! Two stinkin' years. I'm lucky to be alive." He banged his fist on the suitcase.

"It's OK, Uncle Pete, we're here now," said Liberty, trying to soothe the agitated man.

"Did we win it?" he asked.

"Win what?"

UNCLE PETE

Peter da Vine's career in oil exploration ended immediately after his sojourn in China. He became a gardener at the Brooklyn Botanic Garden, New York, specializing in orchids.

"The Great War, of course!"

"Er, kinda," answered Liberty. "A couple of years back. Find any oil?"

"Oh, sure. And gas too. That geologist, Franklin. He sends me round the twist. Singing those lunatic songs. Every night! I've had to build him a new house. He lives over there now. We don't talk; we've not talked for eighteen months. I want out. Out. D'you hear me? OUT! I don't care about being on the board any more. I hate oil. I hate the smell of oil! I hate the *word* oil!"

"D'you have gasoline?" asked Liberty.

"Gasoline! Gallons of the stuff. That's about all I've got."

"What about coffee?"

"Coffee? Sure I've got coffee."

"Come on, Uncle Pete, let's go inside for a bit. Xi, see if you can find a stove. I need a good strong coffee."

The interior of the house was as broken-down as its occupant. He slumped on a wooden chair, clutching his suitcase against his chest. Xi and Doug found a kettle and started to make a pot of coffee, while Becca investigated the larder.

"When y'all meant to go back to America?" asked Liberty.

"I was told to wait here until the order came to return. I've always obeyed orders."

"I think it's time you went home, Uncle Pete." Liberty took a pad of paper from the sideboard and found a pencil. She scribbled a note, and found an envelope. "Here's an order."

Pete's eyes filled with tears. "An order home?"

"Xi, why don't you go and see if Mr Franklin's in. I'd like a chat with him."

Uncle Pete looked edgy at the mention of Franklin. His eyes flicked around the room and he began to drum his fingers on top of the case. Liberty took a sip from the cup that Doug had placed beside her, and immediately spat it out.

"What in the name of all things good is *that*?"

"Coffee. Straight from the tin," said Doug.

"You get a taste for it," said Pete. "It's from Minsk."

"They grow coffee in Minsk?"

Becca pulled out two tins. "Wait. All of your food is Russian."

"Franklin gets the stuff," said Pete. "Buys it from their trucks when they stop over from Kashgar."

"Have you heard of a General Pugachev? Or a man called Dante?" said Becca.

"Is Pugachev here? Has he found out where I live?"

"Do you know where Pugachev is?"

"Some ruined city south-west of Korla. He's training an army. Drills them day and night. They captured me. I escaped and walked for three days. It was a whole week before I found my truck again. The things I saw..."

"Did Pugachev have other prisoners?" tried Liberty.

"Yeah. Some, I guess."

"Anyone called MacKenzie?"

"Didn't get any names."

"Did anyone mention Ur-Can?"

"No. No conversation. Not allowed."

"A husband and wife? The woman would be American. A New Yorker like you."

"Oh, sure. She was allowed to walk about. The other guy, her husband, he was kinda locked in a mud-hut cave. They didn't treat him too well. Not as bad as me. Thought I was spying on them! They buried me in a pit, d'you see? Just my head stickin' up. The scorpions, they crawled across my face. I escaped from the sand on the third night. The New Yorker ... the woman. She helped me. She asked me to go for help. 'Help?' I said. '*Help?* From who? There ain't nobody out here to help!'"

Becca looked over at Doug. Even this fragment of news was enough to make them both smile broadly. "Doug! They're still alive!"

Uncle Pete pocketed Liberty's scribbled note and walked briskly to the door. "Make yourselves at home, why don't you? Would you excuse me."

Liberty sat back and sniffed the coffee again, grimacing and trying another sip. She opened the window to chuck it away, and as she did so, cried out, "Uncle Pete! Hey, Uncle Pete! Come back!"

Her shouts were drowned out as Pete started his biplane, pulled the chocks away and jumped aboard.

From Doug's sketchbook: Uncle Pete – up to his neck in the desert. (DMS 8/53)

Liberty rushed to the door. "Pete!" she called, but it was too late. He waved the note in triumph and began his take-off run, sending clouds of exhaust fumes and dust billowing into the house.

"I have my orders home!" he yelled.

They watched him take off and climb, heading west.

Xi ran over from the direction of Franklin's house. "There's no one there. The place is empty apart from this." He held out a page torn from a history book. "It was pinned to a chair."

"I think we just found Franklin," said Liberty. She read the caption beneath the illustration: "*Benjamin Franklin, 1706–90, statesman of the United States.* There was no Franklin here, just a crazy da Vine. Let's start refuellin'. As soon as it's done, we'll take off. This place gives me the creeps."

It was midday now and Doug, hunkered down in the navigator's seat, calculated with his chart that they were an hour's flying time from Korla. Becca picked up Doug's binoculars and focused them ahead. The heat haze from the desert below had cut visibility considerably. She wiped her eyes and refocused. She was certain she could see something ahead and a little below them.

She handed the binoculars to Doug for a second opinion. He nodded, fixing on the distant object.

"The airship, I think. You can just make out the tail."

Liberty took the binoculars and checked. "That's them all right. They're flyin' at reduced height and speed. They've adjusted the trim, but she's still nose up."

"What's their bearing?" asked Doug.

"Near enough the same as ours. Seventy-five degrees magnetic."

"They're still bound for Korla."

"We have to get there first," said Becca.

"We'll overtake them," shouted Liberty. "I'll make sure we're out of machine-gun range. They don't have the speed to catch us."

Over the next twenty minutes the glimmer on the horizon took shape. Liberty levelled at the same height, and moved dead astern, where the airship had a blind spot. Doug checked to see if there was a lookout in the rear machine-gun position, but it was empty.

"They're makin' less than forty knots to our eighty," yelled Liberty. "Looks like they've lost a couple of engines." She winked at Doug, then squinted ahead. "We've only got about another sixty miles to Korla. I should be able to see it by now, but the visibility's dire over there."

"That's strange," said Doug. "The airship's altering course. Have they seen us?"

Liberty checked around. "Sandstorm! Blown up out of nowhere. That's why I couldn't see Korla. Look at that thing!"

A rolling wave of dust bubbled and boiled as the storm raced across the desert at terrifying speed.

SANDSTORMS

Sandstorms are a powerful and terrifying desert phenomenon. They can range from small "dust devils" of a few feet in diameter, to towering, fast-moving walls of dust up to 20,000 feet high. They have been known to shift whole sand dunes, destroy farmland and bury entire cities.

Liberty gunned the engines and yanked back the control column. "It must have a forty-mile front. Things could get rough in this old boat. We need to put on some height. Trouble is, this crate climbs like a ... well, like an old Limey bomber."

Xu and Xi were looking nervously at the storm. "Qui'l'bharat. The desert is angry!

From Doug's sketchbook: Caught in the sandstorm. (DMS 8/57)

There will be rocks as big as your head in there. We must not enter the storm cloud, Liberty."

"I'm doin' my best, guys, but we don't have a lotta choice."

Liberty battled to climb away from the storm, but within minutes the first wisps of dust had surrounded the plane. Moments later the sunlight was blocked out as they were engulfed by the dense cloud. Stones and boulders struck the airframe and wings, ripping through the thin fabric.

"We're being shredded," yelled Liberty. Almost as she said it, the starboard engine was struck, and part of the airscrew ripped off.

The plane lurched as Liberty struggled to level off. A rock hit the tail, then one of the wing struts splintered in two. The starboard engine coughed and died.

"Becca, gimme a hand here," bellowed Liberty.

Becca too battled with the control column, but the altimeter showed that they were dropping rapidly towards the desert.

"Strap yourselves in. We're gonna crash-land."

The port engine failed. The clammer of the rocks against the hull was deafening as they hit the storm cloud's heart.

Liberty concentrated on the instruments. "Any time now. Any time now…"

They didn't see the dunes as they hit. They clipped one, ripping off a section of the starboard wing. As the plane slewed to the right, the undercarriage struck another dune and was instantly smashed off. They bellyflopped and pitched forward, the port wing tip digging in and making the fuselage lurch sideways. With a wrenching jolt, they careered over the crest of a steep dune and shuddered to a halt with the tail section at a near vertical angle.

"Out! Out!" screamed Liberty, vaulting out of her seat to the safety of the dune below. "There's fuel everywhere!"

Doug, shaken but not injured, could smell the strong petroleum vapour even through the storm. The starboard engine suddenly exploded in a ball of orange-red flame, setting fire to the wing and fuselage. Xu and Xi were thrown to the ground as they fought to save their Sujing battle equipment. Doug jumped down and pulled them both clear, and Becca scrabbled down to help.

"Over here!" yelled Liberty, battling against the storm to hang on to a piece of engine cowling. "Help me dig this into the dune – we can shelter under it. Not such a great landing this time, hey, Doug?"

"I wonder how the airship fared?"

"No chance," said Liberty, shaking her head. "Give me wings every time."

Chapter Fourteen

Becca's diary: 12th August 1920
Sinkiang

The storm raged for the rest of the day, and most of the night. An hour before dawn the wind suddenly died and the air was still again. In the absolute silence it seemed impossible that such a catastrophic event had ever happened.

Doug has been trying to calculate our exact position from the charts. He thinks Korla lies not more than fifty miles to the north. His navigation equipment has survived, and at midday he hopes to get a precise fix using the sextant.

From Doug's sketchbook: The Vimy half buried in the sand dune. (DMS 8/58)

Sujing well and water locator strips. (MA 746.188 SUJ)

Xu and Xi have told us not to move about in the heat of the sun. If we do, we will die. We must conserve energy and water. They say we must travel at night when it's cooler.

Liberty has been gathering our supplies. We have some water, and the Russian food harvested from mad Uncle Pete's should last us a few days.

Xu and Xi pulled thin strips of paper from the lining of their armour. On these, they claim, are drawn secret Sujing wells and water sources. If Doug's navigation is correct, the first lies twelve miles away. How they'll be able to find anything in this wilderness is beyond me. They say that they have been taught to smell water, and that it'll be easy.

Nothing here looks easy. Nothing at all.

They left the plane at dusk and began to walk towards the first well. Doug took compass bearings, but an average course was all they could hope for as it was impossible to walk in a straight line through the dunes.

Xu and Xi looked to the night sky for direction. This, Doug quickly realized, was far easier and more accurate. He'd never seen stars look so bright, and the stillness of the air and the startling clarity of the constellations put him in an almost dreamlike state. Walking made his legs ache as the sand sapped energy with every step.

His concentration shifted to the Sujing twins, who were weighed down with the mysterious battle equipment. In addition to their swords, they each carried a package wrapped in sacking and worn like a backpack. The shape suggested they contained sections of piping, but Doug's enquiries had met with no satisfactory answer as to what they might be. That wasn't all. They each had a menacing-looking composite bow and a quiver of arrows slung over their shoulders. None of the arrows had a typical arrowhead, but a small tubular container with a sharpened end rather like a firework rocket.

At a little after three in the morning Xu and Xi found the well. Doug was impressed.

"You can smell the water," Xi whispered excitedly as they dug in the marshy ground with their bare hands. Drops of water slowly began to fill the hole. After a couple of minutes, Xi tasted a cupped handful. "Yes. Good. Fill your bottles."

"What's the other smell around here?" asked Liberty, sniffing a musty scent in the air.

"It could be the marsh … or my lucky socks. The heat's really making them stink," said Doug with some pride.

"We'll move on up to that higher ground there and take a breather. The old cowgirl in me says there could be quicksand about with all this water."

They climbed a little way from the well and sat on a group of low humps, resting their feet.

"Shoot!" shouted Liberty, jumping up. "There's someone takin' a nap down here." She lightly kicked the sleeping figure.

Xi sprang up, shocked. "Sujing Quantou!"

"Dead Sujing Quantou," added Liberty. "Dried out like a mummy. This is a darn graveyard…"

"An unfinished graveyard," came a voice from behind them. It was a voice they knew well.

"This, Rebecca and Douglas, is all that remains of your parents' expedition. These Sujing died well over a year ago. But hell's teeth – *what* are you doing here?"

Captain Fitzroy MacKenzie strode forward out of the darkness. He was absolutely furious. "You are meant to be in America with Aunt Margaret! Where's my tiger?"

"In India," muttered Becca.

"India? What's she doing there?"

"And you two," came another familiar voice, "are meant to be at Khotan guarding *The 99 Elements*."

Master Aa loomed out of the shadows.

The Captain - furious!

From Doug's sketchbook. (DMS 8/63)

The captain pointed his walking stick at them. "How, exactly, did you get here; and how, Miss da Vine, do you come to be with them? Are you to blame for this outrage?"

"Hey now, Skip, I was takin' these two right back to America, when we got chased onto a flying gas bag death trap—" Liberty's voice rose in irritation.

"Shh..." Master Aa butted in. "The Kalaxx are but three dunes hence; you must speak softly. It is fortunate you have stumbled into us, not them."

Becca's voice was strained. "We came to find you. Mother and Father are alive. They've been captured by General Pugachev, who has found Ur-Can. And soon all four gyrolabes will be there as well."

"Utter nonsense!" snapped the captain.

"I don't think so, Uncle," said Doug softly. "We believe we know where Ur-Can is. It's near Daotang."

The captain gave a stifled laugh. "I suppose I should have known – you two found the southern gyrolabe, so why not Ur-Can as well?"

"Are the Kalaxx heading for Daotang?" Doug asked.

"Now you have told us this, I must assume they are. Their route was making no sense, but now ... this is excellent work." Doug was surprised at this rare compliment from Master Aa. "We have been on the Kalaxx's trail from Korla, where they tortured and killed a man called Dante. The locals told us he was Pugachev's contact. Pugachev must have his headquarters in the ruins of Daotang."

"So all the bad guys will soon be in one place," remarked Liberty. "After all your efforts, Skip, those gyrolabes are scootin' toward this godforsaken sandpit like homin' pigeons to their roost."

The captain gave Liberty a hard stare but didn't rise to her attack. "You know where the eastern and southern gyrolabes are, I take it?"

Becca and Doug nodded. "We were brought here aboard the Coterie's airship. Crozier and Vanvort have them."

Master Aa sighed deeply. "For now, we must continue to bury the dead," he said solemnly. He picked up a near mummified body, carried it to an open grave, and with help from one of his fighters carefully laid it in the ground.

"Our intention was to find your parents," said the captain. "Our imperative now must be to recover as many gyrolabes as we can. If Pugachev succeeds in obtaining all the gyrolabes and starts the machine, your parents' usefulness to him will be greatly diminished. More importantly, we hold the future of the human race in our hands."

"Then we're going to Ur-Can with you?" asked Doug hopefully.

"Against my better judgement, yes," sighed the captain. "There is no other choice. Enough MacKenzies have been lost in this desert."

CHAPTER FIFTEEN

Becca's diary: 13th August 1920
Approximately 5 miles from Daotang

Nothing can live in a place as dead as this for long. Even to breathe here seems like hard work. It's as if the desert listens to you. The silence gets into your mind and searches out every weakness and anxiety and plays upon it. My fear is that we're too late. That after all we've been through we won't make it to our parents in time. General Pugachev is clearly a ruthless and dangerous man.

We have been here at the well all day waiting for the Kalaxx to move. Master Aa thinks they will go tonight, and we will follow them.

Doug and I have passed the time talking to our old shipmates and catching up on news. It's wonderful that we're all together

Chambois Captain M Gasmus Ives

Slippery Sam Fast Frankie

Ten Dinners

From Doug's sketchbook: Catching up with old shipmates. (DMS 8/65)

*again, and somehow their quiet chatter and humour has given me
the illusion of safety in this godforsaken place. Chambois has been
explaining how the captain offered him the chance to join the expedition. As he is still wanted for murder – a charge no one here
believes for a minute is true – he cannot return to Europe. "I am a
man on the run; I thought I might as well see the world while I'm
running," he joked. It's obvious, though, that he longs to return
home to clear his name and continue his research.*

*Master Aa's scout is certain that the Kalaxx are preparing to
move at dusk. In the dying light of the afternoon, the Sujing warriors are filling their water bottles and sharpening their swords. I
just want to start walking. To find Mother and Father. Now. Before
it's too late.*

Doug watched as the Kalaxx climbed a sand dune half a mile
away. Their figures were clearly visible in the moonlight.

A flare shot up into the night sky.

"Keep down," Master Aa whispered urgently.

The Kalaxx suddenly seemed to be running for cover. The
white glare of the lazily descending parachute flare picked out
every detail.

"Have they seen us?" Doug asked.

"No, it is they who have been discovered."

As the captain spoke, three more flares burst high in the
sky. The seventy or so Kalaxx were caught in a natural bowl
created by the dunes. What followed was nothing short of a
massacre, as Pugachev's men opened fire from the top of the
bowl with machine guns, ripping apart the still night air with
a furious hail of bullets. There was nowhere for the Kalaxx to

From Doug's sketchbook: The destruction of the Kalaxx. (DMS 8/69)

hide, and they fell in clusters, their swords useless, their blood spilling onto the hot desert earth. In the blink of an eye, the remnants of the disgraced northern chapter of the Sujing Quantou ceased to exist.

For a while nobody spoke. Doug was dumbfounded, his mouth dry with fear. A flare drifted down trailing smoke, burned for several seconds on the ground and died.

The captain broke the stunned silence. "My condolences, Master Aa."

"But they were your enemy," whispered Doug.

"Enemies or not, it is a miserable night."

What shocked Doug most was the speed and efficiency of the machine-gun attack. He had never once imagined what it might be like to advance into a relentless storm of bullets with nowhere to find cover. He fought the urge to be sick. "Is that what modern warfare is like, Uncle?"

"Mostly, these days, Douglas. There is no honour in it," sighed the captain. "A bad end for any soldier."

As they spoke, several figures in Russian uniform came forward from the shadows and began to search the Kalaxx bodies, carelessly kicking over the corpses until one of them held up what they were looking for – a spherical object in an antique mahogany case.

"Curses!" hissed the captain. "Pugachev's men have taken the northern gyrolabe. Have they no respect for the dead?"

"No – and none for the living," whispered Master Aa. "Quickly, we must withdraw deeper into the desert without delay."

A drift of smoke, spotted by the Sujing scouts against the early dawn light, guided the party to what was left of the airship. Its angular remains lay shredded on the side of a pyramidal sand dune.

Liberty examined a piece of charred gas cell. "She must've exploded as she hit the ground."

"Oh no." Becca blinked back tears. "The maharaja, Snave – they were still on board."

Master Aa led them closer. "There may have been survivors, Rebecca; there are footprints everywhere."

Liberty made for the cargo area with Doug by her side.

She whistled. "They sure hit the ground hard. I don't fancy anyone's chances."

Becca stuck with the captain and Master Aa. They walked further forward to inspect the wrecked control gondola.

"There were horses here," said the captain.

Master Aa dropped to the ground and inspected the prints. "These were made as the storm was subsiding."

The captain swung about and said sharply, "My goodness. Rebecca, do not look forward."

But Becca had already seen it. A tangle of bodies lay clustered at the front of the wreckage: limbs twisted askew, faces disfigured. They had caught the full blast of the explosion when the ship crashed.

From Doug's sketchbook: The wrecked airship. (DMS 8/70)

She turned away, nausea surging upwards from her stomach so that she had to clamp her hand over her mouth. She took a deep breath and quickly caught up with Doug and Liberty, who were pushing their way towards the cargo compartment with Xu and Xi's help. A tangle of rigging wires and the remnants of gas cells slowed their progress.

"The explosion must've been nothing more than a flash," said Liberty. "It didn't have a chance to take hold before the storm blew it out... Would y'all look at that!"

"*Lola!*" exclaimed Doug.

"Well, I finally got the ol' gal back." Liberty's voice was flat. Her aircraft lay trapped beneath a lattice of metalwork and debris. "Two singed and broken wings. Smashed undercart. Prop's shattered." She jumped up and clambered into the cockpit. "She was a real special plane, Doug. I had her built just like I wanted her, engine an' all."

"She'll never fly again, Liberty."

"You're right there, coz." She patted the top wing tenderly and inspected the remains. But her look of sadness quickly dissipated as she nodded her head a couple of times, deep in thought. "But you know, I've got ideas for another plane. One that hasn't had Crozier's grubby paws all over it. *Lola II.* Bigger engine, faster controls, more streamlined..." Liberty's head disappeared below the cockpit line, but Doug could still hear her. "We'll lose the lobster pot radiators..."

Xi stooped down and pulled something out from under the aircraft's float. It was a jacket made of a fine quality white linen with a label stitched to the inside pocket: *Rosson of Savile Row, Tailors, London.* Now scorched and blackened, there were traces of dried blood around the elbow. Xi mouthed the word "Crozier" and looked warily around.

"Hey!" shouted Liberty, sounding puzzled, "*Lola*'s ignition is switched on. Someone must've tried to take off before the ship crash-landed."

The compartment in the aircraft's float was open and Xi found a jumble of wires lying beside it. Doug thought hard. What had his old enemy been up to?

Becca looked about and saw the singed remains of a celestial globe which had once contained a gyrolabe. "Perhaps he was trying to fly the gyrolabes out ahead of the storm? He didn't make it."

Xi inspected the prints on the ground. "He survived, though. He sat here after the crash for several minutes, smoked a cigar and took off his jacket. He opened this locker and…"

Doug reached in and pulled out a steel flask-shaped object. It was heavy, and manufactured with great precision. It had been resting in a wooden cradle.

"What y'all found?" asked Liberty, jumping down onto *Lola*'s broken wing.

Doug turned the object round. There were some dials on the neck: SAFETY SWITCH. YIELD. DELAY SETTINGS. "I think … I think it's a … a zoridium bomb."

"Put it down, Doug," said Becca, moving back.

Doug carefully replaced the device in its cradle, then noticed a second, empty cradle beside it.

A terrific mechanical screech and a balloon of flame suddenly burst from the dune four hundred yards away. Becca was the first to see it through the tangle of metalwork. "Liberty, look!"

"Qui'l'bharat!" exclaimed Xu and Xi in unison.

"Shoot! That ain't no desert djinn. That's a bake-me-alive

flame-thrower! And there's two more comin' from the dune behind us."

"And a fourth there," yelled Doug. "We're surrounded."

Master Aa and the captain rapidly arranged their meagre forces in an arc in front of the wrecked airship.

"Find cover," ordered Liberty. "Quick, clamber up inside *Lola's* fuselage."

"There won't be room for all of us."

Liberty kicked open a cargo compartment built into the starboard float. "Can you get in there, Doug?"

"We must stand and fight," said Xi.

"*What?* Y'all gonna fight twenty-foot flames?"

The Sujing twins seemed uncertain. Hiding from an enemy went against everything they'd been taught.

"You'll be more useful to Master Aa alive than burnt to toast," said Doug.

Becca jumped into the forward pilot's seat with Liberty. "What in the name…" Her words trailed off as they glimpsed the first of the flame-thrower devices through the wreckage. It was mounted pannier-style on a horse, the rider wearing some sort of protective suit with the delivery lance tucked under his right arm. He fired another hellish blast, shooting flames forty feet in front of him, the bizarre weapon roaring, his horse rearing up in terror.

"Sure beats the Liberator," mumbled Liberty as she and Becca hastily ducked down.

Doug couldn't see much from his position in the float, but he felt burning air gust over him, thick with the stench of petrol.

Master Aa was issuing orders to the Sujing warriors to fan out and draw their swords ready for battle. There was a

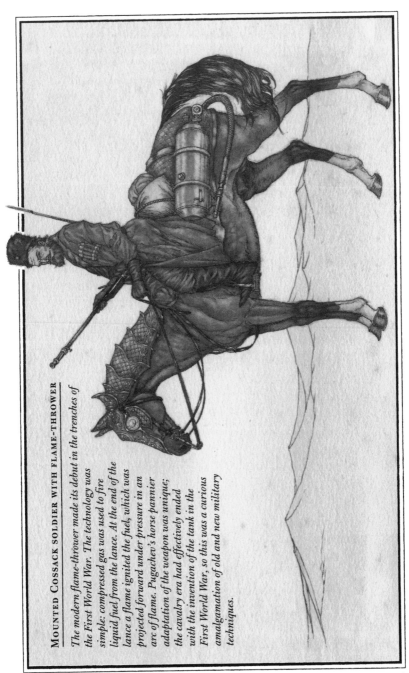

Mounted Cossack soldier with flame-thrower

The modern flame-thrower made its debut in the trenches of the First World War. The technology was simple: compressed gas was used to fire liquid fuel from the lance. At the end of the lance a flame ignited the fuel, which was projected forward under pressure in an arc of flame. Pugachev's horse pannier adaptation of the weapon was unique; the cavalry era had effectively ended with the invention of the tank in the First World War, so this was a curious amalgamation of old and new military techniques.

whoosh as more bursts of flame set fire to the desert air. Becca heard a horse whinny close by, then all went quiet.

"If you fight, Sujing," shouted a commanding Russian voice, "we will cook you like skewered meat. Your swords are no match for flame-throwers and bullets. Surrender or we will kill you all."

Becca could just hear the captain's voice. "They are sure to do it."

"Surrender, Captain?" Master Aa's voice boomed. "We are Sujing Quantou warriors!"

"If we stand and fight," said the captain coldly, "in a minute's time we will be as dead as the Kalaxx and your brothers we buried yesterday. Now is not our time to die, Master Aa. We must find another way."

Master Aa called out an order. After a moment's hesitation, this was followed by the sharp metallic clatter of swords dropping to the ground.

"What's happening?" whispered Liberty.

Becca peered up over the edge of the cockpit. She saw Master Aa march forward towards the line of advancing horses. He stopped and plunged his sword into the sand, then stepped back two paces. For the first time in two thousand years the Sujing Quantou had surrendered.

CHAPTER SIXTEEN

After hiding in *Lola*'s remains for two hours, the young MacKenzies, Liberty, Xu and Xi followed the tracks of Pugachev's men and their captives for five miles until they reached the ruined city of Daotang. They cautiously crawled onto a section of broken wall rendered useless as a defence by the advancing sand that had banked up against it. Stretched out in front of them was the once vast city which had been abandoned for over a thousand years.

Liberty crawled forward. "That's where Pugachev's staked his claim." Dwarfed by the desert were lines of tents, a parade ground, huts, artillery and horses.

Doug took his father's sketch map from his pocket. "The karez must still be carrying water if Pugachev's men are able to live out here."

Xu pointed. "Look there – do you see the line of humps in the ground heading north? They are the service holes for the karez—"

From Doug's sketchbook: Pugachev's camp in the
ruined city of Daotang. (DMS 8/74)

Xi interrupted his brother. "I see our brothers, Master Aa and the captain."

"Where?"

"In the ruins of the temple."

"Give me the binoculars," ordered Becca. She focused on a small group of figures at the far side of the encampment surrounded by armed guards. Desperately she sought her parents. The heat haze blurred the image and she blinked twice. "What do we do now?"

Xu took a turn with the binoculars and checked over the defences. "We must split up. Xi and I must rescue our brothers and sisters. We will hunt for your parents as well."

Xi continued. "Becca and Doug, you must find Ur-Can. Climb down into the karez through one of the service holes. Rescue your parents if they are there. You must capture at least one gyrolabe, then the machine cannot be started. Liberty will help you."

Liberty shrugged. "Looks like I ain't got a choice in the matter. Again."

They slid down from the wall and into the shadow of a rock. Xu and Xi began to unwrap their mysterious bundles.

"This will give us the advantage," said Xi.

"What is it?" asked Doug as three sections of heavy bronze tubing were revealed.

"It is a fire cannon. What you might call a mortar. The pieces screw together."

"Double lethal!" said Doug.

Xu carefully opened his bundle to reveal fifty cylindrical charges. "When we fire these, those Cossack dogs will think an army is attacking them."

Once the cannon had been assembled, Xi removed one of

THE WESTERN CHAPTER OF THE SUJING QUANTOU

This extract describing the fighting techniques of the western chapter of the Sujing Quantou (based at Khotan) is taken from expedition notes made in 1875 by explorer Hugh Travers, HGS, entitled "Anxi to Kashgar".

Our assailants struck in desert country some twenty miles west of Charkilik in the Sinkiang. They were a band of one hundred well-armed Chinese rebels from an uprising farther east, whose villainy had driven them to territory they were unacquainted with. Nonetheless, I feared my escort of twelve western-chapter Sujing would be no match for such an army.

We were ambushed in a shallow gully cut by a long-dried-up stream. A half-dozen bandits on either side of us launched their attack with musket fire, intent on funnelling us towards a trap farther ahead – namely, the main body of their force lying ready where the gully narrowed. I was later told that these marked the line beyond which the Sujing would never retreat in battle. These weapons and their headgear were borne in honour of their Greek ancestors.

Fearsome in lacquered armour, the Sujing charged into battle astride their fine Arabian horses, guiding them with knee and spur so as to allow their hands freedom to take up bows. Their explosive arrows found target amongst our opponents in the scattering of rocks ahead, causing them to spring up from their hiding places and reveal their positions and numbers.

The Sujing fighter who rode beside me had hung back at the line. She united a type of mortar – known to the Sujing as a fire cannon – from her saddle, and rapidly loosed off a shot in support of her advancing comrades. This brutal weapon belched out a projectile high into the sky, which landed in a cloud of azure smoke and flame amongst the rear echelons of the bandit horde. The warrior reloaded and fired once more before her fellow Sujing closed on the enemy, whereupon she set off to single-handedly dispatch the bandits on our flanks.

The Sujing reached the enemy, firing their bows without pause until their quivers were empty of arrows. Next they took up a type of long-handled halberd called a guan dao, which they wielded about them in a mesmerizing, near acrobatic display as my escort forged in amongst the rocks like a deadly storm tide.

The few bandit survivors were left to flee the field of battle without chase, though it would have been a trifle for the Sujing to finish them. This act of mercy was another Sujing tradition, which fostered respect for the fighting prowess of the order amongst their enemies.

From start to finish, the bitter little action lasted less than three minutes. Alas, the hapless rebel bandits had chosen a prey whose centuries-long experience of desert combat had never been bettered. They paid dearly for their error. (MA 46.99 HGS)

JI – HALBERD (below): *A simpler, lighter weapon than the guan dao (above), this ancient Chinese weapon was adopted by the Sujing during their long fighting history. Both of these weapons had a sharp pointed counterweight on the end of the shaft to be used as an alternative point of attack against the enemy. The Sujing kept the ji as a reserve weapon and employed it only if their guan dao had been damaged or lost in battle.*

GUAN DAO (OR KWAN DAO) – HALBERD (above): *This versatile ancient Chinese weapon could be used either on horseback or on foot. The sharp crescent moon blade, combined with the Sujing's expertise in martial arts, made it their weapon of choice for close quarter combat. The V notch allowed the fighter to lock or catch opponents' blades and disarm them with a twisting motion. Tassels were tied to the blade to distract the enemy.*

XYSTON – LANCE: *A Greek lance was carried by the western Sujing to celebrate and honour their ancestral link to the army of Alexander the Great, from whom they were descended.*

JIAN – SWORD (left): *This straight, double-edged sword with steel blade was rarely used in combat. Guild sources note: Being horsemen, the western Sujing find their swords ill-suited to cavalry fighting, preferring to employ their long halberds at close quarters. It is probable that jian were carried in a purely ceremonial capacity; the exquisite workmanship of the blade, hilt and lacquered scabbard contrasts starkly with the plainer guan dao and ji.*

ARROWS: *The quiver contained three arrow variants: highly explosive Daughter of the Sun-tipped; less powerful gunpowder-tipped; and non-explosive metal-tipped. These were fired from a composite bow carried on the saddle; this was manufactured from wood, bone and animal sinew to provide exceptional power, accuracy and range; it had a draw weight of approximately 180 pounds and was designed for use on horseback.*

FIGHTING TECHNIQUES: *The western Sujing at Khotan developed a distinctly different fighting style from their eastern cousins based in Shanghai, finding horses and halberds more suited to their desert terrain and over the centuries the jian had been elevated to purely ceremonial status. In contrast, the eastern chapter rarely used the guan dao, jian or ji, instead developing their own modes of combat: short dagger, martial techniques influenced by the swords of all of these weapons and eastern chapter fighting styles.*

Japan. During the Khotan challenges, however, Sujing fighters had to demonstrate mastery of all of these weapons and and battle disciplines of chemistry, guan dao, ji-jian, battle discus and explosive archery, xyston, unarmed combat and horsemanship.

(MA 746.137 SU)

WESTERN SUJING FIRE CANNON

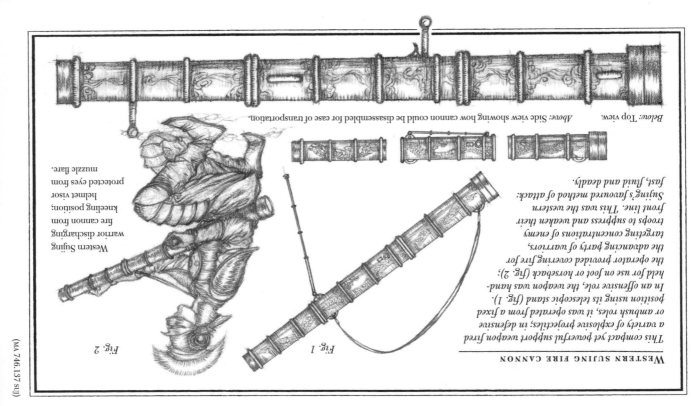

This compact yet powerful support fired weapon fired a variety of explosive projectiles; in defensive or ambush roles, it was operated from a fixed position using its telescopic stand (fig. 1). In an offensive role, the weapon was hand-held for use on foot or horseback (fig. 2); the operator provided covering fire for the advancing party of warriors, targeting concentrations of enemy troops to suppress and weaken their front line. This was the western Sujing's favoured method of attack: fast, fluid and deadly.

Fig. 1

Fig. 2

Western Sujing warrior discharging fire cannon from kneeling position; helmet visor protected eyes from muzzle flare.

Below: Top view.

Above: Side view showing how cannon could be disassembled for ease of transportation.

---

his fighting swords and gave it to Becca. "Our ways divide, but our alliance is strong. Take this as a symbol of our bond of friendship. Good luck."

They all shook hands with great ceremony, and Xu handed Doug one of his swords with a bow.

"If you get out, make for Korla," said Xu. "It's a day's walk. Do not come and look for us. Do you understand?"

Doug's face twisted into a slow grin. "Sujing Cha?"

"Sujing Cha!" the twins replied, slamming their eye guards down into battle position.

Doug, Becca and Liberty skirted the rough ground at the edge of the dune field and ran towards the karez they hoped would lead them to Ur-Can. The line of humps sat like large mole-hills spaced roughly every hundred yards, signalling the subterranean irrigation tunnel running beneath.

Liberty led the way, following the wall of what must have been some kind of agricultural terrace, tumbled and broken but providing enough cover to shield them from view.

"Oh, darn it, that's all we need!" she cursed, suddenly pulling up short.

Julius Pembleton-Crozier squatted in the doorway of a nearby ruined building, Liberty's blunderbuss in hand, grinning like some dreadful gargoyle. His face had been badly burnt on one side and was livid red with blisters.

Becca drew her sword, ready to fight, while Doug struggled to hide his father's sketch map.

Liberty put up her hand. "Stop, Becca. He'll shoot."

"You can bet your bottom dollar on that, Miss da Vine."

From Doug's sketchbook. (DMS 8/79)

Crozier –
still alive!

"So you survived the crash," said Becca.

"Keep your voice down, or you'll get us all killed," he hissed. "There are patrols everywhere. That airship damn well nearly did for me. It blew up when we struck the ground and nearly sautéed me to a crisp."

"Don't suppose you know what happened to the raj and that fancy butler of his?" asked Liberty.

Pembleton-Crozier shrugged.

Becca considered their old enemy. At his feet rested a bundle wrapped in the canvas of one of the airship's hammocks. "What happened to the gyrolabes?"

"Funny you should ask that, Rebecca." He dabbed at his blistered face and seemed thoughtful for a moment. "I tried to get them out in your plane, Miss da Vine, but alas, I didn't make it. I lost consciousness when we crashed and came round to see Pugachev's men leaving." He adjusted a bloodied bandage wrapped round his left hand. "They must have taken them. Now I'm here to reclaim them. They're mine, after all."

"You against five thousand Cossacks?" laughed Liberty. "You're crazier than I thought."

"I have some advantage over them." He nodded at a pile of thin chain mail beside him. "I've got an armoured suit – they had no idea what it was when they went a-plundering. Oh, and they left your trusty blunderbuss," he added, examining the gun. "Obviously thought it was some kind of antique wall decoration."

"I'll put her on your tab – along with poor ol' *Lola*," said Liberty.

"I intend to take Ur-Can no matter what." Pembleton-Crozier jabbed his thumb in the direction of Daotang. As he did so, he slowed, then stopped. "But ... but of course! Ur-Can isn't over there, is it?"

"It must be," blustered Becca. "Right in the middle of the ruins."

"So why are you running *away* from the city, towards the desert? There's nothing out there, is there...?"

Crozier turned his attention to Doug. "You were trying to hide something. What was it, eh? Come on, turn out your pockets. You'd better give me those swords while you're at it."

Reluctantly Becca and Doug complied. But Becca wanted to know what Crozier was hiding, and managed to dislodge the canvas bundle with her foot. A spherical metal object rolled out.

"What's that?"

"My insurance policy," muttered Crozier deviously.

"Looks like a bomb," said Liberty. "You plannin' to blow this place to hell?"

"If I have to, yes. I'll be wearing the suit, of course, so I'll be fine. Can't vouch for the rest of you." His eyes skimmed over the map; he oriented it to the landscape and glanced at the karez. He grinned. "Well, well, Ur-Can is near at hand indeed. But what am I to do with you three? I'd shoot you, da Vine, if it wasn't for the noise and my shortage of ammunition. However, the MacKenzies may be useful."

"You cheap horse thief. How'd I ever get mixed up in your lunatic world?" spat Liberty. "These kids are just lookin' for their parents and I'm tryin' to help them."

"Well, I've some news for you on that front."

Pembleton-Crozier's tone was sly again as he nodded in the direction of the shadows behind him. Doug shielded his eyes, and in the gloom discerned the crumpled shape of a man slumped on the ground, chained to a post.

Becca cautiously stepped forward. She reached out to touch the worn and ripped shirt barely covering the man's shoulder. Slowly she turned him over and gazed upon a bearded, unkempt face, the skin blistered and desiccated by the intense heat of the desert. "Father?"

Father - we barely recognised him

From Doug's sketchbook. (DMS 9/05)

The man gave the faintest of gasps. Doug crouched beside Becca and pulled the water bottle from his bag. Lifting his father's head, he poured a little liquid on his parched lips. Hamish MacKenzie spluttered and swallowed.

His red-rimmed eyes opened slowly and his first words were a harsh whisper. "Nothing…" He lifted his hand, chained at the wrist, and touched Becca's face with trembling fingers. "Nothing but a desert dream." His eyes closed again, wincing with pain.

"Father, it's us. Becca and Doug."

"Impossible ... they are in Srinagar with the Jukeses..."

Doug poured more of the precious water over his father's face. "We're here."

Becca tried to find some way to release him. His manacled wrists were chafed and red raw from the metal. A second set of manacles lay empty beside him.

"Where is Mother?" asked Becca urgently.

"Ur-Can..." He stretched out his hand and clutched the bottle of water. He took three long gulps.

"Slowly now," said Becca, taking the bottle. "Too much will kill you."

They were suddenly aware of Crozier standing impatiently over them.

"Enough of this touching family reunion. We could be discovered at any minute. Douglas, put those manacles on Miss da Vine. The key's in the lock."

"I won't."

Crozier levelled the blunderbuss at Hamish. "He's hardly worth a blast, but I will if I have to."

"Julius? You here too?" said Hamish, coughing. He seemed more alert, his dim eyes fixing on the blunderbuss, then on Becca and Doug.

"You stinkin' snake in the grass, no-good thievin' rustler," Liberty hissed at Crozier.

"The key, Douglas, there's a good fellow."

With Liberty safely restrained, Crozier pulled on the armoured suit, never taking his eyes off his captives. The metal was lightweight and of a surprisingly thin gauge. It was flexible too, the joints and articulations made of a very fine mesh. All in all it looked flimsy and far too light to be effective. But when it was switched on, the molecule invigorator bolted to a plate on the back of the suit would make the metal twenty-five times stronger.

Pembleton-Crozier wrapped the bomb in the canvas hammock. "Carry this, Douglas. I have the detonator, so don't think you'll be able to use it."

And with that he raised the blunderbuss and shoved Becca and Doug into the relentless heat of the desert.

Becca had always pictured finding her parents together. She'd never imagined that they'd find only one of them, and anxiety about her mother gnawed at her insides. She contemplated her father's terrible condition in silence as she trudged across the desert in front of Crozier, wondering if he could survive. Would she ever see them both alive and well, somehow restored from this ordeal?

After tracking the karez for about half a mile, they reached a service hole that had apparently been enlarged.

"This must be it," muttered Crozier, stuffing the map into his pocket. Three rungs of a wooden ladder protruded from the ground, surrounded by footprints.

"You first, Rebecca. Then you, Douglas. Walk along the tunnel and don't try any tricks, d'you hear?"

Becca clambered down into the dark of the karez, followed by Doug, who landed with a splash in a steady stream of water. There wasn't much space and the air was stale and hot. Crozier climbed down cautiously, letting his eyes adjust to the gloom.

"You two, stay in front of me. Start walking."

The young MacKenzies set a fast pace, running their hands

From Doug's sketchbook: Becca is forced into the karez. (DMS 9/14)

along the rock wall to guide them. The airless tunnel offered
no chance of escape, and the bomb tucked under Doug's left
arm was heavy and cumbersome. After a while they rested
beneath the fresh air of another service hole, while Crozier
studied the map.

"There should be a sharp turn ahead."

In the gloom they could just make out the rock edge as
the tunnel changed direction abruptly. They waded forward
slowly, hoping there wouldn't be a guard. Pembleton-
Crozier peered round the rock, then looked back at Doug
with a grin.

"Well, if your map's correct, old boy, Ur-Can should be
just along that tunnel running off to the right."

Wild beasts, not butterflies, cavorted in Doug's stomach as he studied the tunnel ahead. The material of its construction was metallic, yet emitted a strange, soft light. Pembleton-Crozier cocked the blunderbuss and pushed the young MacKenzies towards the entrance. Doug nervously pulled up his lucky socks and then stepped into the ancient tunnel leading to Ur-Can.

CHAPTER SEVENTEEN

The tunnel plunged steeply downwards. Pembleton-Crozier advanced cautiously, testing that the floor, sides or roof wouldn't give way. They continued walking downhill for perhaps ten minutes in silence. The strange luminescence of the walls neither diminished nor brightened. Finally they reached a fork, and Crozier elected to take the right-hand tunnel. Becca edged closer to Doug, the terror clear in her eyes.

Then quite abruptly they came upon a domed chamber with evidence of recent occupation. Empty food tins lay stacked neatly in the corner. In the middle of the room was a desk and two chairs. Engineering equipment lay on a laboratory bench to one side. All about were books on mathematics, many in Russian. Becca grabbed one of the notebooks from a pile on the desk and looked at the handwriting. It was her mother's, although it seemed rather shaky. Doug inspected some schematic drawings lying on the other side of the desk.

"Someone's made a plan."

It was clear from these sketches that Ur-Can was monstrously large.

"What is the machine?" asked Doug, lost in the complexity of it all. "What's it for?"

Crozier jabbed a finger at a circular room on the plan. *"Gyrolabe cartouches and portal chamber,"* he read. "That's where we need to be. The entrance is one floor down."

"What about our mother?" Becca demanded.

Crozier ignored her and flicked a switch inside a panel

on the front of his suit. The suit began to hum with electricity. He took the plan from the desk and looked about him. "This way," he said, spotting a staircase.

Pembleton-Crozier moved stealthily down the steps, Becca and Doug following, until they reached a walkway that passed through a tangle of ducts descending into darkness below. The material they were manufactured from was different from the walls and emitted no light. Doug tapped it, and found it to be more akin to stone than metal.

Crozier led them into another chamber with niches set into the walls, like stone beds. Many were occupied by skeletons covered with garlands of flowers, the bones and flowers well preserved in the parched air.

As Crozier studied the plan, Doug inspected a corpse. "Did they die down here, sis?"

"How would I know?" snapped Becca. She'd never liked skeletons, and here were about a hundred of them. At the back of her mind was the thought that one of them might be their mother.

Suddenly they heard the distant echo of voices.

"Come on," hissed Crozier.

A doorway led into the portal chamber as depicted on the plan. This was the heart of Ur-Can.

The circular chamber was almost a hundred feet across, and, gazing upwards, Doug could discern no ceiling in the vast cathedral-like space. All he knew was that somewhere, far above them, was the desert.

Ahead was a twenty foot high metal buttress, one of four positioned around the periphery of the chamber. In the gloomy light, this provided excellent cover and Crozier motioned for them to creep towards it. They crouched down and observed a pair of shadowy figures standing near the centre of the room talking heatedly.

Forming an inner circle were four oval cartouches, thirty feet high by twenty wide. These were spotlit from above and on each was carved a Tembla compass symbol.

"That's not possible..." Crozier muttered to himself as he squinted into the gloom. "He appears to have the southern gyrolabe."

Doug followed his gaze to where the southern gyrolabe rested in some sort of hinged stand; if canted upwards the gyrolabe would connect with an ornate portal at the centre of the cartouche.

From Doug's sketchbook: The cartouche chamber. (DMS 9/19)

Crozier was incredulous. "I don't understand…"

The two figures walked over towards the western cartouche.

"That's Pugachev," whispered Pembleton-Crozier feverishly as a man stepped into the harsh beam of light. "I've seen his photograph."

Pugachev appeared younger than Becca had pictured him, but he radiated an icy aura of command. He looked almost gallant in his faded Cossack cavalry uniform, and walked with an arrogant swagger. His voice was clear and controlled.

"Zorid insists there will be enough power. Do you agree? Will the machine activate now?"

"Zorid?" whispered Becca. "I thought he was dead."

Then the young MacKenzies heard a voice they knew well. "I've no doubt you will try, General. This is our best estimation. There are no guarantees."

Becca and Doug gasped as their mother stepped forward into the light. Sunburnt, dressed in the ragged remains of her travelling clothes, she was in such a miserable condition that it took a moment to be certain it was her. Becca grabbed Doug's arm, and he scrunched up his eyes to check again. Their mother was in better shape than their father, but she was clearly weak; her body was hunched and emaciated and her hair wild and sun bleached. Doug sprang up, ready to rush to her aid, but Pembleton-Crozier stopped him.

"Stay down!" he ordered through clenched teeth.

Becca looked at her brother and wondered if her mother would even recognize him. Doug had grown at least a foot in height. But there was a change beyond this; they were no longer the children her parents had known. The adventures that had led them from Shanghai to Sinkiang had transformed them both beyond all measure.

From Doug's
sketchbook.
(DMS 9/24)

 Mother!

Nevertheless, Becca found herself smiling. She was over-whelmingly happy to see her mother again. A wave of relief flooded through her: they were still alive. The wave sucked back again … but how were they all going to escape this?

Crozier clicked the hammers back on the blunderbuss and grabbed the canvas package containing the bomb, then slammed the visor down on his helmet. His voice came out distorted.

"I came here to bargain with Pugachev but I can see he's leagues ahead. It's time for me to take control of Ur-Can."

Pembleton-Crozier strode towards Pugachev prepared to do battle, brandishing the blunderbuss and the bomb. His bizarre metal suit hummed with electricity and emitted a sinister glow in the half-light; across his back were strapped the two Sujing swords confiscated from Becca and Doug. Pugachev, alert and edgy like a fierce bird of prey, caught sight of the figure approaching and fired a round from his pistol, but not a single bullet penetrated the suit.

Crozier lifted his visor. "Hold your fire, Pugachev."

"Julius?" stammered Elena.

"Who is this?" demanded Pugachev.

"Julius Pembleton-Crozier," she answered dutifully.

"Of course. The foolish Englishman. My men said you had died in the desert. It was very good of you to bring me the eastern gyrolabe."

"What about the other one?" said Doug, glancing at his sister. "Crozier said the Russians took both from the airship, but he was puzzled when he saw the southern gyrolabe. It must be a fake."

"I bet he's hidden the real one, the sly old dog," whispered Becca. "Back at that ruin with Father…"

"Why are you here, Pembleton-Crozier?" asked Pugachev.

"I've come to offer you a deal, General. My unique weapon designs, such as this impenetrable armoured suit, in exchange for Ur-Can."

"The suit is impressive."

"This suit and this bomb are part of a whole new generation of armament. The bomb is powered by Daughter of the Sun – known to you as zoridium – and has the capacity to destroy beyond imagination; it's powerful enough to bring the roof down on this place, I assure you."

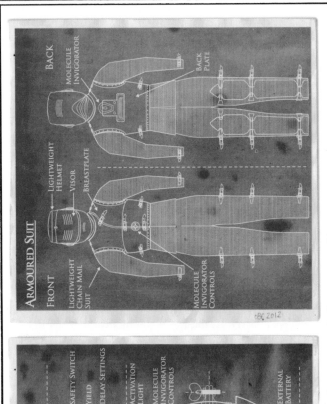

PRELIMINARY BLUEPRINTS OF SOME OF THE COTERIE OF ST PETERSBURG'S ZORIDIUM ARMAMENT

These blueprints show the workings of the armoured suit and zoridium bomb used by Pembleton-Crozier in his single-handed assault on Ur-Can.

Pugachev narrowed his eyes. "Mm. I've heard rumours of your scientific exploits."

"All of the Coterie's weapon designs are in the advanced stages of development. You want Moscow? I could hand it to you on a plate."

Pugachev shrugged off the offer with a look of derision. "What if I don't want to give you Ur-Can?" There was a cold, sardonic note in his voice. "What if I already have my own, radical plans for the capture of Moscow – plans way beyond *your* imagination?"

"Your little army out there would be unstoppable with these new weapons."

"My little army, as you put it, will be unstoppable *without* your intervention, Mr Pembleton-Crozier. Each week our numbers swell as word reaches Russia that we are to attack the Bolsheviks and return the Romanov bloodline to its rightful place. A year ago there were just five hundred of us. Now we are over five thousand. Very soon Ur-Can will do my bidding and the whole world will tremble at my power. Do you really think I need *your* help?"

"But nobody knows what Ur-Can does – not even the Sujing," countered Crozier, a hint of curiosity creeping into his voice.

"Again you are mistaken, Crozier. Your mind is perhaps too small for these matters. I" – Pugachev tapped his chest with his index finger – "I know what Ur-Can is. I alone know what it is capable of doing. It is at the very centre of my plans. I have no interest in your … trinkets."

THE RUSSIAN REVOLUTION AND THE BOLSHEVIKS

In 1917 Russia underwent a series of social and economic upheavals which resulted in the overthrow of old imperial Russia, ruled by Romanov tsars or emperors. The Bolshevik party took control and established the beginnings of Soviet socialism.

Crozier's face flushed deeply as he tried to control his rage at Pugachev's insults. "You bluff, Pugachev. The Coterie knows more than you think – Ur-Can is useless without all four gyrolabes, and I know you don't have them."

Pugachev laughed tersely. "How can you be so sure?"

"Because I am still in possession of one."

"But, Julius, Zorid has manufactured a replica southern gyrolabe," interjected Elena. "The general thinks he no longer needs the original."

"Making gyrolabes is a dangerous business," warned Pembleton-Crozier. "The Coterie tried to create a replica, but never managed to contain the gravity vortex on such a small scale."

"Indeed. Zorid's first experiments using three replicas and one original were unsuccessful," admitted Pugachev. "However, now, with three of the originals, it is certain to succeed."

"You'd be mad to try it, General. The results could be catastrophic."

"Please, Crozier, you must inspect the cartouches." Pugachev changed tack with a look of cunning. "Do you know what information each one carries? Can you comprehend it? Step closer and take a look."

Crozier was suspicious. "I'll stay here, if it's no bother."

"Please, come and inspect the original 99 Elements. Isn't that the very source your secret Guild has tried to protect for so many centuries?"

"Pah," Crozier spat. "The Guild, maybe. The Coterie has far more ambition."

The pair reminded Doug of two predatory animals sizing each other up before a fight. "If I were Pugachev," he whispered, "I'd try to find a way to beat that suit, not stand there chatting."

Becca shook her head. "Pugachev wants to know where that last gyrolabe is. He's luring Crozier in."

As if to prove her point the Russian went on. "Come. Let me reveal the secret of Ur-Can to you, Mr Julius Pembleton-Crozier. A secret far more potent than anything you might have deduced in all your years of research. Tell him, Mrs MacKenzie. Tell him what we know; what he *doesn't* know, and never could."

From Doug's sketchbook: Pugachev and Crozier try to outwit each other. (DMS 9/29)

A dark smile broke across Pugachev's face as he drew Crozier into his trap of forbidden knowledge.

Pembleton-Crozier hesitantly approached the cartouches. Elena held up her hand as if to warn him of something.

"Tell him," repeated Pugachev, aiming his pistol at her.

When she spoke it was with a trembling voice. "Ur-Can is a gift from the Tembla – it is a machine capable of saving the human race from extinction. The Tembla's ancestors had been responsible for nearly wiping out mankind. This machine was built by the survivors to help the planet recover if such a catastrophe should ever happen again."

"Is it the same as the first machine?"

"No. Quite different. The original Toba machine was a monstrous generator – an overambitious test to see exactly how powerful Daughter of the Sun science had become." She looked about her. "This machine is meant to save us. The Tembla knew from the Toba disaster that something as simple as dust in the atmosphere could cause the extinction of mankind."

Elena pointed at the western cartouche. "Here the Tembla write that they believed the dinosaurs had died out after an asteroid hit the earth, sending clouds of dust into the atmosphere and blotting out the sun. They knew we could suffer the same fate. The causes might be natural, like another asteroid collision or a violent volcano, but they also knew from their own terrible history that man's overreaching scientific ambition could seal our fate in the same way. The western quarter warns endlessly that our survival is by no means certain."

"So what does the machine actually *do*?" Crozier interrupted impatiently.

Pugachev stepped forward. "It is a machine capable of repairing the planet's atmosphere."

"Lethal," whispered Doug.

"And how's all this going to help you capture Moscow, old man?" continued Pembleton-Crozier.

"The machine can create a monumental storm – a storm far greater than any hurricane or typhoon."

"I thought this was meant to be a gift," said Crozier nervously.

"Let me finish, Mr Crozier. The centre of the storm is here" – Pugachev gestured to the vast cylindrical space above – "generated by an intense gravity vortex that lowers the atmospheric pressure to an almost perfect vacuum. Any particles of dust in the atmosphere are sucked into the vortex created in this chamber, where they are filtered, collected and pumped into the earth's core, to be absorbed and rendered harmless."

"Double lethal," gulped Doug.

Pembleton-Crozier thought for a moment. "I still don't see how this is going to help you, old boy."

Elena angrily interrupted. "General Pugachev is intending to corrupt Ur-Can for his own ends in a dangerous and wholly irresponsible plan!"

"In *your* opinion, Mrs MacKenzie," replied the general dismissively. "What do you know about agriculture, Mr Pembleton-Crozier?"

"A lot of chaps in muddy boots?"

A flicker of a smile crossed Pugachev's face. "It is nearly harvest time in Russia. The peasants are indeed sharpening their scythes and readying to bring in their crops. For this they need fine weather. I now understand how to control this machine. Once activated, it will take a week for the storm to build to its full potential, becoming a tempest greater than anything in nature. The eye of the storm will be here, at Ur-Can, spreading out until it is nine thousand miles in circumference, consuming Russia and Asia entirely. Nothing will be harvested this year. The people will starve. And when there is famine, chaos reigns, my friend. Chaos is a great advantage to the well prepared.

"My army will hide in the karez tunnels, where there is safety, fresh water and supplies," continued the Russian. "The storm will last a month – then I will invade Russia. The Bolshevik army's stomachs will be empty and their lines of communication in ruins. We will plunge towards Moscow like a knife into the heart of Bolshevik Russia."

"You talk about meddling with the weather like a chap might change his shirt," spluttered Crozier. "You can't just start this machine on a whim, Bolsheviks or no Bolsheviks. I mean, this place may actually prove useful. Now take my Coterie plans—"

"This is no whim!" raged Pugachev, his self-control cast aside in a split second. "The Bolsheviks killed my family. My wife … my five children. Lined up and shot like despised animals! I will take my revenge. I will use Ur-Can to re-store order… Order! To Russia, which has grown sick with Bolshevik poison." He kicked the cartouche and roared, "I will bring death to all Bolsheviks!"

"You cannot control the storm or its effects, Pugachev," said Elena quietly. "By using the machine incorrectly, you may cause a global famine."

"Exactly. And from this chaos I will ensure that Russia rises again, only far, far stronger. Our new economy will be based on zoridium power."

"The Tembla advise use of Ur-Can only after a cataclysmic event, and as a last resort," retorted Elena. "Their warnings about the strength of the storm fill half of the hieroglyphs carved into these cartouches. Your intention to meddle with the machine settings might create a storm that could never be stopped. We just *do not know*!"

Doug watched Crozier pacing, computing the implications of Pugachev's precipitous idea. The Englishman walked a little closer to the Russian, but still kept a good distance from the cartouches. As he did so the vast chamber trembled and shook for several seconds.

"What? Is it already active?"

Pugachev nodded, taking pleasure in Crozier's anxiety. "In some ways, yes. Every hour it shakes. It has grown stronger since we brought the western gyrolabe here."

"I thought the thing would be dormant without all the gyrolabes."

"Another mistake. The Ha-Mi discovered that if this sphere was raised, a small storm could be produced. Here." Pugachev approached a truncated spherical object in the centre of the chamber. "It is most extraordinary. Beneath it are the controls. Come and see."

"We think the Ha-Mi managed to hammer a steel wedge under the sphere," said Elena. "By lifting it, they discovered it would jump ten feet into the air and spin at high speed for several minutes."

"Unsupported? No wires? You jest!" smirked Crozier.

"This is no magician's trick," said Pugachev. "The side effect is very real; the temporary gravity vortex creates massive dust storms outside – a mild indicator of what Ur-Can is capable of. Ignorant Ha-Mi priests believed a djinn lived in the sphere. Many myths grew up about its power, and it was named Qui'l'bharat. They could not properly activate the

GENERAL PUGACHEV

Pugachev's life was one of fanatical dedication to the Romanovs, the Russian royal family. This obsessive loyalty is thought to have evolved during his early upbringing in the royal household of Tsar Nicholas II. Pugachev's father was a low-ranking noble who served as "purchaser and keeper of the emperor's hunting rifles". This role was probably a cover, as the elder Pugachev travelled constantly across Europe; he was at the very least a courier of secret messages, if not a tsarist spy. The Pugachev family prospered under the patronage of the tsar, buying houses in both St Petersburg and Moscow, and the young Pugachev is said to have amused Nicholas II with his ability to play the piano "with unerring skill from the age of five". He went on to have a successful, if brutal, military career, rising rapidly through the ranks of the imperial army. It is known that his wife and children were murdered during the Russian Revolution; the circumstances are lost to history, but it is a psychological probability that this added fuel to the fire of his anti-Bolshevik fanaticism.

machine or operate the controls hidden beneath the sphere because they had no gyrolabes. It was a primitive and incorrect use of Ur-Can, but effective."

Crozier laughed. "Utter rubbish."

"This is how we brought down your airship," said Pugachev.

"That storm *was* colossal," whispered Doug from his hiding place.

Crozier looked shocked. His curiosity finally overwhelmed his caution and he absent-mindedly approached the southern cartouche, running his fingers over the engraved hieroglyphs. "Incredible..."

Pugachev rapidly edged closer to a lever to the left of the sphere. "You're too late, Crozier. You will not hinder my plans now. Only I will control Ur-Can!"

Crozier was suddenly suspicious and swung the blunderbuss round, dropping the bomb.

Pugachev smiled. "The metal of your suit may be an advantage on the battlefield, but not here." He kicked the lever and sprang away.

Pembleton-Crozier lifted the blunderbuss and pulled the trigger, but the ancient weapon refused to fire.

CHAPTER EIGHTEEN

The floor shook as the gyrolabes canted upwards and engaged with their cartouches. Becca turned to her brother, her expression a mixture of fascination, fear and confusion. The four gyrolabes began to spin, unleashing extraordinary power, and the sphere at the centre of the chamber began to rotate.

Pembleton-Crozier fought to recock the hammers of the blunderbuss but his metallic suit was attracted by the strong magnetic force generated by the sphere and he was dragged towards it, unable to resist. Pugachev stood back and watched, a smile playing on his lips as Crozier collided with the sphere and was pinned to its surface. Imprisoned by the suit, he rotated once every two seconds, screaming to be released.

With a sudden jump, the sphere began to levitate, rising twenty feet into the air. Becca and Doug gazed with terrified wonder as beneath the sphere was revealed a perfect representation of planet earth, fifteen feet in diameter, cast in a silvery metal which gleamed with unnatural brilliance. The globe was supported on an axis bar connected to a circular pedestal base.

From Doug's sketchbook: Crozier pinned to the sphere. (DMS 9/37)

Becca grabbed Doug's arm. "Look! Something's happening." She pointed at a panel on the base.

Doug lifted his binoculars and focused on it. Four hexagonal-shaped dials were slowly emerging.

"I think that's the panel from our photograph," she said. "It must be the activation mechanism."

"You're right," said Doug. His attention was drawn to a bewildering array of dials and levers positioned all the way round the top edge of the globe's pedestal. "And they must be the controls to create the storm."

"The gyrolabes are working!" said Pugachev. "I will activate Ur-Can immediately. There is no reason to delay."

He took a piece of paper from his pocket and began to adjust the multitude of dials. Then he pulled out another note and crouched down to set the activation panel.

"Don't do it!" Elena begged, her voice trembling. "This could be catastrophic."

"I'm not interested in your concerns. Moscow is all that matters."

Doug watched through the binoculars as Pugachev clicked round each of the four hexagonal dials to align with a particular hieroglyph.

"Becca, it's Zedd's code – but Pugachev knows the missing symbol. It looks like a backward C."

Pugachev stood up and rechecked his piece of paper, then pulled a second lever on the globe's base. The chamber jolted. The gyrolabes slowed and stopped spinning, then the support arms hinged them away from their cartouches.

Pugachev was triumphant. "Let the storm commence."

The sphere descended and once again concealed Ur-Can's controls. It stopped spinning almost immediately, releasing

Pembleton-Crozier from its influence. He was flung violently away, and slammed into the northern cartouche with such force that he dropped the blunderbuss. It clattered away across the floor while he lay slumped and motionless, stunned by the brunt of the impact.

"Is he dead?" whispered Doug, running to the other side of their hiding place to see.

Pugachev strolled over and inspected the armoured suit. He opened the molecule invigorator compartment and ripped out a handful of wires. The humming stopped. He picked up one of the swords, and kicked the other away.

"Leave us, Mrs MacKenzie. Your task is complete."

"This is an affront to civilization, General. I demand that you stop this. You have no idea what you're unleashing."

"I said *go*." Pugachev brought the razor-sharp sword point up to her throat.

Pugachev threatens Mother

From Doug's sketchbook. (DMS 9/40)

Doug could barely stop himself from rushing forward to tackle him, but all the fight seemed to leave his mother and she walked slowly away looking exhausted and defeated. As she reached a side archway she glanced back at the Russian in despair.

Suddenly a new, deeper note made the fabric of the chamber tremble and shake. Doug and Becca looked down at their feet; only now did they realize that the floor they were standing on was a platform, which was beginning to ascend the chamber at great speed.

"It's going up," shouted Becca over the gathering din. "How do we get off?"

But when they looked down the young MacKenzies saw that they were already more than forty feet in the air. It was too dangerous to jump.

Doug gulped. "We're heading for the surface!"

The circular platform shot upwards with remarkable speed. Still undetected by Pugachev, Doug and Becca clung to the buttress and watched their mother recede into the gloom below.

An iris-shaped aperture began to open at the top of the chamber, illuminated by a series of lights that blinked on. Sand began to tumble downwards, and for a moment Doug feared that they would be buried alive. But Ur-Can's makers had considered this, and pumps activated to suck the sand into the side ducts of the chamber's walls.

The platform broke the surface and lofted skywards. The MacKenzies blinked in the sudden intense brightness of the desert sun. A gale howled about them, choked with sand.

From Doug's sketchbook: The gyrolabe platform ascends. (DMS 9/44)

"We must do something!" spluttered Becca. "We must stop this or Pugachev'll kill us all."

"Perhaps we can re-engage the gyrolabes … reset the controls?" suggested Doug.

"If we put in the wrong symbols we may do more harm. We just don't understand the codes."

"What, then?"

"We have to try to destroy the machine, before the storm builds."

Doug saw his sister wasn't joking. "Crozier's bomb?"

"There's no choice."

"If we can re-engage the gyrolabes and lift the sphere, we can plant the bomb beneath it. Once that's done, we disengage the gyrolabes—"

"—and with luck the blast will be contained by the sphere. It's made of solid metal. D'you think it'll work?"

Doug shrugged. "I've no idea, but it's the only plan we've got."

But Pembleton-Crozier, struggling back to consciousness, had his own ideas. The electronics of his suit still smouldering, he hauled himself up and tried to stagger towards the blunderbuss.

Pugachev pulled out his pistol and fired, penetrating the thin steel of the unpowered suit. The Russian fired again, but he was out of ammunition. He threw the pistol aside and grabbed the blunderbuss before Crozier could reach it, slicing the Sujing sword in his left hand back and forth to test its weight.

Gambling that the blunderbuss wouldn't fire, Crozier ran headlong at the Russian and tackled him to the ground.

Becca and Doug watched their adversaries battling hard.

"Let's go," said Doug.

Becca looked at the gyrolabes and the cartouches, but hesitated. "Will the replica work a second time? Look – it's glowing with heat."

"We have to try," pressed Doug. "I'll get the bomb."

Even as he spoke, the buttress they were hiding behind began to glide inwards towards the sphere, revealing a silver hemispherical node which sparked with electricity. The other buttresses were also on the move.

The platform's ascent had slowed; Doug glanced down feeling slightly nauseous and guessed they had reached an altitude of about a mile. He looked over to where Pembleton-Crozier and Pugachev were still slugging it out, Pugachev now using the Liberator as a club, slamming it into Crozier's metal suit. Around them, burning sparks of lightning arced between the cartouches, buttresses and the newly revealed silver nodes, while the noise and rush of air around the platform intensified.

From Doug's sketchbook: Crozier and Pugachev fight. (DMS 9/48)

Becca sprinted towards the lever that engaged the gyrolabes. Doug scooped up the bomb as he ran after her.

"Here goes," she said, pushing the lever.

The four gyrolabe stands glided upwards to engage the gyrolabes once again in the cartouches. As the sphere began to spin and rise, smoke poured from the replica southern gyrolabe.

Doug checked to see if Pugachev had noticed them, but he and Crozier were fighting for their lives at the edge of the platform. The blunderbuss finally split apart; frustrated, Pugachev wrestled his opponent, punching and clawing to try to push him over the edge to the desert one mile below.

The Russian finally managed to release a catch on Crozier's suit. The Englishman lashed out, but Pugachev dodged and grabbed the armour now hanging from his opponent's leg, then spun him round. With some skill he landed Crozier on one of the silver nodes. Electricity surged through the Englishman, sparking and dancing on the armour, as he cried out in pain.

Pugachev, panting from the fight and laughing heartily at his opponent's distress, suddenly noticed the sphere ascending again. His laughter turned to rage and he cursed in his native Russian.

"He's seen us. Hurry!" Becca called out as Doug tried to fathom the bomb's complex controls. None of the switches seemed to activate the device.

Pugachev ran towards them.

"I'll hold him off," Becca shouted.

They nodded at each other, knowing what they had to do, then Becca raced for the second sword, still lying where Pugachev had kicked it away.

She watched her opponent approach and tested the weight and grip of the Sujing sword; it was light and balanced to perfection, but unlike the rapiers and sabres she was used to. Pugachev grinned; he was overconfident, underestimating her skill. Becca immediately executed a rare Sujing Quantou feint, using a technique Xi had taught her, flicking the blade so quickly that it cracked like a whip. Pugachev was confused, and in that split second, Becca lunged, narrowly missing his arm as he parried and ducked away.

The replica gyrolabe was now white hot and emitting a shrill, screeching noise. Doug still couldn't work out Crozier's bomb. This was no hand grenade. This was a sophisticated weapon – and one whose activation light wouldn't illuminate, even when the controls were switched on.

Becca fought harder than she ever had in her life to counter

Pugachev's attack. He had the advantage of height and power, but in the next three engagements she managed to draw him away from the sphere. She stole a glance at the node that was slowly electrocuting Crozier. All the while, the buttresses closed in on the cartouches in a blaze of lightning and sparks.

There was nothing for it but to try a last, all-out attack. In a flurry of lunges she drove the Russian back towards Crozier, who, to her surprise, reached out a trembling hand and grabbed Pugachev's ankle. Electricity surged through the Russian, making him cry out and drop his sword. He stumbled and fell, dragging the Englishman from the charged node.

From Doug's sketchbook: Becca duels with Pugachev. (DMS 9/51)

Smoke poured from Crozier's armour as they teetered on the brink of the platform. Becca ran towards them, just as Pembleton-Crozier, with a mighty heave, rolled Pugachev over the edge. As he fell the Russian dragged Crozier with him; Crozier slipped over the edge, but grabbed hold of the platform with his left hand while the Russian hung on to his right leg. Pugachev dangled helplessly, staring down at the desert a mile below.

With his free boot, Crozier kicked hard on Pugachev's shoulder. "You should have accepted my deal, old man."

The Russian slipped, then fell to his death, his arms flailing.

Becca caught hold of Pembleton-Crozier's right arm. She gazed into the Englishman's tortured eyes.

"It's no good. That machine roasted me like a turkey. I got that Russian dog, though... Impertinent fellow." Becca tried to pull him up, but he was too heavy. His grip on the platform weakened. "I didn't ... like the sound of Pugachev's plan. Damnable dangerous, even by my standards..." He took a sharp breath.

"Can you help us stop the machine?" asked Becca. "Doug's going to use your bomb."

A wry smile played faintly across Crozier's blistered lips. He slipped a little, and looked up wide-eyed. "You can try, but you'll never make it explode."

"Why not?"

"You're clever. Work it out... Judging by this machine, I think Avalon ... might not be such a good idea... Stop Lucretia, Rebecca. Stop the Coterie." His fingers slipped further.

"Hold on!" yelled Becca.

"Honour, duty or death..."

With that, Pembleton-Crozier fell to the desert below.

Honour, duty - or death   *Douglas MacKenzie, 1920*

CROZIER FALLS FROM THE EDGE OF THE PLATFORM

Becca ran back to the sphere, shaking and weak at the knees. Her arms ached from the strain of holding Crozier.

"Are you all right?" yelled Doug.

"They're both dead. I tried to stop Crozier falling..."

The buttresses were now less than ten feet from the cartouches. The whole platform shook violently as the gravity vortex began to form beneath it.

Becca took a deep breath and looked about her at the gathering storm. "We'll never stop this! How can we?"

Then, with a screeching clunk, the replica gyrolabe caught fire and stopped spinning. Becca watched in horror as all of the gyrolabes automatically swung away

From Doug's sketchbook: The replica gyrolabe catches fire. (DMS 9/55)

from the cartouches; she just had time to pull her brother away from the control panel before the sphere slammed down.

Doug frantically tried every combination of switches on the bomb. "We'll have to hope this is strong enough to crack the sphere *and* the controls now."

Becca shook her head. "The bomb's a dud. Crozier said we'd never be able to make it explode."

"What?" Doug slumped down cross-legged, exhaustion and defeat draining his last reserves of strength. "We were close, Becca. So close." Suddenly all their efforts seemed for nothing. "That's it then, sis. We've failed." Doug sniffed with derision. "That bomb... I'm not surprised it didn't work. Something's been bothering me about it."

Becca slumped down next to her brother. "What?"

"Remember that pile of wires beside *Lola*'s float? Crozier must have disarmed it before he left the airship. Why did he do that? Why didn't he set the thing so it was easy to explode? You know – like a grenade."

"I've no idea, Doug," replied Becca half-heartedly.

"Why, though? He must've had a reason to lug that thing around with him. There's something rattling inside," added Doug, shaking the casing.

Becca's mind raced back to those last moments before Crozier's death. What had he meant when he said *Work it out*? "Give me the bomb, Doug. How do we get this thing apart?"

Doug looked it over. "It's made of two hemispheres held together by fly nut screws. Should be able to undo them. It may be dangerous, though, sis."

Becca wasted no time. "Let's see what Crozier's been hiding in here."

From Doug's sketchbook: Becca investigates Crozier's "bomb". (DMS 9/57)

She carefully undid the screws and split the device in half. Inside, wrapped in a bloodied shirt, was the missing gyrolabe.

"Crozier, you ingenious old rogue," laughed Doug, lifting out the gravity device. "A makeshift carrying case. The best hiding place he could find in a hurry."

"It still leaves us with a problem," said Becca. "How do we stop the machine with a bomb, when the bomb isn't a bomb at all?"

"Now we have all the gyrolabes, we can lift the sphere and reset the dials."

"Reset them to what, though?"

"Pugachev used a four-symbol code to activate the machine. Three of the symbols were identical to those Ezekiel Zedd saw, and the ones on the maharaja's uncle's upper lip."

"Yes, so what?"

"Pugachev must have got the missing symbol from somewhere," reasoned Doug.

"Where from? Mother?"

Doug thought for a moment. "He said the machine became stronger after he obtained the western gyrolabe."

Becca's mind suddenly clicked. "Yes, of course. Xu and Xi said the western chapters of *The 99 Elements* dealt specifically with the survival of the human race. Ur-Can was built to save mankind from natural and man-made disasters. So it would make sense for the *western* gyrolabe to have special significance."

"But where would the Tembla hide the symbol?"

"In *The 99 Elements*?"

They thought for a moment, then said at exactly the same time, "On the western gyrolabe!"

Both MacKenzies jumped up and ran to the western gyrolabe. They lifted it out and examined it carefully. Elaborate engraving seemed to camouflage and confuse their search, but Becca finally found a minute code sequence engraved on the underside of one of the meridians.

"There, that's it. But there are only three symbols! We need four."

"No, look – there's a blank space where the third symbol would go."

"Where's your sketchbook?"

Doug was already flicking through the pages to find his

drawings of the hieroglyphs recorded by Ezekiel Zedd and tattooed on the sage's lips. He found the sketch and held it next to the gyrolabe so Becca could see.

"Look at Zedd's symbols, the ones on the sage's upper lip. The first hieroglyph and the last are the same as on the gyrolabe – they match!" he said excitedly. "The blank in Zedd's code is where the second symbol should be…"

"And the blank on the western gyrolabe is where the third symbol should be."

Doug examined the engraved hieroglyphs on the gyrolabe. "Yes! The symbol missing from the upper tattoo – the second symbol on the gyrolabe – is the reversed C shape we saw Pugachev input into the machine. This is how he knew. If we combine these two sets of codes we have all four symbols. We have the activation sequence!"

Becca checked a second time to be sure. "The first and last symbols are the same on the tattoo and the gyrolabe. The middle two symbols come from the tattoo and the gyrolabe."

"Pugachev must have found Ezekiel Zedd's symbols in Mother's notebooks. And when he sacked the Khotan temple and stole the western gyrolabe, he had the final symbol."

"But this is no good. We need to *stop* the machine."

"What about the second sequence? The one on the old man's bottom lip? What did Xu and Xi say?" said Doug, thinking fast. "You know, about *The 99 Elements*? The southern chapters are the sum of all the Tembla's fears."

"I suppose the sum of all their fears would be precisely this. A lunatic using Tembla science for his own ends. They knew the machine could cause a catastrophe in the wrong hands."

Both turned and stared at the southern gyrolabe still lying

on the floor beside the bomb casing where they'd left it. Becca looked at Doug. He nodded and grinned. He quickly hitched up his lucky socks.

"Come on!" urged Becca, sprinting for it.

It was Doug who found the hieroglyphs this time, on the outer meridian.

"Three symbols and another blank. It's the same system." He placed his sketchbook alongside and this time they cracked the code quickly. Doug scribbled down the missing second symbol from the gyrolabe to complete the tattoo code from the dead sage's lower lip.

"We have it, Doug! We have the complete four-symbol code."

Doug was suddenly cautious. "We don't know what this new code will do to the machine."

"We have to give it a try. What other choice is there?"

He nodded. "We'll need to extract the Daughter of the Sun from the replica and charge the top and bottom nodes of the real one."

The replica gyrolabe was white hot, impossible to touch. Doug quickly retrieved the canvas hammock, poured some of his water on it then wrapped it round the gyrolabe. He pulled it from its stand; the canvas steamed and caught fire. He dropped the heavy bundle to the floor and stamped on the flames, grinning at his sister.

The buttresses were six inches from the cartouches now, and such fierce heat and light were radiating from them that it was difficult to see. Doug poured the last of his water over the replica to cool it, then gingerly extracted the heavy grains of Daughter of the Sun and handed them to Becca. The metal burned the tips of her fingers, but she knew she

CRACKING THE TEMBLA CODES

1) Elena MacKenzie was the first to discover that Ezekiel Zedd's mysterious symbols were an incomplete activation code for Ur-Can.

2) Becca and Doug discovered this same code tattooed on the inside of the sage's upper lip.

Code from sage's upper lip BLANK

3) Becca and Doug discovered a second code sequence unknown to the Guild tattooed on the sage's lower lip. This also had a missing second symbol.

Code from sage's lower lip BLANK

4) The missing symbols were found on the western and southern gyrolabes, which in each instance showed the second symbol but not the third. This fail-safe system ensured that only someone with knowledge of both sets of codes could complete the two four-symbol sequences. The combination of both codes to fill in the blanks gave a simple solution in each case.

COMPLETE UR-CAN ACTIVATION CODE

Incomplete code from sage's upper lip

Incomplete code from western gyrolabe

Solution: combination of both codes

COMPLETE UR-CAN DEACTIVATION CODE

Incomplete code from sage's lower lip

Incomplete code from southern gyrolabe

Solution: combination of both codes

had to complete the task. She loaded the northern pole, then turned the gravity device upside down and charged the southern pole.

It was ready.

With Doug's help Becca lifted the real gyrolabe into the stand and clicked it in place. She ran to the sphere and pushed the silver lever back. The gyrolabes glided home and started to spin.

The sphere also began to spin again. "Come on! Come on!" Becca yelled at it: the buttresses were almost touching the cartouches now. "Give me your sketchbook, Doug. I'll get ready to reset the machine."

The sphere spun faster and faster and finally lifted to reveal the control panel once again. The hexagonal dials eased out of the panel with infuriating leisureliness.

"Is there time?" shouted Doug over the crackle of arcing electricity.

"Get ready to set those two controls; I'll do the others."

Becca's fingers were already tensed against the first dial. Sketchbook clasped in her left hand, she twisted the first to its new setting, then the second. Doug turned his two dials, completing the new combination.

"That's it."

The buttresses were now touching the cartouches. The platform floor vibrated alarmingly.

"All set. Now the control lever," ordered Becca.

The MacKenzies looked at each other and took a deep breath, then pulled the lever together. The platform jolted. The hexagonal dials sank back into the panel.

"Did we do it?" asked Doug.

For one heart-stopping moment, nothing seemed to change.

Electricity still crackled between the buttresses and intense heat and light flashed around them.

Then the gyrolabes swung away from the cartouches. Becca pushed her brother away from the control panel as the sphere stopped spinning and slammed down.

"Look!" exclaimed Doug. "The buttresses are moving back!"

"We did it," shouted Becca. "We did it! The sequence worked!"

To their relief the platform began slowly to descend.

But Doug and Becca's triumph was short-lived. Below them raged a vicious battle.

"Xu and Xi!" shouted Becca.

They ran to the edge of the platform to get a better view of Daotang. The storm clouds surging and circling around them offered partially obscured glimpses of the ruined city. "They must have launched an attack!"

Doug took out his binoculars and searched for their friends, but it was impossible to make out what was going on. Suddenly they were cast into shadow as the platform reached the ground and continued on its course downwards into the dark mechanical heart of Ur-Can.

CHAPTER NINETEEN

The platform slowed as it returned to its original position deep below the desert. Doug and Becca blinked as their eyes adjusted to the gloom.

"Children?" Their mother rushed towards them, her mouth agape. "Becca, Doug? It *was* you I saw. I thought I'd gone out of my mind. But how...?"

The young MacKenzies looked at each other. Doug suddenly felt guilty, as if he had done something wrong. The only word that came to mind was "sorry", so he said it.

"Sorry?" repeated his mother.

"We shouldn't be here really," he replied.

"I'm glad you are. Well, it would be nice to say hello to you both properly."

"Er ... um ... it's nice to see you again," tried Doug rather formally. He sniffed, wiping his nose on his sleeve. "We've ... we've missed you." He bent down to pick up the remains of Liberty's blunderbuss and fiddled with the broken trigger.

Becca scowled. Suddenly she had no idea what to say to her mother either. There was so much to tell, to explain and to ask that it was impossible to know where to start. A strange and uneasy silence fell.

Doug finally spluttered out to his sister, "Well. *You* say something."

His mother gazed at him with tears in her eyes. "Give me a hug, Douglas MacKenzie, and you too, Becca."

Doug put his arms awkwardly around his mother then

quickly pulled away, glancing towards the tunnel entrance. There was an outside chance someone might see.

"You two. I'm your mother! Look a little more pleased to see me."

Becca, still unsure exactly what to say, stuck to the pressing matters at hand. "We need to rescue Father and our friends. They're in great danger."

"Children, how … how did you stop the machine? Where are Pugachev and Julius?"

"We used a code. Pugachev and Pembleton-Crozier are dead."

"Dead? Both of them?" Elena looked horrified.

"Yep," said Doug. "They finished each other off. Good riddance."

"What code did you use?" she asked anxiously.

Becca looked at Doug, who found the page in his sketchbook. "We guessed it was the deactivation code. We were right, I think."

An awkward reunion

From Doug's sketchbook. (DMS 9/60)

Elena glanced at the symbols, swiftly deciphering the Tembla hieroglyphs.

"This … this is not a deactivation code. This is the code to destroy Ur-Can."

"Well, we're sorry!" said Becca with sudden indignation, her voice much more forthright than she'd meant it to be. "We had to think fast. What else were we meant to do up there?"

Elena blinked and looked impressed. "No, no… You did the right thing. It's absolutely the only way you could have stopped the machine. It just leaves us with a problem." As she spoke, the sphere kicked up again and started to spin. "Ur-Can will self-destruct and bury itself. As it does so it will create a storm. Nothing as big as the storm Pugachev had in mind, but it will be devastating."

"Qui'l'bharat?" asked Doug.

"Of enormous proportions. We must get out of here."

At that moment, Liberty ran into the chamber followed by the maharaja. She gave a whoop. "You made it!"

"Elena, I am so glad we've found you," exclaimed the maharaja, rushing forward to greet her.

"Maharaja." Elena beamed. "You're here too?"

"Thank goodness you're alive, Raj," said Becca. "How did you escape, Liberty?"

"The raj here and his trusty butler gave me a hand."

"How's Father?" asked Doug.

"Snave's tryin' to coax him back to life. He'll pull through."

With a rueful look, Doug handed her the broken blunderbuss. "I'm not sure the Liberator will."

"Who ... who is this?" asked Elena suspiciously.

"Liberty da Vine. Aviatrix adventurer for hire. In my spare time I like to run educational tours of Asia for your kids. Keeps us all occupied and outta trouble."

Elena looked alarmed.

"She's our friend," said Becca. "It's a long story."

The chamber shook violently.

"The gyrolabes," shouted Doug, "we have to take them."

Becca was anxious to get away. "But they're useless now."

"If this machine is going to destroy itself, then they're about to become the rarest scientific objects on the planet. We can't leave them!"

"Doug's right," agreed Elena. "We should save them."

They quickly removed the four gyrolabes from their stands and emptied out the Daughter of the Sun to lighten them. Doug picked up the singed replica gyrolabe for good measure. The whole of Ur-Can started to shake violently, and deep beneath them they heard a rush of air.

Doug hesitated and smiled across at his sister. "Glad I'm wearing my lucky socks."

"So am I," said Becca. "Now let's get out of here."

As they ran through the tunnels back to the surface, every stone in the ancient underground city seemed to quake with foreboding as the great Tembla machine began the process of self-destruction.

Doug was first out of the karez and reached down to assist the others. The resourceful Snave appeared on horseback leading eight Cossack horses, four of them armed with the huge flame-throwers they'd seen earlier.

"How the—?" began Liberty.

"Ah, Snave," said the maharaja as smoothly as ever. "Jolly good timing."

"Sir, take a horse." The butler turned to Elena with a polite bow. "Mrs MacKenzie. Rebecca, Douglas – I'm happy to report that Mr MacKenzie is much improved. I managed to obtain this equipment from a detachment of Russians who were ... resting."

For once, Liberty was speechless.

"Look. The sphere!" Becca exclaimed as the metallic globe shot up out of the desert and hovered portentously above

Ur-Can. Electricity danced wildly about its surface, and high in the sky wisps of cloud began to form and rotate. Immense bolts of electricity forked down to the ground, reaching out into the desert in a circle that described the limits of the subterranean machine's influence. The horses, already restless, fought to escape.

From Doug's sketchbook: Ur-Can begins to self-destruct. (DMS 9/65)

They felt the ground move beneath their feet as a series of blasts caused the sand to shift and shimmy. A huge section of the desert floor in front of them cascaded downwards as if a trapdoor had been released. Doug was torn between fear and curiosity; suddenly he could see a colossal section of the machine's workings – hundreds of ducts and pipes, all manufactured from the strange iridescent metal he'd seen inside the tunnels.

As the sand beneath them began to avalanche into the chasm, they turned and ran for their lives.

Their father was waiting at the door of the ruined building, clutching a water bottle and looking much revived. As he saw his family approach he tried to stand to greet them.

Becca and Doug were first there. "Father!"

"Did you stop the machine?"

Becca nodded. "Yes, but now Ur-Can is destroying itself. We must get away."

Supporting their father on either side, they started to run as fast as they could.

"Which way?" shouted Liberty as they reached the ruined walls of Daotang.

"Head north-east for Korla," yelled Elena.

A rattle of machine-gun fire made everyone glance over the broken city wall.

"The Russians are fighting an unknown opponent," Snave explained. "I suggest we use this timely diversion to get away as fast as we can."

"But that's the captain and crew – and the Sujing!" Doug said indignantly. "They're our friends; we can't just leave them."

Snave coughed. "I've a mind the Russians are winning,

in light of their larger numbers and modern weapons. I had
a look, sir; the tall fellows and their associates are giving a
good account of themselves, make no mistake. Fighting like
lions."

Doug pulled his binoculars from his bag to assess the state
of the battle. The situation was confused, the air choked with
sand, dust and smoke. Outnumbered, the Sujing Quantou
and the crew from the *Expedient* clung to a defensive perim-
eter around the remains of a fortified temple, and were
fighting with great tenacity; Xu and Xi were using their fire
cannon to hold back Pugachev's forces, while two other
Sujing kept up a barrage of exploding arrows from their composite bows. Huge scarlet and azure explosions ripped into
the Russian cavalry, but the Sujing's limited ammunition
could only mean this advantage was temporary.

"We have to send a message," said Becca.

"Good idea, sis. I'll need something shiny." Doug looked
about him, then quickly opened his jacket, ripped the shoulder lining and pulled out a small gold bar that had been sewn
inside. He gave it a quick polish on his trousers and flashed
EXPEDIENT in Morse towards the temple. He was suddenly
aware of his parents standing beside him.

Hamish looked at his son with utter incomprehension.
"You know Morse?"

"And I suppose it would be too much to ask how you
know Fitzroy and his crew and where on *earth* you got a bar
of gold?" added Elena.

"Um ... it's a long story. We sailed with them aboard
Expedient... Wait!"

A distant glimmer flashed back, long and short dashes
glinting in the sun.

REPORT.

Doug flashed out a reply: UR-CAN SECURED. PARENTS SAFE. PREPARE FOR STORM.

The response was immediate: POSITION UNTENABLE. MAKE FOR KORLA. WILL COVER YOUR RETREAT. GOOD LUCK AND GOODBYE. FITZROY.

"It's over," said Doug. "They are defeated."

"Good luck and goodbye be damned," said Becca. "They're our friends. We *have* to save them!"

"I'm with you there, coz." Liberty grabbed the binoculars. "Xu and Xi are someplace in that crazy Russian bear pit."

The wind gusted about them and plum-black storm clouds began to gather in the sky above. Dust and sand whipped up into their eyes and stung their skin.

Becca pointed in the direction of the machine. "Look – look at Ur-Can."

Within seconds, the whirlwind – the merciless desert djinn of Sujing legend – began to form around the sphere.

"The storm will be unlike anything in nature," warned Elena. "We must get away from here now."

Hamish looked at the battle, then at his children. He coughed. "I agree with your mother. It's too dangerous."

Becca flushed with rage. "Dangerous? *Dangerous?* Have you *any* idea what we've been through to get here? Yes, it'll be dangerous – it's *all* been dangerous! – but we won't abandon the friends who have risked everything for us. You two wouldn't be standing here if it wasn't for the people over there fighting for their lives!"

Doug nodded. He was as resolute as his sister.

Liberty gave Hamish and Elena her coldest stare. "They're right."

"Yes, well, you're as hot-headed as I was at your age. MacKenzies through and through, there's no mistaking it. Have you kept up with your swordsmanship?"

Doug nodded. "Becca's the expert."

"Very well," said Hamish gruffly. "Now's your time. Both of you."

"Hamish, you ride with me," said Elena. "Doug, put the gyrolabes in the saddlebags and help your father onto that horse."

"Saddle up and tie those spare steeds together," barked Liberty. "We'll need all the transport we can lay our hands on." She hooked her foot into the stirrup of her horse and swung up with the swagger of a cowboy. "Raj, Snave, why don't y'all take a flame-throwing cayuse each?"

"But you can't ride, Doug," Elena exclaimed as she settled in the saddle. Doug had always hated horses.

Becca swung up onto her horse and offered her brother a hand. "Take my sword as well. I'll ride; you defend us."

Liberty
back in the saddle

From Doug's sketchbook. (DMS 9/67)

"Will you two be all right on your own?" worried Elena.

"*Now* she asks," whispered Doug in his sister's ear. They pulled down their flying goggles to cover their eyes.

"Gentleman, ready your flame-throwers," Liberty yelled. "We'll cut straight through them in a V-shaped formation. Frighten the life outta them."

Behind them, the sphere descended slowly into the centre of Ur-Can. The storm intensified, howling and screaming as the sky turned black. Liberty took a last look back and cried, "Yeehah… Git up there!"

Chapter Twenty

The Cossacks ranged around the temple were surprised by the sudden attack. Liberty steered her horse with the reins clenched between her teeth, leaving both hands free to broadside Pugachev's men with the flame lance. The curtain of fire generated by the three flame-throwers was accelerated by the gale-force wind. The Russians scattered in the face of this wild inferno, allowing the horses to make quick progress.

From Doug's sketchbook: Liberty charges at the Cossacks. (DMS 9/71)

Becca concentrated hard on riding. The saddle was like nothing she had ever ridden on before, and having Doug behind her made the whole exercise uncomfortable and difficult.

About halfway to the temple, Liberty turned to the right and blasted a Cossack artillery post with a long burst of flame.

Carts and ammunition boxes instantly caught light and began to explode with dull thumps.

Liberty turned and yelled, "Becca, Doug – keep your heads down. Watch out for machine-gun fire."

Then Becca saw the first of the Sujing near the gate of the temple. It was Master Aa using double swords to drive back three Russians. A tear in the dust cloud revealed the open gateway ahead, so Becca tucked down as low as she could and spurred the horse onwards. The gateway flashed by and she reined in, coming to a halt in a swirl of dust.

They'd reached a small courtyard protected by high walls.

"Is everyone here?" shouted Liberty, checking about her as she circled around.

Doug clambered down, still clutching his swords. "Mr Ives!"

"Sure is good to see you two," said the coxswain. He had a deep cut to his forehead and was breathing hard.

"We're here to rescue you and the others," yelled Becca.

"Rescue?" He laughed. "You two never could take an order. You've gotten in here sure enough, but gettin' *out* is gonna be a whole different story."

The captain hurried over from the gatehouse, but suddenly stopped short and pointed his stick at Doug and Becca's parents. "Hamish. Elena. Hell's teeth, you really are alive."

"Fitzroy!" cried Elena, running to embrace him.

"We really will be dead if we don't get away from here," said Hamish, shaking his brother's hand. "We have horses, Fitzroy. We can escape."

"I told you to make a run for Korla. We have hardly any weapons. There's no way out of here – we're all dead men."

These words struck Doug hard. He'd never heard the captain talk about defeat – ever.

Liberty assessed the situation. "The storm's gettin' worse. I'm gonna give them a hand up on the walls. Raj, Snave – defend the gateway. We may be able to break out under cover of the storm. Becca and Doug, find your parents some shelter."

"Give these to Xu and Xi," said Becca, taking the two Sujing swords from her brother and handing them to Liberty.

Three artillery shells exploded in quick succession, blasting chunks from the mud-brick walls. Liberty's horse reared up. She aimed a blast of flame through the new hole in their defences and charged up a well-worn staircase to the top of the crenellated wall. Becca grabbed the two saddlebags containing the gyrolabes and handed one to her brother.

From Doug's sketchbook: Liberty blasts her way through the defences. (DMS 9/75)

"This way," said Elena. "There's a cellar where we were kept prisoner. We'll be safe enough there."

She led them into the remains of the crumbled building, where dilapidated stairs led downwards to a vaulted cellar lit by a dim lantern. They helped Hamish in and slammed the door shut. The air inside was still after the cacophony of the battle. The young MacKenzies gazed at three pitiful camp beds. A neat stack of books occupying a niche in the wall seemed to have been their parents' only possessions.

"Now you're safe we'll get back out there and help," said Becca. "We can't sit here and hope for the best—"

She was interrupted by an extremely tall man kicking the door open. He was carrying Slippery Sam on his back; Sam was unconscious and blood poured from a head wound.

"Is he dead?" asked Doug, seeing his old shipmate.

"This man is alive but badly injured," said the giant in a Russian accent.

Becca, certain the stranger was one of Pugachev's men, chided herself for giving both the swords away. "Keep back, Doug, he's a Cossack."

"No, no, he's a friend," said Elena.

Doug pulled a camp bed into the centre of the room, giving the Russian somewhere to lay the casualty.

The stranger spoke. "A huge hurricane is building in the desert. We cannot hold out; Pugachev's men are too strong and too numerous."

Becca couldn't stand being in the cellar a moment longer. She turned and ran for the door with Doug just behind her.

The storm was astounding – Becca couldn't see more than two feet in front of her. In vain she wiped her flying goggles. She saw Chambois running towards her clutching a rifle.

"The captain has told us to shelter in the cellar. The Sujing are covering our retreat, though many of them are dead."

"We have to find Xu and Xi," replied Becca, and the MacKenzies broke away and ran into the dust storm before Chambois could stop them.

They found the wall where Doug had last seen the twins. Becca made out faint figures, then a burst of flame in the gathering darkness. Disorientated, she stumbled about trying to find the steps leading to the top of the wall.

Then, quite suddenly, Doug bumped into Master Aa, who swung his sword round to attack, but pulled up short when he recognized them. His eyes were half closed against the sand and he had a deep knife wound across one cheek.

"Where are Xu and Xi?" Becca yelled.

"I am looking for them."

Three dead Sujing fighters were slumped at the top of the steps. With a shock, Becca realized that one was Ba'd Ak. She fought a wave of nausea. Master Aa stopped and bent down, gently closing Ba'd Ak's eyes, his lips moving in a brief prayer.

He straightened up to his full height. "The battlefield is not a place to grieve. We must find the twins."

Becca struggled to stand upright as the storm howled and moaned, and Doug tried to shield them against the rocks and stones hurled by the wind. Then she saw Xu, crouching in the lee of the wall. He was tying a bandage around his brother's lower leg. The fire cannon lay discarded, out of ammunition. Becca shook him by the shoulder, relieved the twins were alive.

"I cannot walk!" shouted Xi, his eyes full of pain. He spat sand out of his mouth. "Injured in my first real battle! I, the Sujing prodigy—"

"Where's Liberty?" interrupted Doug.

"I do not know. She was holding the south wall, fighting as hard as a Sujing master."

"We will move Xi to the cellar," ordered Master Aa. "Lean on your brother; I will guide the way."

They set off bent double against the storm, stumbling towards the steps. They reached Ba'd Ak, who seemed to radiate a calmness that contrasted sharply with the violence of the scene raging about them. Master Aa sheathed his swords and lifted his dead wife in his mighty arms.

"We were the last left fighting," yelled Xu to Becca. "It is a terrible day for the Sujing Quantou. Cut down with machine guns, like the Kalaxx."

As they reached the stairs to the cellar Master Aa suddenly crashed to the ground, still holding his dead wife. At first Becca thought he had tripped – then she saw the neat hole in his armour, where he'd been shot in the back. Xu turned and sliced his sword into the sandstorm, cutting down a Cossack.

Xi dropped to the ground and tried to pull Master Aa to safety. They managed to get him and then Ba'd Ak to the doorway, where there was some shelter from the wind. Xi pulled the armour from Master Aa's back, and found the bullet hole.

"Leave me. There is nothing you can do."

"Do not say that!" snapped Xi, stuffing Master Aa's Sujing sash into the wound to stem the bleeding.

"Xi ... Xi, you are the Sujing Quantou prodigy. You will lead the eastern chapter. It is ordained." Master Aa clutched

From Doug's sketchbook: Master Aa cradling the body of Ba'd Ak. (DMS 9/79)

Xi's shoulder, fighting for breath. "Bury me... Bury me beside Ba'd Ak at Ur-Can."

Master Aa's grip loosened. He reached out a trembling hand to stroke Ba'd Ak's cheek, then his face relaxed into an expression of serenity.

"No!" yelled Xi. *"No!"*

Becca spun round, aware that someone was approaching through the dust. It was the captain and the crew from the *Expedient.*

"They've been killed." Becca could hardly speak, her voice choked with tears. "Both of them."

"We'll all be dead if we don't get inside," said the captain, kneeling respectfully to close Master Aa's eyes. "They were great warriors."

"Help us," said Xi. "Help us carry them out of the storm."

"Are there any Sujing still alive out there?"

"No," said Xu, looking at his brother. "We are the last. The last of the Sujing Quantou Order."

As the storm raged outside, Doug and Becca felt helpless as to how to comfort the grieving Xu and Xi. The young Sujing had begun chanting and praying for Master Aa and Ba'd Ak as soon as they had found safety in the cellar. The two bodies lay at rest in a dark corner lit by a single candle. Doug and Becca had tried to help their friends, but Xi made it clear that they were not to be disturbed until the ceremony was completed. They would bury the bodies at dawn, in the Sujing manner, and for that they would need assistance.

So in the opposite corner the MacKenzie family began to talk, speaking stiffly at first, none of them knowing where to start. But the conversation soon flowed as it had done so many times around the kitchen table in Lucknow. In the flickering lantern light of that long night, the young MacKenzies told wild stories of Chinese pirates and finger-bone necklaces; of typhoons and volcanoes; of shipwrecks and airships ... and of a pungent pair of socks with remarkable lucky powers.

In another corner Liberty talked to the captain. "D'you think zoridium would make a good power source for an airplane engine?"

"Excellent, I should think."

She unscrewed a tiny phial hidden in her flying goggles.

"Good, because I've been carrying these few grains of the

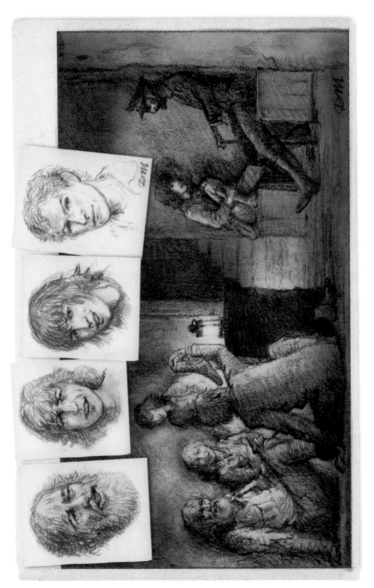

THE FAMILY BACK TOGETHER AT LAST, WITH MANY TALES TO TELL

(MA 239.200 MAC)

darn stuff around with me since Foochow. I grabbed them while Crozier and Capulus were brawlin'.'"

"Have you indeed? Ha!" The captain chuckled, then looked across at her from under heavy eyebrows. "I've a question to ask you, Miss da Vine. Would you consider joining the Hon—"

"Wait! Don't even say it, Skip! I'm not joinin' your spooky old gang. No, sir. Not ever. Not for all the zoridium in China."

"Ah, well. I just thought I'd ask. We've had our differences, but you're a remarkable woman, Liberty – a remarkable pilot, I mean."

"Yeah, yeah, I know. I've got a question for you too, Skip – who d'you think the giant is? The Russian guy talkin' to Chambois."

"Oh, that's obvious," said the captain, tilting his hat down over his eyes. He crossed his arms and settled himself for a doze.

"It ain't obvious to *me*."

From Doug's sketchbook: Zorid and Chambois. (DMS 9/85)

"He is the missing Professor Zorid. Pugachev was making him work as hard as Hamish and Elena. His meddling with zoridium – the Sujing's Daughter of the Sun – accelerated his growth, just as it did with the Sujing. It's a nasty side effect if you breathe the vapours too much. You should be careful."

"So Chambois can clear his name?" asked Liberty.

"Well, yes. He can hardly be convicted of murder if the man he's accused of killing is still alive, albeit rather taller than before."

"Actually, it's time I had a chat with Chambois." She put her fingers in her mouth and whistled at the Frenchman. "Hey, Luc, y'all know anything about airplane engines?"

He rubbed his hands over weary eyes. "A little, Liberty, yes."

"I'm buildin' a new plane – *Lola II*. Wanna design me a new breed of engine – one that can be fired up on zoridium?"

PROFESSOR ZORID

Zorid had been tasked by the tsar with assessing the research papers and Daughter of the Sun confiscated from the original Coterie of St Petersburg. During the Russian Revolution of 1917 he left Moscow for Switzerland with the remains of the Coterie's Daughter of the Sun supplies, and further quantities he'd discovered during an imperial expedition to Sinkiang with Pugachev in 1912.

Pugachev and Zorid split in disagreement over what to do with the original Coterie's secrets. Zorid's subsequent proclamation that he'd discovered "zoridium" (Daughter of the Sun) made him a target for the new revived Coterie of St Petersburg, who attempted to assassinate him and frame Chambois for the murder. Injured but not killed in the explosion, Zorid fled Switzerland, but was captured by Pugachev's agents and taken against his will to work at Ur-Can.

KINDLY RECEIPT

THE VICARAGE,
BRIGHAM-UPON-TROUT

April 15th

Sir,

After reading your article "The Unparalleled Violence of Sandstorms", I hastened to write to you of my recent experiences in the Sinkiang region of China, where I have been studying ancient wall paintings for a monograph I plan to publish next year.

I was nearing Korla, where I hoped to discover further evidence of Buddhist fresco work, when my guide became animated to the point of rudeness and shouted a curious name repeatedly - "Qui'l'bharat". Conversation with a traveller I later met at Anxi revealed this to be a desert djinn or spirit much feared for its ferocity.

The sandstorm blew up from the direction of the desert; the danger was in its silence - if I'd had my back to it, I should never have seen it before it was upon me. Away to my left, the horizon softened and blurred as if touched by a watercolourist's brush. After some minutes this became a solidly discernible buff-coloured cloud, much like a tidal bore or eagre seen in rivers.

We rode hard until we reached a forlorn scattering of abandoned buildings and took cover to watch the fermenting storm. The cloud advanced with great rapidity now, a tumbling wave of amber dust reaching towards us in the shape of some fantastic lion's paw. Oh! to have felt the force of it - but I surely would have perished in its sublime caress. The fierce, gusting wind rasped against us, as sand and dust twisted high into the atmosphere, eclipsing the sky to midnight's blackness...

Such a commotion is usually witnessed only in the dark fury of our most volatile oceans - on land, I assure you, the barren desert magnified its grandeur a thousandfold, impressing upon me the...

P.T.O.

Chapter Twenty-One

By dawn the storm had died completely. The *Expedient*'s men had checked the ruins of Daotang for Pugachev's army, but it was quickly apparent the Cossacks had either fled or become victims of the angry desert.

In the gathering light, Becca walked up to the broken city walls where her uncle was perched on a rock smoking his pipe and waiting for the sunrise.

"Those young Sujing have been busy," commented the captain.

"The crew have been helping them dig the graves," replied Becca sadly. "Doug's been giving them a hand too."

"So I saw. Ur-Can is also buried. It's almost as if it were never there." Becca looked at the huge mound of sand now covering the site. "A freakishly violent storm, wouldn't you say, Rebecca? Tembla science is quite extraordinary."

"It *was* quite extraordinary," she corrected. "Doug and I just wrecked the world's best defence against global catastrophe."

"Pugachev would have destroyed us all," argued the captain, relighting his pipe. "You did the right thing."

There was silence for a moment as they considered the huge new sand dune.

"What a waste, though," he said thoughtfully. "How I would have loved to see the interior of Ur-Can. Those cartouches. The original *99 Elements…*"

Doug sauntered up and slumped in the sand beside them. The sun suddenly broke on the horizon, casting crimson rays over the dunes. "The desert looks like the sea in this light," he said, rubbing his hands together. "The sandy crests could almost be waves."

"Do you know, I was thinking exactly the same thing, nephew! And yet here we are at the most landlocked place on the globe. Imagine that. The most useless place for a sea captain to be in all the world." Their uncle gave a rare laugh. "No hint of the briny. I miss it. I've been away for too long."

"A shame your ship is at the bottom of the Celebes Sea," commented Doug. "There's always Borelli's submarine, I suppose."

"There is, but I shall be selling that heap of rubbish as soon as I can. I must pick you up on a point of fact, however."

Doug had never heard the captain speak in such a friendly manner.

"*Expedient* was the Guild's ship. My own ship, the *Juno*, is a topsail schooner – as pretty a vessel as you'll ever see. She's being ice strengthened in an English shipyard as we speak. Ur-Can is destroyed, but there is still much work to do. Expeditions to plan; missions to carry out. The Coterie are still active; Pembleton-Crozier's death will not stop them. If your parents consent, I should be honoured if you would both accompany me on future voyages. Honoured indeed."

Becca laughed. "After all the trouble we've caused?"

"You shook things up. Got results. Will you join the Guild now, niece?"

"I'll think about it." Becca turned her face to the rising sun. She saw figures moving on the dune over Ur-Can. "Is that Xu and Xi?"

"Yes, they're just finishing the burial ritual," explained Doug.

The twins were raising a makeshift flagpole on top of the new dune. The first rays of sun fell on the fresh graves of their fallen comrades, covering the summit of Ur-Can. A sudden breeze caught the flag, made of Master Aa's long red Sujing Quantou sash. It fluttered out on the wind revealing a downturned ram's horn symbol, stark against the sunrise.

Xu and Xi mounted their horses. Xi stood up in his stirrups, cupped his hands round his mouth and shouted, "I am Master Xi, leader of the Sujing Quantou, the finest fighters in all China. We are the last surviving detachment of Alexander the Great's army, disciples of *The 99 Elements*, and guardians of the Ur-Can mysteries. Our blades run with the blood of our enemies. We are bowed but not defeated. We will rise again." He pulled one of his fighting swords from its scabbard and raised it high above his head. "Sujing Cha!"

Sujing Cha! Xu and Xi's final farewell

From Doug's sketchbook. (DMS 9/92)

And with that they both charged down the dune and headed eastwards, kicking up a fine plume of dust. Before they disappeared from view, Xu turned and waved. He raised a gyrolabe in his left hand, its ancient metalwork flashing and glinting in the first desert light.

"Didn't even say goodbye," muttered Doug.

His sister thought differently. "That was the finest goodbye I've ever seen."

"Mother said she'd cook breakfast. Only Uncle Pete's tinned stuff, but it'll be all right."

"I'll walk down with you, Douglas," said the captain brightly.

"Coming with us, sis?" asked Doug, pulling up his socks.

Becca smiled. "You two go on ahead. I want to watch the flag a little longer."

"Suit yourself. I'm starving."

THE CONCLUSION OF THE
GUILD TRILOGY

APPENDICES

THE GREAT MECHANISM AT UR-CAN

The Ur-Can machine measured a colossal 1.39 miles (2,250 metres) wide by 2.7 miles (4,374 metres) deep – see inset of the Eiffel Tower for a visual scale.

The storm bowl was positioned at the very top of the machine just beneath the desert's surface. The focus of the storm was the intake duct, which sucked air and particulate matter from the atmosphere at 5,000 miles an hour when running at full operating speed. At the bottom of this duct were the cartouche chamber and controls. Either side of this upper section were the storm initiator ducts which generated the first stages of the storm.

At the heart of the machine were four super-gyrolabes arranged around the intake duct and powered by Daughter of the Sun. These created immensely strong gravity vortices powerful enough to bore like a drill through the earth's crust and mantle (as demonstrated by the machine at Sulphur Island – see Book II). To achieve this, the four gravity vortices emanating from the southern nodes of the super-gyrolabes were focused downwards into the central intake duct.

The filtering system separated the particulate matter from the air. The clean air was then channelled outwards through ducts to eight peripheral clean air exit portals 122.5 miles distant from Ur-Can. The particulate matter was fed into the gravity vortices, which forced the matter downwards under intense pressure into the earth's core.

Owing to the extreme physical stresses of the process, the machine could run for a maximum of five days. Chambois speculated that the circular body and network of clean air ducts were designed to act as a plug to any resurgent lava once the machine had stopped.

The diagram to the bottom left illustrates the predicted situation thirty-six hours after initiation of the machine. Of interest is the control platform positioned above the eye of the storm.

(Material and technical details for this section taken from notes made by Doug MacKenzie and Luc Chambois in the 1930s.)

NOTE: The Ha-Mi discovered that they could create storms by causing the sphere in the cartouche chamber to raise itself into the air. This was an erroneous use of the machine which activated only the primary initiator sequence designed to generate the first stages of the storm. Without the four gyrolabes, they could never have fully activated the machine.